DATE DUE

THE UNTAMED

D1002551

THE UNTAMED

By
MAX BRAND

Introduction to the Bison Book Edition
by William A. Bloodworth, Jr.

University of Nebraska Press
Lincoln and London

First Bison Book printing: 1994
Most recent printing indicated by the last number below:
10   9   8   7   6   5   4   3   2   1

Library of Congress Cataloging-in-Publication Data
Brand, Max, 1892–1944.
The untamed / by Max Brand; introduction to the Bison Book edi-
tion by William A. Bloodworth, Jr.
p.   cm.
ISBN 0-8032-1248-8
ISBN 0-8032-6117-9 (pbk.)
I. Title.
PS3511.A87U58   1994
813'.52—dc20
94-13997   CIP
∞   *81574*

INTRODUCTION

by William A. Bloodworth, Jr.

With popular novels we have a habit of ignoring origins. Many of Zane Grey's novels, for instance, were first published in women's magazines, *Ladies' Home Journal* among them. Max Brand's *The Untamed,* which as a Pocket Books paperback in 1955 helped satisfy the American hunger for western novels and movies at that time, first appeared as a six-part serial in *All-Story Weekly,* beginning in December 1918. *All-Story Weekly* was a publication of the Munsey Company, which also published *Argosy, Railroad Man's Magazine, Woman,* and *Cavalier.* These were so-called pulp magazines, printed on inexpensive, unglazed paper.

All-Story Magazine ran only fiction and was Munsey's effort to provide literary entertainment to an audience of general readers. Each of the company's other magazines aimed at a more specific clientele. Editing was geared to public taste, but the sheer volume of fiction needed for a weekly publication widened the editorial net. Since the pulps were more dependent for profit on the appeal of their copy than they were on advertising revenue—as a comparison of their text-filled pages with the advertising-laden pages of later "slick" magazines like *Saturday Evening Post* will quickly show—they were open to new material that promised more sales and subscriptions.

Only conditions such as these allowed the publication of

The Untamed in 1918. Although the story was by setting and character a western, it was unlike anything previously offered by that genre of popular fiction. Instead of the romantic vistas of Zane Grey, *The Untamed* pictured an unnatural terrain, a "junk-shop of the world" ruled by rattlesnakes. Instead of a cowboy shaped by the experience of the ranching frontier, the hero of *The Untamed* is a Pan-like creature of mysterious origins, as much wild animal as human being. It is as though Max Brand, at the beginning, took to their farthest extremes all the western heroes, Shane included, by other writers who would follow. Dan Barry, the protagonist, has more in common with the world of E. L. Doctorow's *Welcome to Hard Times* than that of *The Virginian* or *Riders of the Purple Sage.*

Since his first western novel expanded known borders, Max Brand created his own unfenced range for hundreds of western stories that would follow. Eventually there would be almost four hundred Max Brand titles—short stories, single-issue novelettes, and serials—published in pulp magazines, with many also issued in book form, as *The Untamed* was in 1919. Some, including *The Untamed,* made it to the screen as well, the most famous instance being *Destry Rides Again* in its 1939 version with James Stewart and Marlene Dietrich.

Max Brand also strained against western expectations by being a fiction himself. Although pseudonyms occasionally had been attached to earlier western stories, the tradition stressed personal involvement with western places and events. Owen Wister, a frequent visitor in Wyoming, drew details from life and infused his stories, especially *The Virginian,* with attitudes learned from wealthy ranchers. Zane Grey felt strong personal ties to the West following a trip to Arizona after his own wedding, and he wrote fondly of specific places he had visited.

Max Brand could offer no similarly compelling personal connection with the West because he was merely a by-line, one of at least eighteen such pen names used by Frederick Schiller Faust, whose own association with the West was one of flight and distance. Faust was born in Seattle, reared and orphaned in the San Joaquin Valley of California, experience that scarred him internally and gave him no reason to sentimentalize the West. He made his way on borrowed money to the University of California as a student in 1911, filled with poetic intensity and desires for literary fame. He published over fifty poems in the Berkeley literary magazine, the *Occident*, and grew famous on campus for his writing of poetry, drama, and humor, some of which was critical of the university administration. He also fell victim to alcohol. In 1915 the president of the university refused, on technical academic grounds but likely also out of frustration with Faust's behavior, to grant him his degree.

Consequently, Faust set off with a friend for the revolution building in India, got only as far as Hawaii, went then to Canada, where he joined the Canadian Army in hopes of reaching the battleground in Europe. He failed in this effort, finally going AWOL in Nova Scotia and making his way to New York City with no possessions beyond the clothes on his back and some ten thousand lines of a narrative poem about Tristram and Isolde. In New York his poetic hopes grew when he gained access through acquaintances to such literati as Henry Seidel Canby and Stephen Vincent Benét. But he published only two poems. One paid him fifty dollars, the other nothing. Early in 1917 a letter of introduction directed him to the office of a Munsey editor, Robert Hobart Davis. Upon Davis's invitation he tried his hand at fiction and within a few hours produced an 8,000-word story about a remorseful gangster with a heart of gold. Suddenly the world of popular stories opened before him, luring him with its per-word payments and creating for his poetic interests a conflict that would haunt him for the rest of his life.

By mid-1918 Faust had produced for Munsey a variety of stories about criminals, miners, eighteenth-century swordsmen, twentieth-century revolutionaries, and veterans of the war "over there" that he still yearned to join. He had used two pen names—"Max Brand" (first in June 1917) and "John

Frederick"—to hide his own overly German name. He had also returned to California to marry his college sweetheart, housed her in ever-increasing luxury in New York City, seen the birth of their first child, and enlisted in the United States Army in another futile effort to enter the war. His life was boiling with ambition and desire, all funded by the popular stories he wrote for Munsey magazines.

Sometime in the summer of 1918, while stationed at a Virginia army camp, he began writing *The Untamed*. Before then he had written four other stories—none of them a novel-length serial—set in the West and evocative of Zane Grey's settings and characters. In one of these, for instance, the heroine, freshly arrived in Nevada from the East, looks out her hotel room to see "the wild outlines of the mountains . . . imperious with purple. She smiled as she stared, for her heart wandered as freely as her eyes." For *The Untamed,* however, he changed course entirely, writing a story where the first act of a mysterious hero is to grab a rattlesnake with his bare hand and cut off its head. Zane Grey, Owen Wister, and other western novelists had written about the power of the West to redeem and regenerate Americans, especially those corrupted by eastern values. Frederick Faust was interested only in action and adventure; his sources were imagination, classical mythology, and his uncanny ability to create stories. His protagonists, as in *The Untamed,* were not held to the same moral expectations, the same transformations of character, as were other western heroes. When Dan Barry rides off at the end of *The Untamed,* he is the same wild and amoral character who severs the snake's head at the beginning of the story.

Following *The Untamed,* Faust wrote two sequels—*The Night Horseman* and *The Seventh Man*—before putting Dan Barry away. He also entered into a long association with another pulp house, Street & Smith, publisher of *Western Story Magazine,* the most successful venture of its kind in American magazine history. Throughout the twenties and early thirties Faust wrote large portions of the magazine—eventually 306 titles, all but seven of them novelettes or book-length serials. He also continued to write in other genres for other magazines: mystery, detection, romance, historical adventure, and even some slick and highbrow fiction. For almost twenty years he produced the equivalent of a full-length novel, on average, every three weeks—all while leading a lavish life, much of it spent at a rented villa in Florence, Italy. Throughout his career he suffered from a weak heart, alcohol abuse, and a continuing desire to be a poet along classical lines. In 1938 he moved from Florence to Hollywood, where he wrote for several movie studios. His most enduring Hollywood work was a series of stories and novels about a young physician named Doctor Kildare, later of television fame in the form of Richard Chamberlain.

In 1944, unhappy in Hollywood, still eager to see a war, he managed to get an assignment from *Harper's* as a battlefield correspondent. He was almost fifty-two years old when he left for a final, fatal trip to Italy. He was killed in action in May 1944, dying a death befitting a Max Brand hero.

A half-century after his death, Frederick Faust remains— as Max Brand—an important American popular writer. His importance is due in large measure to sheer impact and the countless millions of readers and viewers his works touched. He was clearly a shaper of attitudes towards the West even though he was out of step with most of his literary cohorts in that venture. His was a West of fantasy, fantastic conflict, and constant action; in the pages of his novels, never more apparent than in *The Untamed,* the West is a place without consistent value unto itself. Two years before his death he wrote to a Berkeley professor, an old friend, about his stories, preferring to call them "tales" rather than "fiction." A writer of tales, such as himself, he wrote, "freely abandons all attempts to give an exact replica of life, of reality, and writes the reader out the door . . . into the world of open conceiving." The world of *The Untamed* certainly allows its readers the latitude to conceive of a western hero unattached to history or even ordinary human emotions.

It was a remarkable first book in April 1919 when it appeared in a G. P. Putnam hardcover. Today it remains remarkable, an exploitation of the western as much as an example of it, a strange adventure of violence and innocence inextricably combined in a single character. There is nothing else quite like it, not even amid the hundreds of other Max Brand westerns.

Fortunately, the work of Max Brand—née Frederick Faust—has attracted increasing attention in recent years from persons other than casual readers and fans. Robert Easton's biography, *Max Brand: The Big "Westerner"* (Norman: University of Oklahoma Press, 1970) tells the story of his life well. William F. Nolan's *Max Brand: Western Giant* (Bowling Green, Ohio: Bowling Green State University Popular Press, 1985) is an indispensable guide and bibliography. Chapters in Christine Bold's *Selling the Wild West: Popular Western Fiction, 1860–1960* (Bloomington and Indianapolis: University of Indiana Press, 1987) and Cynthia S. Hamilton's *Westerns and Hard-Boiled Detective Fiction* (Iowa City: University of Iowa Press, 1987) deal with Faust's role in popular culture. My *Max Brand* (New York: Twayne Publishers, 1993) offers a view of his entire career. But as with any writer worth reading, the best guide is the writer's own work. Nowhere is this more true than with *The Untamed*.

CONTENTS

THE UNTAMED

THE UNTAMED

CHAPTER I

PAN OF THE DESERT

EVEN to a high-flying bird this was a country to be passed over quickly. It was burned and brown, littered with fragments of rock, whether vast or small, as if the refuse were tossed here after the making of the world. A passing shower drenched the bald knobs of a range of granite hills and the slant morning sun set the wet rocks aflame with light. In a short time the hills lost their halo and resumed their brown. The moisture evaporated. The sun rose higher and looked sternly across the desert as if he searched for any remaining life which still struggled for existence under his burning course.

And he found life. Hardy cattle moved singly or in small groups and browsed on the withered bunch grass. Summer scorched them, winter humped their backs with cold and arched up their bellies with famine, but they were a breed schooled through generations for this fight against nature. In this junk-shop of the world, rattlesnakes were rulers of the soil. Overhead the buzzards, ominous black specks pendant against the white-hot sky, ruled the air.

It seemed impossible that human beings could live in this rock-wilderness. If so, they must be to other men what the lean, hardy cattle of the hills are to the corn-fed stabled beeves of the States.

Over the shoulder of a hill came a whistling which might have been attributed to the wind, had not this day been deathly calm. It was fit music for such a scene, for it seemed neither of heaven nor earth, but the soul of the great god Pan come back to earth to charm those nameless rocks with his wild, sweet piping. It changed to harmonious phrases loosely connected. Such might be the exultant improvisations of a master violinist.

A great wolf, or a dog as tall and rough coated as a wolf, trotted around the hillside. He paused with one foot lifted and lolling, crimson tongue, as he scanned the distance and then turned to look back in the direction from which he had come.

The weird music changed to whistled notes as liquid as a flute. The sound drew closer. A horseman rode out on the shoulder and checked his mount. One could not choose him at first glance as a type of those who fight nature in a region where the thermometer moves through a scale of a hundred and sixty degrees in the year to an accompaniment of cold-stabbing winds and sweltering suns. A thin, handsome face with large brown eyes and black hair, a body tall but rather slenderly made—he might have been a descendant of some ancient family of Norman nobility; but could such proud gentry be found riding the desert in a tall-crowned sombrero with chaps on his legs and a red bandana handkerchief knotted around his throat? That first glance made the rider seem strangely out of place in such surroundings. One might even smile at the contrast, but at the second glance the smile would fade, and at the third, it would be replaced with a stare of interest. It was impossible to tell why one respected this man, but after a time there grew a suspicion of unknown strength in this lone rider, strength like that of a machine which is stopped but only needs a spark of fire to plunge it into irresistible action. Strangely enough, the youthful figure seemed in tune with that region of mighty dis-

tances, with that white, cruel sun, with that bird
of prey hovering high, high in the air.

It required some study to guess at these qualities of the rider, for they were such things as a
child feels more readily than a grown man; but
it needed no expert to admire the horse he be-
strode. It was a statue in black marble, a steed
fit for a Shah of Persia! The stallion stood barely
fifteen hands, but to see him was to forget his
size. His flanks shimmered like satin in the sun.
What promise of power in the smooth, broad
hips! Only an Arab poet could run his hand over
that shoulder and then speak properly of the
matchless curve. Only an Arab could appreciate
legs like thin and carefully drawn steel below the
knees; or that flow of tail and windy mane; that
generous breast with promise of the mighty heart
within; that arched neck; that proud head with
the pricking ears, wide forehead, and muzzle, as
the Sheik said, which might drink from a pint-pot.

A rustling like dried leaves came from among
the rocks and the hair rose bristling around the
neck of the wolflike dog. With outstretched
head he approached the rocks, sniffing, then
stopped and turned shining eyes upon his master,
who nodded and swung from the saddle. It was
a little uncanny, this silent interchange of glances

between the beast and the man. The cause of the dog's anxiety was a long rattler which now slid out from beneath a boulder, and giving its harsh warning, coiled, ready to strike. The dog backed away, but instead of growling he looked to the man.

Cowboys frequently practise with their revolvers at snakes, but one of the peculiarities of this rider was that he carried no gun, neither six-shooter nor rifle. He drew out a short knife which might be used to skin a beef or carve meat, though certainly no human being had ever used such a weapon against a five-foot rattler. He stooped and rested both hands on his thighs. His feet were not two paces from the poised head of the snake. As if marvelling at this temerity, the big rattler tucked back his head and sounded the alarm again. In response the cowboy flashed his knife in the sun. Instantly the snake struck but the deadly fangs fell a few inches short of the riding boots. At the same second the man moved. No eye could follow the leap of his hand as it darted down and fastened around the snake just behind the head. The long brown body writhed about his wrist, with rattles clashing. He severed the head deftly and tossed the twisting mass back on the rocks.

Then, as if he had performed the most ordinary act, he rubbed his gloves in the sand, cleansed his knife in a similar manner, and stepped back to his horse. Contrary to the rules of horse-nature, the stallion had not flinched at sight of the snake, but actually advanced a high-headed pace or two with his short ears laid flat on his neck, and a sudden red fury in his eyes. He seemed to watch for an opportunity to help his master. As the man approached after killing the snake the stallion let his ears go forward again and touched his nose against his master's shoulder. When the latter swung into the saddle, the wolf-dog came to his side, reared, and resting his fore-feet on the stirrup stared up into the rider's face. The man nodded to him, whereat, as if he under-stood a spoken word, the dog dropped back and trotted ahead. The rider touched the reins and galloped down the easy slope. The little episode had given the effect of a three-cornered conversa-tion. Yet the man had been as silent as the animals.

In a moment he was lost among the hills, but still his whistling came back, fainter and fainter, until it was merely a thrilling whisper that dwelt in the air but came from no certain direction.

His course lay towards a road which looped

whitely across the hills. The road twisted over a low ridge where a house stood among a grove of cottonwoods dense enough and tall enough to break the main force of any wind. On the same road, a thousand yards closer to the rider of the black stallion, was Morgan's place.

CHAPTER II

In the ranch house old Joseph Cumberland frowned on the floor as he heard ·his daughter say: "It isn't right, Dad. I never noticed it before I went away to school, but since I've come back I begin to feel that it's shameful to treat Dan in this way."

Her eyes brightened and she shook her golden head for emphasis. Her father watched her with a faintly quizzical smile and made no reply. The dignity of ownership of many thousand cattle kept the old rancher's shoulders square, and there was an antique gentility about his thin face with its white goatee. He was more like a quaint figure of the seventeenth century than a successful cattleman of the twentieth.

"It *is* shameful, Dad," she went on, encouraged by his silence, "or you could tell me some reason."

"Some reason for not letting him have a gun?" asked the rancher, still with the quizzical smile.

8

"Yes, yes!" she said eagerly, "and some reason for treating him in a thousand ways as if he were an irresponsible boy."

"Why, Kate, gal, you have tears in your eyes!"

He drew her onto a stool beside him, holding both her hands, and searched her face with eyes as blue and almost as bright as her own. "How does it come that you're so interested in Dan?"

"Why, Dad, dear," and she avoided his gaze, "I've always been interested in him. Haven't we grown up together?"

"Part ways you have."

"And haven't we been always just like brother and sister?"

"You're talkin' a little more'n sisterly, Kate."

"What do you mean?"

"Ay, ay! What do I mean! And now you're all red. Kate, I got an idea it's nigh onto time to let Dan start on his way."

He could not have found a surer way to drive the crimson from her face and turn it white to the lips.

"Dad!"

"Well, Kate?"

"You wouldn't send Dan away!"

Before he could answer she dropped her head against his shoulder and broke into great sobs.

He stroked her head with his calloused, sunburned hand and his eyes filmed with a distant gaze.

"I might have knowed it!" he said over and over again; "I might have knowed it! Hush, my silly gal."

Her sobbing ceased with magic suddenness.

"Then you won't send him away?"

"Listen to me while I talk to you straight," said Joe Cumberland, "and accordin' to the way you take it will depend whether Dan goes or stays. Will you listen?"

"Dear Dad, with all my heart!"

"Humph!" he grunted, "that's just what I don't want. This what I'm goin' to tell you is a queer thing—a mighty lot like a fairy tale, maybe. I've kept it back from you years an' years thinkin' you'd find out the truth about Dan for yourself. But bein' so close to him has made you sort of blind, maybe! No man will criticize his own hoss."

"Go on, tell me what you mean. I won't interrupt."

He was silent for a moment, frowning to gather his thoughts.

"Have you ever seen a mule, Kate?"

"Of course!"

"Maybe you've noticed that a mule is just as strong as a horse——"

"Yes."

"—but their muscles ain't a third as big?"

"Yes, but what on earth——"

"Well, Kate, Dan is built light an' yet he's stronger than the biggest men around here."

"Are you going to send him away simply because he's strong?"

"It doesn't show nothin'," said the old man gently, "savin' that he's different from the regular run of men—an' I've seen a considerable pile of men, honey. There's other funny things about Dan maybe you ain't noticed. Take the way he has with hosses an' other animals. The wildest man-killin', spur-hatin' bronchos don't put up no fight when them long legs of Dan settle round 'em."

"Because they know fighting won't help them!"

"Maybe so, maybe so," he said quietly, "but it's kind of queer, Kate, that after most a hundred men on the best hosses in these parts had ridden in relays after Satan an' couldn't lay a rope on him, Dan could jest go out on foot with a halter an' come back in ten days leadin' the wildest devil of a mustang that ever hated men."

"It was a glorious thing to do!" she said.

Old Cumberland sighed and then shook his head.

"It shows more'n that, honey. There ain't any man but Dan that can sit the saddle on Satan. If Dan should die, Satan wouldn't be no more use to other men than a piece of haltered lightnin'. An' then tell me how Dan got hold of that wolf, Black Bart, as he calls him."

"It isn't a wolf, Dad," said Kate, "it's a dog. Dan says so himself."

"Sure he says so," answered her father, "but there was a lone wolf prowlin' round these parts for a considerable time an' raisin' Cain with the calves an' the colts. An' Black Bart comes pretty close to a description of the lone wolf. Maybe you remember Dan found his 'dog' lyin' in a gully with a bullet through his shoulder. If he was a dog how'd he come to be shot——"

"Some brute of a sheep herder may have done it. What could it prove?"

"It only proves that Dan is queer—powerful queer! Satan an' Black Bart are still as wild as they ever was, except that they got one master. An' they ain't got a thing to do with other people. Black Bart'd tear the heart out of a man that so much as patted his head."

"Why," she cried, "he'll let me do anything with him!"

"Humph!" said Cumberland, a little baffled;

"maybe that's because Dan is kind of fond of you, gal, an' he has sort of introduced you to his pets, damn 'em! That's just the pint! How is he able to make his man-killers act sweet with you an' play the devil with everybody else."

"It wasn't Dan at all!" she said stoutly, "and he *isn't* queer. Satan and Black Bart let me do what I want with them because they know I love them for their beauty and their strength."

"Let it go at that," growled her father. "Kate, you're jest like your mother when it comes to arguin'. If you wasn't my little gal I'd say you was plain pig-headed. But look here, ain't you ever felt that Dan is what I call him—different? Ain't you ever seen him get mad—jest for a minute —an' watched them big brown eyes of his get all packed full of yellow light that chases a chill up and down your back like a wrigglin' snake?"

She considered this statement in a little silence.

"I saw him kill a rattler once," she said in a low voice. "Dan caught him behind the head after he had struck. He did it with his bare hand! I almost fainted. When I looked again he had cut off the head of the snake. It was—it was terrible!"

She turned to her father and caught him firmly by the shoulders.

"Look me straight in the eye, Dad, and tell me just what you mean."

"Why, Kate," said the wise old man, "you're beginnin' to see for yourself what I'm drivin' at! Haven't you got somethin' else right on the tip of your tongue?"

"There was one day that I've never told you about," she said in a low voice, looking away, "because I was afraid that if I told you, you'd shoot Black Bart. He was gnawing a big beef bone and just for fun I tried to take it away from him. He'd been out on a long trail with Dan and he was very hungry. When I put my hand on the bone he snapped. Luckily I had a thick glove on and he merely pinched my wrist. Also I think he realized what he was doing for otherwise he'd have cut through the glove as if it had been paper. He snarled fearfully and I sprang back with a cry. Dan hadn't seen what happened, but he heard the snarl and saw Black Bart's bared teeth. Then—oh, it was terrible!"

She covered her face.

"Take your time, Kate," said Cumberland softly.

" 'Bart,' called Dan," she went on, "and there was such anger in his face that I think I was more afraid of him than of the big dog.

"Bart turned to him with a snarl and bared his teeth. When Dan saw that his face turned —I don't know how to say it!"

She stopped a moment and her hands tightened.

"Back in his throat there came a sound that was almost like the snarl of Black Bart. The wolf-dog watched him with a terror that was uncanny to see, the hair around his neck fairly on end, his teeth still bared, and his growl horrible.

" 'Dan!' I called, 'don't go near him!'

"I might as well have called out to a whirlwind. He leaped. Black Bart sprang to meet him with eyes green with fear. I heard the loud click of his teeth as he snapped—and missed. Dan swerved to one side and caught Black Bart by the throat and drove him into the dust, falling with him.

"I couldn't move. I was weak with horror. It wasn't a struggle between a man and a beast. It was like a fight between a panther and a wolf. Black Bart was fighting hard but fighting hope-lessly. Those hands were settling tighter on his throat. His big red tongue lolled out; his struggles almost ceased. Then Dan happened to glance at me. What he saw in my face sobered him. He got up, lifting the dog with him, and flung away the lifeless weight of Bart. He began to brush the dust from his clothes, looking down as if he were ashamed. He asked me if the dog had hurt me when he snapped. I could not speak for a moment. Then came the most horrible part. Black Bart, who must have been nearly killed, dragged himself to Dan on his belly, choking and whining, and licked the boots of his master!"

"Then you *do* know what I mean when I say Dan is—different?"

She hesitated and blinked, as if she were shutting her eyes on a fact. "I *don't* know. I know that he's gentle and kind and loves you more than you love him." Her voice broke a little. "Oh, Dad, you forget the time he sat up with you for five days and nights when you got sick out in the hills, and how he barely managed to get you back to the house alive!"

The old man frowned to conceal how greatly he was moved.

"I haven't forgot nothin', Kate," he said, "an' everything is for his own good. Do you know what I've been tryin' to do all these years?"

"What?"

"I've been tryin' to hide him from himself! Kate, do you remember how I found him?"

"I was too little to know. I've heard you tell

a little about it. He was lost on the range. You found him twenty miles south of the house."

"Lost on the range?" repeated her father softly. "I don't think he could ever have been lost. To a hoss the corral is a home. To us our ranch is a home. To Dan Barry the whole mountain-desert is a home! This is how I found him. It was in the spring of the year when the wild geese was honkin' as they flew north. I was ridin' down a gulley about sunset and wishin' that I was closer to the ranch when I heard a funny, wild sort of whistlin' that didn't have any tune to it that I recognized. It gave me a queer feelin'. It made me think of fairy stories—an' things like that! Pretty soon I seen a figure on the crest of the hill. There was a triangle of geese away up overhead an' the boy was walkin' along lookin' up as if he was followin' the trail of the wild geese.

"He was up there walkin' between the sunset an' the stars with his head bent back, and his hands stuffed into his pockets, whistlin' as if he was goin' home from school. An' such whistlin'."

"Nobody could ever whistle like Dan," she said, and smiled.

"I rode up to him, wonderin'," went on Cumberland.

"'What're you doin' round here?' I says.

"Says he, lookin' at me casual like over his shoulder: 'I'm jest takin' a stroll an' whistlin'. Does it bother you, mister?'

"'It doesn't bother me none,' says I. 'Where do you belong, sonny?'

"'Me?' says he, lookin' sort of surprised, 'why, I belong around over there!' An' he waved his hand careless over to the settin' sun.

"There was somethin' about him that made my heart swell up inside of me. I looked down into them big brown eyes and wondered—well, I don't know what I wondered; but I remembered all at once that I didn't have no son.

"'Who's your folks?' says I, gettin' more an' more curious.

"He jest looked at me sort of bored.

"'Where does your folks live at?' says I.

"'Oh, they live around here,' says he, an' he waved his hand again, an' this time over towards the east.

"Says I: 'When do you figure on reachin' home?'

"'Oh, most any day,' says he.

"An' I looked around at them brown, naked hills with the night comin' down over them. Then I stared back at the boy an' there was something that come up in me like hunger. You see, he was lost; he was alone; the queer ring of his whistlin' was still in my ears; an' I couldn't help rememberin' that I didn't have no son.

"'Then supposin' you come along with me,' says I, 'an' I'll send you home in a buckboard tomorrow?'

"So the end of it was me ridin' home with the little kid sittin' up before me, whistlin' his heart out! When I got him home I tried to talk to him again. He couldn't tell me, or he wouldn't tell me where his folks lived, but jest kept wavin' his hand liberal to half the points of the compass. An' that's all I know of where he come from. I done all I could to find his parents. I inquired and sent letters to every rancher within a hundred miles. I advertised it through the railroads, but they said nobody'd yet been reported lost. He was still mine, at least for a while, an' I was terrible glad.

"I give the kid a spare room. I sat up late that first night listenin' to the wild geese honkin' away up in the sky an' wonderin' why I was so happy. Kate, that night there was tears in my eyes when I thought of how that kid had been out there on the hills walkin' along so happy an' independent.

"But the next mornin' he was gone. I sent my cowpunchers out to look for him.

"'Which way shall we ride?' they asked.

"I don't know why, but I thought of the wild geese that Dan had seemed to be followin'.

"'Ride north,' I said.

"An' sure enough, they rode north an' found him. After that I didn't have no trouble with him about runnin' away—at least not durin' the summer. An' all those months I kept plannin' how I would take care of this boy who had come wanderin' to me. It seemed like he was sort of a gift of God to make up for me havin' no son. And everythin' went well until the next fall, when the geese began to fly south.

"Sure enough, that was when Dan ran away again, and when I sent my cowpunchers south after him, they found him and brought him back. It seemed as if they'd brought back half the world to me, when I seen him. But I saw that I'd have to put a stop to this runnin' away. I tried to talk to him, but all he'd say was that he'd better be movin' on. I took the law in my hands an' told him he had to be disciplined. So I started thrashin' him with a quirt, very light. He took it as if he didn't feel the whip on his shoulders, an' he smiled. But there came up a yellow light in his eyes that made me feel as if a man was standin' right behind me with a bare knife in his hand an' smilin' jest like the kid was doin'. Finally I simply backed out of the room, an' since that day there ain't been man or beast ever has put a hand on Whistlin' Dan. To this day I reckon he ain't quite forgiven me."

"Why!" she cried, "I have never heard him mention it!"

"That's why I know he's not forgotten it. Anyway, Kate, I locked him in his room, but he wouldn't promise not to run away. Then I got an inspiration. You was jest a little toddlin' thing then. That day you was cryin' an awful lot an' I suddenly thought of puttin' you in Dan's room. I did it. I jest unlocked the door quick and then shoved you in an' locked it again. First of all you screamed terrible hard. I was afraid maybe you'd hurt yourself yellin' that way. I was about to take you out again when all at once I heard Dan start whistlin' and pretty quick your cryin' stopped. I listened an' wondered. After that I never had to lock Dan in his room. I was sure he'd stay on account of you. But now, honey, I'm gettin' to the end of the story, an' I'm goin' to give you the straight idea the way I see it.

"I've watched Dan like—like a father, almost. I think he loves me, sort of—but I've never got over being afraid of him. You see I can't forget how he smiled when I licked him! But listen to me, Kate, that fear has been with me all the time—an' it's the only time I've ever been afraid of any man. It isn't like being scared of a man, but of a panther.

"Now we'll jest nacherally add up all the points we've made about Dan—the queer way I found him without a home an' without wantin' one—that strength he has that's like the power of a mule compared with a horse—that funny control he has over wild animals so that they almost seem to know what he means when he simply looks at them (have you noticed him with Black Bart and Satan?)—then there's the yellow light that comes in his eyes when he begins to get real mad—you an' I have both seen it only once, but we don't want to see it again! More than this there's the way he handles either a knife or a gun. He hasn't practiced much with shootin' irons, but I never seen him miss a reasonable mark— or an unreasonable one either, for that matter. I've spoke to him about it. He said: 'I dunno how it is. I don't see how a feller can shoot crooked. It jest seems that when I get out a gun there's a line drawn from the barrel to the thing I'm shootin' at. All I have to do is to pull the trigger—almost with my eyes closed!' Now,

Kate, do you begin to see what these here things point to?"

"Tell me what you see," she said, "and then I'll tell you what I think of it all."

"All right," he said. "I see in Dan a man who's different from the common run of us. I read in a book once that in the ages when men lived like animals an' had no weapons except sticks and stones, their muscles must have been two or three times as strong as they are now—more like the muscles of brutes. An' their hearin' an' their sight an' their quickness an' their endurance was about three times more than that of ordinary men. Kate, I think that Dan is one of those men the book described! He knows animals because he has all the powers that they have. An' I know from the way his eyes go yellow that he has the fightin' instinct of the ancestors of man. So far I've kept him away from other men. Which I may say is the main reason I bought Dan Morgan's place so's to keep fightin' men away from our Whistlin' Dan. So I've been hidin' him from himself. You see, he's my boy if he belongs to anybody. Maybe when time goes on he'll get tame. But I reckon not. It's like takin' a panther cub—or a wolf pup—an tryin' to raise it for a pet. Some day it gets the taste of blood, maybe its own blood, an' then it goes mad and becomes a killer. An' that's what I fear, Kate. So far I've kept Dan from ever havin' a single fight, but I reckon the day'll come when someone'll cross him, and then there'll be a tornado turned loose that'll jest about wreck these parts."

Her anger had grown during this speech. Now she rose.

"I won't believe you, Dad," she said. "I'd sooner trust our Dan than any man alive. I don't think you're right in a single word!"

"I was sure loco," sighed Cumberland, "to ever dream of convincin' a woman. Let it drop, Kate. We're about to get rid of Morgan's place, an' now I reckon there won't be any temptation near Dan. We'll see what time'll do for him. Let the thing drop there. Now I'm goin' over to the Bar XO outfit an' I won't be back till late tonight. There's only one thing more. I told Morgan there wasn't to be any gun-play in his place today. If you hear any shootin' go down there an' remind Morgan to take the guns off'n the men."

Kate nodded, but her stare travelled far away, and the thing she saw was the yellow light burning in the eyes of Whistling Dan.

CHAPTER III

It was a great day and also a sad one for Morgan. His general store and saloon had been bought out by old Joe Cumberland, who declared a determination to clear up the landscape, and thereby plunged the cowpunchers in gloom. They partially forgave Cumberland, but only because he was an old man. A younger reformer would have met armed resistance. Morgan's place was miles away from the next oasis in the desert and the closing meant dusty, thirsty leagues of added journey to every man in the neighbourhood. The word "neighbourhood," of course, covered a territory fifty miles square.

If the day was very sad for this important reason, it was also very glad, for rustling Morgan advertised the day of closing far and wide, and his most casual patrons dropped all business to attend the big doings. A long line of buckboards and cattle ponies surrounded the place. Newcomers gallopped in every few moments. Most of them did not stop to tether their mounts, but simply dropped the reins over the heads of the horses and then went with rattling spurs and slouching steps into the saloon. Every man was greeted by a shout, for one or two of those within usually knew him, and when they raised a cry the others joined in for the sake of good fellowship. As a rule he responded by ordering everyone up to the bar.

One man, however, received no more greeting than the slamming of the door behind him. He was a tall, handsome fellow with tawny hair and a little smile of habit rather than mirth upon his lips. He had ridden up on a strong bay horse, a full two hands taller than the average cattle pony, and with legs and shoulders and straight back that unmistakably told of a blooded pedigree. When he entered the saloon he seemed nowise abashed by the silence, but greeted the turned heads with a wave of the hand and a good-natured "Howdy, boys!" A volley of greetings replied to him, for in the mountain-desert men cannot be strangers after the first word.

"Line up and hit the red-eye," he went on, and leaning against the bar as he spoke, his habitual smile broadened into one of actual invitation. Except for a few groups who watched the gambling in the corners of the big room, there was a general movement towards the bar.

"And make it a tall one, boys," went on the genial stranger. "This is the first time I ever irrigated Morgan's place, and from what I have heard today about the closing I suppose it will be the last time. So here's to you, Morgan!"

And he waved his glass towards the bartender. His voice was well modulated and his enunciation bespoke education. This, in connection with his careful clothes and rather modish riding-boots, might have given him the reputation of a dude, had it not been for several other essential details of his appearance. His six-gun hung so low that he would scarcely have to raise his hand to grasp the butt. He held his whisky glass in his left hand, and the right, which rested carelessly on his hip, was deeply sunburned, as if he rarely wore a glove. Moreover, his eyes were marvellously direct, and they lingered a negligible space as they touched on each man in the room. All of this the cattlemen noted instantly. What they did not see on account of his veiling fingers was that he poured only a few drops of the liquor into his glass.

In the meantime another man who had never before "irrigated" at Morgan's place, rode up.

His mount, like that of the tawny-haired rider, was considerably larger and more finely built than the common range horse. In three days of hard work a cattle pony might wear down these blooded animals, but would find it impossible to either overtake or escape them in a straight run. The second stranger, short-legged, barrel-chested, and with a scrub of black beard, entered the barroom while the crowd was still drinking the health of Morgan. He took a corner chair, pushed back his hat until a mop of hair fell down his forehead, and began to roll a cigarette. The man of the tawny hair took the next seat.

"Seems to be quite a party, stranger," said the tall fellow nonchalantly.

"Sure," growled he of the black beard, and after a moment he added: "Been out on the trail long, pardner?"

"Hardly started."

"So'm I."

"As a matter of fact, I've got a lot of hard riding before me."

"So've I."

"And some long riding, too."

Perhaps it was because he turned his head suddenly towards the light, but a glint seemed to come in the eyes of the bearded man.

"Long rides," he said more amiably, "are sure hell on hosses."

"And on men, too," nodded the other, and tilted back in his chair.

The bearded man spoke again, but though a dozen cowpunchers were close by no one heard his voice except the man at his side. One side of his face remained perfectly immobile and his eyes stared straight before him drearily while he whispered from a corner of his mouth: "How long do you stay, Lee?"

"Noon," said Lee.

Once more the shorter man spoke in the manner which is learned in a penitentiary: "Me too. We must be slated for the same ride, Lee. Do you know what it is? It's nearly noon, and the chief ought to be here."

There was a loud greeting for a newcomer, and Lee took advantage of the noise to say quite openly: "If Silent said he'll come, he'll be here. But I say he's crazy to come to a place full of range riders, Bill."

"Take it easy," responded Bill. "This hangout is away off our regular beat. Nobody'll know him."

"His hide is his own and he can do what he wants with it," said Lee. "I warned him before."

"Shut up," murmured Bill, "Here's Jim now, and Hal Purvis with him!"

Through the door strode a great figure before whom the throng at the bar gave way as water rolls back from the tall prow of a ship. In his wake went a little man with a face dried and withered by the sun and small bright eyes which moved continually from side to side. Lee and Bill discovered their thirst at the same time and made towards the newcomers.

They had no difficulty in reaching them. The large man stood with his back to the bar, his elbows spread out on it, so that there was a little space left on either side of him. No one cared to press too close to this sombre-faced giant. Purvis stood before him and Bill and Lee were instantly at his side. The two leaned on the bar, facing him, yet the four did not seem to make a group set apart from the rest.

"Well?" asked Lee.

"I'll tell you what it is when we're on the road," said Jim Silent. "Plenty of time, Haines."

"Who'll start first?" asked Bill.

"You can, Kilduff," said the other. "Go straight north, and go slow. Then Haines will follow you. Purvis next. I come last because I got here last. There ain't any hurry—What's this here?"

"I tell you I seen it!" called an angry voice from a corner.

"You must of been drunk an' seein' double, partner," drawled the answer.

"Look here!" said the first man, "I'm willin' to take that any way you mean it!"

"An' I'm willin'," said the other, "that you should take it any way you damn please."

Everyone in the room was grave except Jim Silent and his three companions, who were smiling grimly.

"By God, Jack," said the first man with ominous softness, "I'll take a lot from you but when it comes to doubtin' my word——"

Morgan, with popping eyes and a very red face, slapped his hand on the bar and vaulted over it with more agility than his plumpness warranted. He shouldered his way hurriedly through the crowd to the rapidly widening circle around the two disputants. They stood with their right hands resting with rigid fingers low down on their hips, and their eyes, fixed on each other, forgot the rest of the world. Morgan burst in between them.

"Look here," he thundered, "it's only by way of

a favour that I'm lettin' you boys wear shootin' irons today because I promised old Cumberland there wouldn't be no fuss. If you got troubles there's enough room for you to settle them out in the hills, but there ain't none at all in here!"

The gleam went out of their eyes like four candles snuffed by the wind. Obviously they were both glad to have the tension broken. Mike wiped his forehead with a rather unsteady hand.

"I ain't huntin' for no special brand of trouble," he said, "but Jack has been ridin' the red-eye pretty hard and it's gotten into that dried up bean he calls his brain."

"Say, partner," drawled Jack, "I ain't drunk enough of the hot stuff to make me fall for the line you've been handing out."

He turned to Morgan.

"Mike, here, has been tryin' to make me believe that he knew a feller who could drill a dollar at twenty yards every time it was tossed up."

The crowd laughed, Morgan loudest of all.

"Did you anyways have Whistlin' Dan in mind?" he asked.

"No, I didn't," said Mike, "an' I didn't say this here man I was talkin' about could drill them every time. But he could do it two times out of four."

"Mike," said Morgan, and he softened his disbelief with his smile and the good-natured clap on the shoulder, "you sure must of been drinkin' when you seen him do it. I allow Whistlin' Dan could do that an' more, but he ain't human with a gun."

"How d'you know?" asked Jack, "I ain't ever seen him packin' a six-gun."

"Sure you ain't," answered Morgan, "but I have, an' I seen him use it, too. It was jest sort of by chance I saw it."

"Well," argued Mike anxiously, "then you allow it's possible if Whistlin' Dan can do it. An' I say I seen a chap who could turn the trick."

"An' who in hell is this Whistlin' Dan?" asked Jim Silent.

"He's the man that caught Satan, an' rode him," answered a bystander.

"Some man if he can ride the devil," laughed Lee Haines.

"I mean the black mustang that ran wild around here for a couple of years. Some people tell tales about him being a wonder with a gun. But Morgan's the only one who claims to have seen him work."

"Maybe you did see it, and maybe you didn't," Morgan was saying to Mike noncommittally,

3

"but there's some pretty fair shots in this room, which I'd lay fifty bucks no man here could hit a dollar with a six-gun at twenty paces."

"While they're arguin'," said Bill Kilduff, "I reckon I'll hit the trail."

"Wait a minute," grinned Jim Silent, "an' watch me have some fun with these short-horns."

He spoke more loudly: "Are you makin' that bet for the sake of arguin', partner, or do you calculate to back it up with cold cash?"

Morgan whirled upon him with a scowl, "I ain't pulled a bluff in my life that I can't back up!" he said sharply.

"Well," said Silent, "I ain't so flush that I'd turn down fifty bucks when a kind Christian soul, as the preachers say, slides it into my glove. Not me. Lead out the dollar, pal, an' kiss it farewell!"

"Who'll hold the stakes?" asked Morgan.

"Let your friend Mike," said Jim Silent carelessly, and he placed fifty dollars in gold in the hands of the Irishman. Morgan followed suit. The crowd hurried outdoors.

A dozen bets were laid in as many seconds. Most of the men wished to place their money on the side of Morgan, but there were not a few who stood willing to risk coin on Jim Silent, stranger though he was. Something in his unflinching eye, his stern face, and the nerveless surety of his movements commanded their trust.

"How do you stand, Jim?" asked Lee Haines anxiously. "Is it a safe bet? I've never seen you try a mark like this one!"

"It ain't safe," said Silent, "because I ain't mad enough to shoot my best, but it's about an even draw. Take your pick."

"Not me," said Haines, "if you had ten chances instead of one I might stack some coin on you. If the dollar were stationary I know you could do it, but a moving coin looks pretty small."

"Here you are," called Morgan, who stood at a distance of twenty paces, "are you ready?"

Silent whipped out his revolver and poised it. "Let 'er go!"

The coin whirled in the air. Silent fired as it commenced to fall—it landed untouched.

"As a kind, Christian soul," said Morgan sarcastically, "I ain't in your class, stranger. Charity always sort of interests me when I'm on the receivin' end!"

The crowd chuckled, and the sound infuriated Silent.

"Don't go back jest yet, partners," he drawled. "Mister Morgan, I got one hundred bones which holler that I can plug that dollar the second try."

"Boys," grinned Morgan, "I'm leavin' you to witness that I hate to do it, but business is business. Here you are!"

The coin whirled again. Silent, with his lips pressed into a straight line and his brows drawn dark over his eyes, waited until the coin reached the height of its rise, and then fired—missed—fired again, and sent the coin spinning through the air in a flashing semicircle. It was a beautiful piece of gun-play. In the midst of the clamour of applause Silent strode towards Morgan with his hand outstretched.

"After all," he said. "I knowed you wasn't really hard of heart. It only needed a little time and persuasion to make you dig for coin when I pass the box."

Morgan, red of face and scowling, handed over his late winnings and his own stakes.

"It took you two shots to do it," he said, "an' if I wanted to argue the pint maybe you wouldn't walk off with the coin."

"Partner," said Jim Silent gently, "I got a wanderin' hunch that you're showin' a pile of brains by not arguin' this here pint!"

There followed that little hush of expectancy

which precedes trouble, but Morgan, after a glance at the set lips of his opponent, swallowed his wrath.

"I s'pose you'll tell how you did this to your kids when you're eighty," he said scornfully, "but around here, stranger, they don't think much of it. Whistlin' Dan"—he paused, as if to calculate how far he could safely exaggerate—"Whistlin' Dan can stand with his back to the coins an' when they're thrown he drills four dollars easier than you did one—an' he wouldn't waste three shots on one dollar. He ain't so extravagant!"

CHAPTER IV

SOMETHING YELLOW

THE crowd laughed again at the excitement of Morgan, and Silent's mirth particularly was loud and long.

"An' if you're still bent on charity," he said at last, "maybe we could find somethin' else to lay a bet on!"

"Anything you name!" said Morgan hotly.

"I suppose," said Silent, "that you're some rider, eh?"

"I c'n get by with most of 'em."

"Yeh—I suppose you never pulled leather in your life?"

"Not any hoss that another man could ride straight up."

"Is that so? Well, partner, you see that roan over there?"

"That tall horse?"

"You got him. You c'n win back that hundred if you stick on his back two minutes. D'you take it?"

Morgan hesitated a moment.   The big roan was
footing it nervously here and there, sometimes
throwing up his head suddenly after the manner of
a horse of bad temper.   However, the loss of that
hundred dollars and the humiliation which accompanied it, weighed heavily on the saloon owner's
mind.

"I'll take you," he said.

A high, thrilling whistle came faintly from the
distance.

"That fellow on the black horse down the
road," said Lee Haines, "I guess he's the one that
can hit the four dollars?   Ha! ha! ha!"

"Sure," grinned Silent, "listen to his whistle!
We'll see if we can drag another bet out of the
bar-keep if the roan doesn't hurt him too bad.
Look at him now!"

Morgan was having a bad time getting his foot
in the stirrup, for the roan reared and plunged.
Finally two men held his head and the saloon-
keeper swung into the saddle.   There was a little
silence.   The roan, as if doubtful that he could
really have this new burden on his back, and still
fearful of the rope which had been lately tethering
him, went a few short, prancing steps, and then,
feeling something akin to freedom, reared straight
up, snorting.   The crowd yelled with delight, and

the sound sent the roan back to all fours and racing
down the road.   He stopped with braced feet, and
Morgan lurched forwards on the neck, yet he
struck to his seat gamely.   Whistling Dan was not
a hundred yards away.

Morgan yelled and swung the quirt.   The
response of the roan was another race down the
road at terrific speed, despite the pull of Morgan
on the reins.   Just as the running horse reached
Whistling Dan, he stopped as short as he had done
before, but this time with an added buck and a
sidewise lurch all combined, which gave the effect
of snapping a whip—and poor Morgan was hurled
from the saddle like a stone from a sling.   The
crowd waved their hats and yelled with delight.

"Look out!" yelled Jim Silent.   "Grab the
reins!"

But though Morgan made a valiant effort the
roan easily swerved past him and went racing down
the road.

"My God," groaned Silent, "he's gone!"

"Saddles!" called someone.   "We'll catch
him!"

"Catch hell!" answered Silent bitterly.   There
ain't a hoss on earth that can catch him—an' now
that he ain't got the weight of a rider, he'll run
away from the wind!"

"Anyway there goes Dan on Satan after him!"

"No use! The roan ain't carryin' a thing but the saddle."

"Satan never seen the day he could make the roan eat dust, anyway!"

"Look at 'em go, boys!"

"There ain't no use," said Jim Silent sadly, "he'll wind his black for nothin'—an' I've lost the best hoss on the ranges."

"I believe him," whispered one man to a neighbour, "because I've got an idea that hoss is Red Peter himself!"

His companion stared at him agape.

"Red Pete!" he said. "Why, pal, that's the hoss that Silent——"

"Maybe it is an' maybe it ain't. But why should we ask too many questions?"

"Let the marshals tend to him. He ain't ever troubled this part of the range."

"Anyway, I'm goin' to remember his face. If it's really Jim Silent, I got something that's worth tellin' to my kids when they grow up."

They both turned and looked at the tall man with an uncomfortable awe. The rest of the crowd swarmed into the road to watch the race.

The black stallion was handicapped many yards at the start before Dan could swing him around after the roan darted past with poor Morgan in ludicrous pursuit. Moreover, the roan had the inestimable advantage of an empty saddle. Yet Satan leaned to his work with a stout heart. There was no rock and pitch to his gait, no jerk and labour to his strides. Those smooth shoulders were corded now with a thousand lines where the steel muscles whipped to and fro. His neck stretched out a little—his ears laid back along the neck—his whole body settled gradually and continually down as his stride lengthened. Whistling Dan was leaning forward so that his body would break less wind. He laughed low and soft as the air whirred into his face, and now and then he spoke to his horse, no yell of encouragement, but a sound hardly louder than a whisper. There was no longer a horse and rider—the two had become one creature—a centaur—the body of a horse and the mind of a man.

For a time the roan increased his advantage, but quickly Satan began to hold him even, and then gain. First inch by inch; then at every stride the distance between them diminished. No easy task. The great roan had muscle, heart, and that empty saddle; as well, perhaps, as a thought of the free ranges which lay before him and liberty from the accursed thraldom of the bit and reins and galling spurs. What he lacked was that small whispering voice—that hand touching lightly now and then on his neck—that thrill of generous sympathy which passes between horse and rider. He lost ground steadily and more and more rapidly. Now the outstretched black head was at his tail, now at his flank, now at his girth, now at his shoulder, now they raced nose and nose. Whistling Dan shifted in the saddle. His left foot took the opposite stirrup. His right leg swung free.

The big roan swerved—the black in response to a word from his rider followed the motion—and then the miracle happened. A shadow plunged through the air; a weight thudded on the saddle of the roan; an iron hand jerked back the reins.

Red Pete hated men and feared them, but this new weight on his back was different. It was not the pressure on the reins which urged him to slow up; he had the bit in his teeth and no human hand could pull down his head; but into the blind love, blind terror, blind rage which makes up the consciousness of a horse entered a force which he had never known before. He realized suddenly that it was folly to attempt to throw off this cling-ing burden. He might as well try to jump out of his skin. His racing stride shortened to a halting gallop, this to a sharp trot, and in a moment more he was turned and headed back for Morgan's place. The black, who had followed, turned at the same time like a dog and followed with jouncing bridle reins. Black Bart, with lolling red tongue, ran under his head, looking up to the stallion now and again with a comical air of proprietorship, as if he were showing the way.

It was very strange to Red Pete. He pranced sideways a little and shook his head up and down in an effort to regain his former temper, but that iron hand kept his nose down, now, and that quiet voice sounded above him—no cursing, no raking of sharp spurs to torture his tender flanks, no whir of the quirt, but a calm voice of authority and understanding. Red Pete broke into an easy canter and in this fashion they came up to Morgan in the road. Red Pete snorted and started to shy, for he recognized the clumsy, bouncing weight which had insulted his back not long before; but this quiet voiced master reassured him, and he came to a halt.

"That red devil has cost me a hundred bones and all the skin on my knees," groaned Morgan, "and I can hardly walk. Damn his eyes. But say, Dan"—and his eyes glowed with an admiration which made him momentarily forget his pains—"that was some circus stunt you done down the road there—that changin' of saddles on the run, I never seen the equal of it!"

"If you got hurt in the fall," said Dan quietly, overlooking the latter part of the speech, "why don't you climb onto Satan. He'll take you back."

Morgan laughed.

"Say, kid, I'd take a chance with Satan, but there ain't any hospital for fools handy."

"Go ahead. He won't stir a foot. Steady, Satan!"

"All right," said Morgan, "every step is sure like pullin' teeth!"

He ventured closer to the black stallion, but was stopped short. Black Bart was suddenly changed to a green-eyed devil, his hair bristling around his shoulders, his teeth bared, and a snarl that came from the heart of a killer. Satan also greeted his proposed rider with ears laid flat back on his neck and a quivering anger.

"If I'm goin' to ride Satan," declared Morgan, " I got to shoot the dog first and then blindfold the hoss."

"No you don't," said Dan. "No one else has ever had a seat on Satan, but I got an idea he'll make an exception for a sort of temporary cripple.

Steady, boy. Here you, Bart, come over here an'
keep your face shut!"

The dog, after a glance at his master, moved
reluctantly away, keeping his eyes upon Morgan.
Satan backed away with a snort. He stopped at
the command of Dan, but when Morgan laid a
hand on the bridle and spoke to him he trembled
with fear and anger. The saloon-keeper turned
away.

"Thankin' you jest the same, Dan," he said,
"I think I c'n walk back. I'd as soon ride a tame
tornado as that hoss."

He limped on down the road with Dan riding
beside him. Black Bart slunk at his heels, sniffing.

"Dan, I'm goin' to ask you a favour—an' a big
one; will you do it for me?"

"Sure," said Whistling Dan. "Anything I
can."

"There's a skunk down there with a bad eye
an' a gun that jumps out of its leather like it had a
mind of its own. He picked me for fifty bucks by
nailing a dollar I tossed up at twenty yards.
Then he gets a hundred because I couldn't ride this
hoss of his. Which he's made a plumb fool of me,
Dan. Now I was tellin' him about you—maybe
I was sort of exaggeratin'—an' I said you could
have your back turned when the coins was tossed

an' then pick off four dollars before they hit the ground. I made it a bit high, Dan?"

His eyes were wistful.

"Nick four round boys before they hit the dust?" said Dan. "Maybe I could, I don't know. I can't try it, anyway, Morgan, because I told Dad Cumberland I'd never pull a gun while there was a crowd aroun'."

Morgan sighed; he hesitated, and then: "But you promised you'd do me a favour, Dan?"

The rider started.

"I forgot about that—I didn't think——"

"It's only to do a shootin' trick," said Morgan eagerly. It ain't pullin' a gun on any one. Why, lad, if you'll tell me you got a ghost of a chance, I'll bet every cent in my cash drawer on you agin that skunk! You've give me your word, Dan."

Whistling Dan shrugged his shoulders.

"I've given you my word," he said, "an' I'll do it. But I guess Dad Cumberland'll be mighty sore on me."

A laugh rose from the crowd at Morgan's place, which they were nearing rapidly. It was like a mocking comment on Dan's speech. As they came closer they could see money changing hands in all directions.

"What'd you do to my hoss?" asked Jim Silent, walking out to meet them.

"He hypnotized him," said Hal Purvis, and his lips twisted over yellow teeth into a grin of satis-, faction.

"Git out of the saddle damn quick," growled Silent. "It ain't nacheral he'd let you ride him like he was a plough-hoss. An' if you've tried any fancy stunts, I'll——"

"Take it easy," said Purvis as Dan slipped from the saddle without showing the slightest anger. "Take it easy. You're a bum loser. When I seen the black settle down to his work," he explained to Dan with another grin, "I knowed he'd nail him in the end an' I staked twenty on you agin my friend here! That was sure a slick change of hosses you made."

There were other losers. Money chinked on all sides to an accompaniment of laughter and curses. Jim Silent was examining the roan with a scowl, while Bill Kilduff and Hal Purvis approached Satan to look over his points. Purvis reached out towards the bridle when a murderous snarl at his feet made him jump back with a shout. He stood with his gun poised, facing Black Bart.

"Who's got any money to bet this damn wolf lives more'n five seconds?" he said savagely.

"I have," said Dan.

"Who in hell are you? What d'you mean by trailing this man-killer around?"

He turned to Dan with his gun still poised.

"Bart ain't a killer," said Dan, and the gentleness of his voice was oil on troubled waters, "but he gets peeved when a stranger comes nigh to the hoss."

"All right this time," said Purvis, slowly restoring his gun to its holster, "but if this wolf of yours looks cross-eyed at me agin he'll hit the long trail that ain't got any end, savvy?"

"Sure," said Dan, and his soft brown eyes smiled placatingly.

Purvis kept his right hand close to the butt of his gun and his eyes glinted as if he expected an answer somewhat stronger than words. At this mild acquiesence he turned away, sneering. Silent, having discovered that he could find no fault with Dan's treatment of his horse, now approached with an ominously thin-lipped smile. Lee Haines read his face and came to his side with a whisper: "Better cut out the rough stuff, Jim. This chap hasn't hurt anything but your cash, and he's already taken water from Purvis. I guess there's no call for you to make any play."

"Shut your face, Haines," responded Silent, in

4

the same tone. "He's made a fool of me by showin' up my hoss, an' by God I'm goin' to give him a man-handlin' he'll never forgit."

He whirled on Morgan.

"How about it, bar-keep, is this the dead shot you was spillin' so many words about?"

Dan, as if he could not understand the broad insult, merely smiled at him with marvellous good nature.

"Keep away from him, stranger," warned Morgan. "Jest because he rode your hoss you ain't got a cause to hunt trouble with him. He's been taught not to fight."

Silent, still looking Dan over with insolent eyes, replied: "He sure sticks to his daddy's lessons. Nice an' quiet an' house broke, ain't he? In my part of the country they dress this kind of a man in gal's clothes so's nobody'll ever get sore at him an' spoil his pretty face. Better go home to your ma. This ain't any place for you. They's men aroun' here."

There was another one of those grimly expectant hushes and then a general guffaw; Dan showed no inclination to take offence. He merely stared at brawny Jim Silent with a sort of childlike wonder.

"All right," he said meekly, "if I ain't wanted around here I figger there ain't any cause why I should stay. You don't figger to be peeved at me, do you?"

The laughter changed to a veritable yell of delight. Even Silent smiled with careless contempt.

"No, kid," he answered, "if I was peeved at you, you'd learn it without askin' questions."

He turned slowly away.

"Maybe I got jaundice, boys," he said to the crowd, "but it seems to me I see something kind of yellow around here!"

The delightful subtlety of this remark roused another side-shaking burst of merriment. Dan shook his head as if the mystery were beyond his comprehension, and looked to Morgan for an explanation. The saloon-keeper approached him, struggling with a grin.

"It's all right, Dan," he said. "Don't let 'em rile you."

"You ain't got any cause to fear that," said Silent, "because it can't be done."

CHAPTER V

FOUR IN THE AIR

DAN looked from Morgan to Silent and back again for understanding. He felt that something was wrong, but what it was he had not the slightest idea. For many years old Joe Cumberland had patiently taught him that the last offence against God and man was to fight. The old cattleman had instilled in him the belief that if he did not cross the path of another, no one would cross his way. The code was perfect and satisfying. He would let the world alone and the world would not trouble him. The placid current of his life had never come to "white waters" of wrath.

Wherefore he gazed bewildered about him. They were laughing—they were laughing unpleasantly at him as he had seen men laugh at a fiery young colt which struggled against the rope. It was very strange. They could not mean harm. Therefore he smiled back at them rather uncertainly. Morgan slapped at his shoulder by way of good-fellowship and to hearten him, but Dan slipped away under the extended hand with a motion as subtle and swift as the twist of a snake when it flees for its hole. He had a deep aversion for contact with another man's body. He hated it as the wild horse hates the shadow of the flying rope.

"Steady up, pal," said Morgan, "the lads mean no harm. That tall man is considerable riled; which he'll now bet his sombrero agin you when it comes to shootin'."

He turned back to Silent.

"Look here, partner," he said, "this is the man I said could nail the four dollars before they hit the dust. I figger you don't think how it can be done, eh?"

"Him?" said Silent in deep disgust. "Send him back to his ma before somebody musses him all up! Why, he don't even pack a gun!"

Morgan waited a long moment so that the little silence would make his next speech impressive.

"Stranger," he said, "I've still got somewhere in the neighbourhood of five hundred dollars in that cash drawer. An' every cent of it hollers that Dan can do what I said."

Silent hesitated. His code was loose, but he did not like to take advantage of a drunk or a crazy man. However, five hundred dollars was five hundred dollars. Moreover that handsome fellow who had just taken water from Hal Purvis and was now smiling foolishly at his own shame, had actually ridden Red Peter. The remembrance infuriated Silent.

"Hurry up," said Morgan confidently. "I dunno what you're thinkin', stranger. Which I'm kind of deaf an' I don't understand the way anything talks except money."

"Corral that talk, Morgan!" called a voice from the crowd, "you're plumb locoed if you think any man in the world can get away with a stunt like that! Pick four in the air!"

"You keep your jaw for yourself," said Silent angrily, "if he wants to donate a little more money to charity, let him do it. Morgan, I've got five hundred here to cover your stake."

"Make him give you odds, Morgan," said another voice, "because——"

A glance from Silent cut the suggestion short. After that there was little loud conversation. The stakes were large. The excitement made the men hush the very tones in which they spoke. Morgan moistened his white lips.

"You c'n see I'm not packin' any shootin' irons," said Dan. "Has anybody got any suggestions?"

Every gun in the crowd was instantly at his service. They were heartily tempted to despise Dan, but as one with the courage to attempt the impossible, they would help him as far as they could. He took their guns one after the other, weighed them, tried the action, and handed them back. It was almost as if there were a separate intelligence in the ends of his fingers which informed him of the qualities of each weapon.

"Nice gun," he said to the first man whose revolver he handled, "but I don't like a barrel that's quite so heavy. There's a whole ounce too much in the barrel."

"What d'you mean?" asked the cowpuncher. "I've packed that gun for pretty nigh eight years!"

"Sorry," said Dan passing on, "but I can't work right with a top-heavy gun."

The next weapon he handed back almost at once.

"What's the matter with that?" asked the owner aggressively.

"Cylinder too tight," said Dan decisively, and a moment later to another man, "Bad handle. I don't like the feel of it."

Over Jim Silent's guns he paused longer than over most of the rest, but finally he handed them back. The big man scowled.

Dan looked back to him in gentle surprise.

"You see," he explained quietly, "you got to handle a gun like a horse. If you don't treat it right it won't treat you right. That's all I know about it. Your gun ain't very clean, stranger, an' a gun that ain't kept clean gets off feet."

Silent glanced at his weapons, cursed softly, and restored them to the holsters.

"Lee," he muttered to Haines, who stood next to him, "what do you think he meant by that? D' you figger he's got somethin' up his sleeve, an' that's why he acts so like a damned woman?"

"I don't know," said Haines gravely, "he looks to me sort of queer—sort of different—damned different, chief!"

By this time Dan had secured a second gun which suited him. He whirled both guns, tried their actions alternately, and then announced that he was ready. In the dead silence, one of the men paced off the twenty yards.

Dan, with his back turned, stood at the mark, shifting his revolvers easily in his hands, and smiling down at them as if they could understand his caress.

"How you feelin', Dan?" asked Morgan anxiously.

"Everything fine," he answered.

"Are you gettin' weak?"

"No, I'm all right."

"Steady up, partner."

"Steady up? Look at my hand!"

Dan extended his arm. There was not a quiver in it.

"All right, Dan. When you're shootin', remember that I got pretty close to everything I own staked on you. There's the stranger gettin' his four dollars ready."

Silent took his place with the four dollars in his hand.

"Are you ready?" he called.

"Let her go!" said Dan, apparently without the least excitement.

Jim Silent threw the coins, and he threw them so as to increase his chances as much as possible. A little snap of his hand gave them a rapid rotary motion so that each one was merely a speck of winking light. He flung them high, for it was probable that Whistling Dan would wait to shoot until they were on the way down. The higher he threw them the more rapidly they would be travelling when they crossed the level of the markman's eye.

As a shout proclaimed the throwing of the coins, Dan whirled, and it seemed to the bystanders that a revolver exploded before he was fully turned; but one of the coins never rose to the height of the throw.   There was a light "cling!" and it spun a dozen yards away.   Two more shots blended almost together; two more dollars darted away in twinkling streaks of light.   One coin still fell, but when it was a few inches from the earth a six-shooter barked again and the fourth dollar glanced sidewise into the dust.   It takes long to describe the feat.   Actually, the four shots consumed less than a second of time.

"That last dollar," said Dan, and his soft voice was the first sound out of the silence, "wasn't good.   It didn't ring true.   Counterfeit?"

It seemed that no one heard his words.   The men were making a wild scramble for the dollars. They dived into the dust for them, rising white of face and clothes to fight and struggle over their prizes.   Those dollars with the chips and neat round holes in them would confirm the truth of a story that the most credulous might be tempted to laugh or scorn.   A cowpuncher offered ten dollars for one of the relics—but none would part with a prize.

The moment the shooting was over Dan stepped quietly back and restored the guns to the owners. The first man seized his weapon carelessly.   He was in the midst of his rush after one of the chipped coins. The other cowpuncher received his weapon almost with reverence.

"I'm thankin' you for the loan," said Dan, "an here's hopin' you always have luck with the gun."

"Luck?" said the other. "I sure *will* have luck with it. I'm goin' to oil her up and put her in a glass case back home, an' when I get grandchildren I'm goin' to point out that gun to 'em and tell 'em what men used to do in the old days. Let's go in an' surround some red-eye at my expense."

"No thanks," answered Dan, "I ain't drinkin'."

He stepped back to the edge of the circle and folded his arms. It was as if he had walked out of the picture. He suddenly seemed to be aloof from them all.

Out of the quiet burst a torrent of curses, exclamations, and shouts. Chance drew Jim Silent and his three followers together.

"My God!" whispered Lee Haines, with a sort of horror in his voice, "it wasn't human! Did you see? Did you see?"

"Am I blind?" asked Hal Purvis, "an' think of me walkin' up an' bracin' that killer like he was a two-year-old kid! I figger that's the nearest I ever come to a undeserved grave, an' I've had some close calls! 'That last dollar wasn't good! It didn't ring true,' says he when he finished. I never seen such nerve!"

"You're wrong as hell," said Silent, "a *woman* can shoot at a target, but it takes a cold *nerve* to shoot at a man—an' this feller is yellow all through!"

"Is he?" growled Bill Kilduff, "well, I'd hate to take him by surprise, so's he'd forget himself. He gets as much action out of a common six-gun as if it was a gatling. He was right about that last dollar, too. It was pure—lead!"

"All right, Haines," said Silent. "You c'n start now any time, an' the rest of us'll follow on the way I said. I'm leavin' last. I got a little job to finish up with the kid."

But Haines was staring fixedly down the road.

"I'm not leaving yet," said Haines. "Look!"

He turned to one of the cowpunchers.

"Who's the girl riding up the road, pardner?"

"That calico? She's Kate Cumberland—old Joe's gal."

"I like the name," said Haines. "She sits the saddle like a man!"

Her pony darted off from some imaginary object in the middle of the road, and she swayed gracefully, following the sudden motion. Her mount came to the sudden halt of the cattle pony and she slipped to the ground before Morgan could run out to help. Even Lee Haines, who was far quicker, could not reach her in time.

"Sorry I'm late," said Haines. "Shall I tie your horse?"

The fast ride had blown colour to her face and good spirits into her eyes. She smiled up to him, and as she shook her head in refusal her eyes lingered a pardonable moment on his handsome face, with the stray lock of tawny hair fallen low across his forehead. She was used to frank admiration, but this unembarrassed courtesy was a new world to her. She was still smiling when she turned to Morgan.

"You told my father the boys wouldn't wear guns today."

He was somewhat confused.

"They seem to be wearin' them," he said weakly, and his eyes wandered about the armed circle, pausing on the ominous forms of Hal Purvis, Bill Kilduff, and especially Jim Silent, a head taller than the rest. He stood somewhat in the background, but the slight sneer with which he watched Whistling Dan dominated the entire picture.

"As a matter of fact," went on Morgan, "it

would be a ten man job to take the guns away from this crew. You can see for yourself."

She glanced about the throng and started. She had seen Dan.

"How did he come here?"

"Oh, Dan?" said Morgan, "he's all right. He just pulled one of the prettiest shootin' stunts I ever seen."

"But he promised my father—" began Kate, and then stopped, flushing.

If her father was right in diagnosing Dan's character, this was the most critical day in his life, for there he stood surrounded by armed men. If there were anything wild in his nature it would be brought out that day. She was almost glad the time of trial had come.

She said: "How about the guns, Mr. Morgan?"

"If you want them collected and put away for a while," offered Lee Haines, "I'll do what I can to help you!"

Her smile of thanks set his blood tingling. His glance lingered a little too long, a little too gladly, and she coloured slightly.

"Miss Cumberland," said Haines, "may I introduce myself? My name is Lee."

She hesitated. The manners she had learned in the Eastern school forbade it, but her Western instinct was truer and stronger. Her hand went out to him.

"I'm very glad to know you, Mr. Lee."

"All right, stranger," said Morgan, who in the meantime had been shifting from one foot to the other and estimating the large chances of failure in this attempt to collect the guns, "if you're going to help me corral the shootin' irons, let's start the roundup."

The girl went with them. They had no trouble in getting the weapons. The cold blue eye of Lee Haines was a quick and effective persuasion.

When they reached Jim Silent he stared fixedly upon Haines. Then he drew his guns slowly and presented them to his comrade, while his eyes shifted to Kate and he said coldly: "Lady, I hope I ain't the last one to congratulate you!"

She did not understand, but Haines scowled and coloured. Dan, in the meantime, was swept into the saloon by an influx of the cowpunchers that left only Lee Haines outside with Kate. She had detained him with a gesture.

CHAPTER VI

LAUGHTER

"Mr. Lee," she said, "I am going to ask you to do me a favour. Will you?"

His smile was a sufficient answer, and it was in her character that she made no pretext of misunderstanding it.

"You have noticed Dan among the crowd?" she asked, "Whistling Dan?"

"Yes," he said, "I saw him do some very nice shooting."

"It's about him that I want to speak to you. Mr. Lee, he knows very little about men and their ways. He is almost a child among them. You seem—stronger—than most of the crowd here. Will you see that if trouble comes he is not imposed upon?"

She flushed a little, there was such a curious yearning in the eyes of the big man.

"If you wish it," he said simply, "I will do what I can."

As he walked beside her towards her horse, she turned to him abruptly.

"You are very different from the men I have met around here," she said.

"I am glad," he answered.

"Glad?"

"If you find me different, you will remember me, whether for better or worse."

He spoke so earnestly that she grew grave. He helped her to the saddle and she leaned a little to study him with the same gentle gravity.

"I should like to see you again, Mr. Lee," she said, and then in a little outburst, "I should like to see you a *lot!* Will you come to my house sometime?"

The directness, the sudden smile, made him flinch. His voice was a trifle unsteady when he replied.

"I *shall!*" He paused and his hand met hers. "If it is possible."

Her eyebrows raised a trifle.

"Is it so hard to do?"

"Do not ask me to explain," he said, "I am riding a long way."

"Oh, a 'long-rider'!" she laughed, "then of course—" She stopped abruptly. It may have been imagination, but he seemed to start when she

5

spoke the phrase by which outlaws were known to each other. He was forcing his eyes to meet hers.

He said slowly: "I am going on a long journey. Perhaps I will come back. If I am able to, I shall."

He dropped his hand from hers and she remained silent, guessing at many things, and deeply moved, for every woman knows when a man speaks from his soul.

"You will not forget me?"

"I shall never forget you," she answered quietly. "Good-bye, Mr. Lee!"

Her hand touched his again, she wheeled, and rode away. He remained standing with the hand she had grasped still raised. And after a moment, as he had hoped, she turned in the saddle and waved to him. His eyes were downward and he was smiling faintly when he re-entered the saloon.

Silent sat at a table with his chin propped in his hand—his left hand, of course, for that restless right hand must always be free. He stared across the room towards Whistling Dan. The train of thoughts which kept those ominous eyes so unmoving must be broken. He sat down at the side of his chief.

"What the hell?" said the big man, "ain't you started yet?"

"Look here, Jim," said Haines cautiously, "I want you to lay off on this kid, Whistling Dan. It won't meant anything to you to raise the devil with him."

"I tell you," answered Silent, "it'll please me more'n anything in the world to push that damned girl face of his into the floor."

"Silent, I'm asking a personal favour of you!"

The leader turned upon him that untamed stare. Haines set his teeth.

"Haines," came the answer, "I'll stand more from you than from any man alive. I know you've got guts an' I know you're straight with me. But there ain't' anything can keep me from man-handlin' that kid over there." He opened and shut his fingers slowly. "I sort of yearn to get at him!"

Haines recognized defeat.

"But you haven't another gun hidden on you, Jim? You won't try to shoot him up?"

"No," said Silent. "If I had a gun I don't know—but I haven't a gun. My hands'll be enough!"

All that could be done now was to get Whistling Dan out of the saloon. That would be simple. A single word would suffice to send the timid man helter-skelter homewards.

The large, lazy brown eyes turned up to Haines as the latter approached.

"Dan," he said, "hit for the timbers—get on your way—there's danger here for you!"

To his astonishment the brown eyes did not vary a shade.

"Danger?" he repeated wonderingly.

"Danger! Get up and get out if you want to save your hide!"

"What's the trouble?" said Dan, and his eyes were surprised, but not afraid.

"The biggest man in this room is after your blood."

"Is he?" said Dan wonderingly. "I'm sorry I don't feel like leavin', but I'm not tired of this place yet."

"Friend," said Haines, "if that tall man puts his hands on you, he'll break you across his knee like a rotten stick of wood!"

It was too late. Silent evidently guessed that Haines was urging his quarry to flee.

"Hey!" he roared, so that all heads turned towards him, "you over there."

Haines stepped back, sick at heart. He knew that it would be folly to meet his chief hand to hand, but he thought of his pledge to Kate, and groaned.

"What do you want of me?" asked Dan, for the pointed arm left no doubt as to whom Silent intended.

"Get up when you're spoke to" cried Silent. "Ain't you learned no manners? An' git up quick!"

Dan rose, smiling his surprise.

"Your friend has a sort of queer way of talkin'," he said to Haines.

"Don't stan' there like a fool. Trot over to the bar an' git me a jolt of red-eye. I'm dry!" thundered Silent.

"Sure!" nodded Whistling Dan amiably, "glad to!" and he went accordingly towards the bar.

The men about the room looked to each other with sick smiles. There was an excuse for acquiescence, for the figure of Jim Silent contrasted with Whistling Dan was like an oak compared with a sapling. Nevertheless such bland cowardice as Dan was showing made their flesh creep. He asked at the bar for the whisky, and Morgan spoke as Dan filled a glass nearly to the brim.

"Dan," he whispered rapidly, "I got a gun behind the bar. Say the word an' I'll take the chance of pullin' it on that big skunk. Then you make a dive for the door.   Maybe I can keep him back till you get on Satan."

"Why should I beat it?" queried Dan, astonished.   "I'm jest beginnin' to get interested in your place.   That tall feller is sure a queer one, ain't he?"

With the same calm and wide-eyed smile of inquiry he turned away, taking the glass of liquor, and left Morgan to stare after him with a face pale with amazement, while he whispered over and over to himself: "Well, I'll be damned! Well, I'll be damned!"

Dan placed the liquor before Silent.   The latter sat gnawing his lips.

"What in hell do you mean?" he said.   "Did you only bring one glass?   Are you too damn good to drink with me?   Then drink by yourself, you white-livered coyote!"

He dashed the glass of whisky into Dan's face. Half blinded by the stinging liquor, the latter fell back a pace, sputtering, and wiping his eyes. Not a man in the room stirred.   The same sick look was on each face.   But the red devil broke loose in Silent's heart when he saw Dan cringe. He followed the thrown glass with his clenched fist. Dan stood perfectly still and watched the blow coming   His eyes were wide and wondering, like those of a child. The iron-hard hand struck him full on the mouth, fairly lifted him from his feet, and flung him against the wall with such violence that he recoiled again and fell forward onto his knees. Silent was making beast noises in his throat and preparing to rush on the half-prostrate figure. He stopped short.

Dan was laughing. At least that chuckling murmur was near to a laugh. Yet there was no mirth in it. It had that touch of the maniacal in it which freezes the blood. Silent halted in the midst of his rush, with his hands poised for the next blow. His mouth fell agape with an odd expression of horror as Dan stared up at him. That hideous chuckling continued. The sound defied definition. And from the shadow in which Dan was crouched his brown eyes blazed, changed, and filled with yellow fires.

"God!" whispered Silent, and at that instant the ominous crouched animal with the yellow eyes, the nameless thing which had been Whistling Dan a moment before, sprang up and forward with a leap like that of a panther.

Morgan stood behind the bar with a livid face and a fixed smile. His fingers still stiffly clutched the whisky bottle from which the last glass had been filled. Not another man in the room stirred from his place. Some sat with their cards raised in the very act of playing. Some had stopped midway a laugh. One man had been tying a boot-lace. His body did not rise. Only his eyes rolled up to watch.

Dan darted under the outstretched arms of Silent, fairly heaved him up from the floor and drove him backwards. The big man half stumbled and half fell, knocking aside two chairs. He rushed back with a shout, but at sight of the white face with the thin trickle of blood falling from the lips, and at the sound of that inhuman laughter, he paused again.

Once more Dan was upon him, his hands darting out with motions too fast for the eye to follow. Jim Silent stepped back a half pace, shifted his weight, and drove his fist straight at that white face. How it happened not a man in the room could tell, but the hand did not strike home. Dan had swerved aside as lightly as a wind-blown feather and his fist rapped against Silent's ribs with a force that made the giant grunt.

Some of the horror was gone from his face and in its stead was baffled rage. He knew the scientific points of boxing, and he applied them. His eye was quick and sure. His reach was whole inches longer than his opponent's. His strength

was that of two ordinary men. What did it avail
him? He was like an agile athlete in the circus
playing tag with a black panther. He was like
a child striking futilely at a wavering butterfly.
Sometimes this white-faced, laughing devil ducked
under his arms. Sometimes a sidestep made his
blows miss by the slightest fraction of an inch.

And for every blow he struck four rained home
against him. It was impossible! It could not
be! Silent telling himself that he dreamed, and
those dancing fists crashed into his face and body
like sledgehammers. There was no science in
the thing which faced him. Had there been trained
skill the second blow would have knocked Silent
unconscious, and he knew it, but Dan made no
effort to strike a vulnerable spot. He hit at
anything which offered.

Still he laughed as he leaped back and forth.
Perhaps mere weight of rushing would beat the
dancing will-o'-the-wisp to the floor. Silent bored
in with lowered head and clutched at his enemy.
Then he roared with triumph. His outstretched
hand caught Dan's shirt as the latter flicked to
one side. Instantly they were locked in each
other's arms! The most meaning part of the
fight followed.

The moment after they grappled, Silent shifted

his right arm from its crushing grip on Dan's body and clutched at the throat. The move was as swift as lightning, but the parry of the smaller man was still quicker. His left hand clutched Silent by the wrist, and that mighty sweep of arm was stopped in mid-air! They were in the middle of the room. They stood perfectly erect and close together, embraced. Their position had a ludicrous resemblance to the posture of dancers, but their bodies were trembling with effort. With every ounce of power in his huge frame Silent strove to complete his grip at the throat. He felt the right arm of Dan tightening around him closer, closer, closer! It was not a bulky arm, but it seemed to be made of linked steel which was shrinking into him, and promised to crush his very bones. The strength of this man seemed to increase. It was limitless. His breath came struggling under that pressure and the blood thundered and raged in his temples. If he could only get at that soft throat!

But his struggling right hand was held in a vice of iron. Now his numb arm gave way, slowly, inevitably. He ground his teeth and cursed. His curse was half a prayer. For answer there was the unearthly chuckle just below his ear. His hand was moved back, down, around! He was helpless

as a child in the arms of its father—no, helpless as
a sheep in the constricting coils of a python.

An impulse of frantic horror and shame and fear
gave him redoubled strength for an instant. He
tore himself clear and reeled back. Dan planted
two smashes on Silent's snarling mouth. A glance
showed the large man the mute, strained faces
around the room. The laughing devil leaped
again. Then all pride slipped like water from the
heart of Jim Silent, and in its place there was only
icy fear, fear not of a man, but of animal power.
He caught up a heavy chair and drove it with all
his desperate strength at Dan.

It cracked distinctly against his head and the
weight of it fairly drove him into the floor. He
fell with a limp thud on the boards. Silent, reeling
and blind, staggered to and fro in the centre of
the room. Morgan and Lee Haines reached Dan
at the same moment and kneeled beside him.

CHAPTER VII

THE MUTE MESSENGER

ALMOST at once Haines raised a hand and spoke to the crowd: "He's all right, boys. Badly cut across the head and stunned, but he'll live."

There was a deep gash on the upper part of the forehead. If the cross-bar of the chair had not broken, the skull might have been injured. The impact of the blow had stunned him, and it might be many minutes before his senses returned.

As the crowd closed around Dan, a black body leaped among them, snarling hideously. They sprang back with a yell from the rush of this green-eyed fury; but Black Bart made no effort to attack them. He sat crouching before the prostrate body, licking the deathly white face, and growling horribly, and then stood over his fallen master and stared about the circle. Those who had seen a lone wolf make its stand against a pack of dogs recognized the attitude. Then without a sound, as swiftly as he had entered the room, he leaped through the door and darted off up the road. Satan, for the first time deserted by this wolfish companion, turned a high head and neighed after him, but he raced on.

The men returned to their work over Dan's body, cursing softly. There was a hair-raising unearthliness about the sudden coming and departure of Black Bart. Jim Silent and his comrades waited no longer, but took to their saddles and galloped down the road.

Within a few moments the crowd at Morgan's place began to thin out. Evening was coming on, and most of them had far to ride. They might have lingered until midnight, but this peculiar accident damped their spirits. Probably not a hundred words were spoken from the moment Silent struck Dan to the time when the last of the cattlemen took to the saddle. They avoided each other's eyes as if in shame. In a short time only Morgan remained working over Dan.

In the house of old Joe Cumberland his daughter sat fingering the keys of the only piano within many miles. The evening gloom deepened as she played with upward face and reminiscent eyes. The tune was uncertain, weird—for she was trying to recall one of those nameless airs which Dan whistled as he rode through the hills.

There came a patter of swift, light footfalls in the hall, and then a heavy scratching at the door.

"Down, Bart!" she called, and went to admit him to the room.

The moment she turned the handle the door burst open and Bart fell in against her. She cried out at sight of the gleaming teeth and eyes, but he fawned about her feet, alternately whining and snarling.

"What is it, boy?" she asked, gathering her skirts close about her ankles and stepping back, for she never was without some fear of this black monster. "What do you want, Bart?"

For reply he stood stock still, raised his nose, and emitted a long wail, a mournful, a ghastly sound, with a broken-hearted quaver at the end. Kate Cumberland shrank back still farther until the wall blocked her retreat. Black Bart had never acted like this before. He followed her with a green light in his eyes, which shone phosphorescent and distinct through the growing shadows. And most terrible of all was the sound which came deep in his throat as if his brute nature was struggling to speak human words. She felt a great impulse to cry out for help, but checked herself. He was still crouching about her feet. Obviously he meant no harm to her.

He turned and ran towards the door, stopped, looked back to her, and made a sound which was nearer to the bark of a dog than anything he had ever uttered. She made a step after him. He whined with delight and moved closer to the door. Now she stopped again. He whirled and ran back, caught her dress in his teeth, and again made for the door, tugging her after him.

At last she understood and followed him. When she went towards the corral to get her horse, he planted himself in front of her and snarled so furiously that she gave up her purpose. She was beginning to be more and more afraid. A childish thought came to her that perhaps this brute was attempting to lure her away from the house, as she had seen coyotes lure dogs, and then turn his teeth against her. Nevertheless she followed. Something in the animal's eagerness moved her deeply. When he led her out to the road he released her dress and trotted ahead a short distance, looking back and whining, as if to beg her to go faster. For the first time the thought of Dan came into her mind. Black Bart was leading her down the road towards Morgan's place. What if something had happened to Dan?

She caught a breath of sharp terror and broke

into a run. Bart yelped his pleasure. Yet a cold horror rose in her heart as she hurried. Had her father after all been right? What power had Dan, if he needed her, to communicate with this mute beast and send him to her? As she ran she wished for the day, the warm, clear sun—for these growing shadows of evening bred a thousand ghostly thoughts. Black Bart was running backwards and forwards before her as if he half entreated and half threatened her.

Her heart died within her as she came in sight of Morgan's place. There was only one horse before it, and that was the black stallion. Why had the others gone so soon? Breathless, she reached the door of the saloon. It was very dim within. She could make out only formless shades at first. Black Bart slid noiselessly across the floor. She followed him with her eyes, and now she saw a figure stretched straight out on the floor while another man kneeled at his side. She ran forward with a cry.

Morgan rose, stammering. She pushed him aside and dropped beside Dan. A broad white bandage circled his head. His face was almost as pale as the cloth. Her touches went everywhere over that cold face, and she moaned little syllables that had no meaning. He lived, but it seemed to her that she had found him at the legended gates of death.

"Miss Kate!" said Morgan desperately.

"You murderer!"

"You don't think that *I* did that?"

"It happened in your place—you had given Dad your word!"

Still she did not turn her head.

"Won,t you hear me explain? He's jest in a sort of a trance. He'll wake up feelin' all right. Don't try to move him tonight. I'll go out an' put his hoss up in the shed. In the mornin' he'll be as good as new. Miss Kate, won't you listen to me?"

She turned reluctantly towards him. Perhaps he was right and Dan would waken from his swoon as if from a healthful sleep.

"It was that big feller with them straight eyes that done it," began Morgan.

"The one who was sneering at Dan?"

"Yes."

"Weren't there enough boys here to string him up?"

"He had three friends with him. It would of taken a hundred men to lay hands on one of those four. They were all bad ones. I'm goin' to tell you how it was, because I'm leavin' in a few minutes

6

and ridin' south, an' I want to clear my trail before I start. This was the way it happened——"

His back was turned to the dim light which fell through the door. She could barely make out the movement of his lips. All the rest of his face was lost in shadow. As he spoke she sometimes lost his meaning and the stir of his lips became a nameless gibbering. The grey gloom settled more deeply round the room and over her heart while he talked. He explained how the difference had risen between the tall stranger and Whistling Dan. How Dan had been insulted time and again and borne it with a sort of childish stupidity. How finally the blow had been struck. How Dan had crouched on the floor, laughing, and how a yellow light gathered in his eyes.

At that, her mind went blank. When her thoughts returned she stood alone in the room. The clatter of Morgan's galloping horse died swiftly away down the road. She turned to Dan. Black Bart was crouched at watch beside him. She kneeled again—lowered her head—heard the faint but steady breathing. He seemed infinitely young—infinitely weak and helpless. The whiteness of the bandage stared up at her like an eye through the deepening gloom. All the mother in her nature came to her eyes in tears.

CHAPTER VIII

RED WRITING

HE stirred.

"Dan—dear!"

"My head," he muttered, "it sort of aches, Kate, as if——"

He was silent and she knew that he remembered.

"You're all right now, honey. I've come here to take care of you—I won't leave you. Poor Dan!"

"How did you know?" he asked, the words trailing.

"Black Bart came for me."

"Good ol' Bart!"

The great wolf slunk closer, and licked the outstretched hand.

"Why, Kate, I'm on the floor and it's dark. Am I still in Morgan's place? Yes, I begin to see clearer."

He made an effort to rise, but she pressed him back.

"If you try to move right away you may get a fever. I'm going back to the house, and I'll bring you down some blankets. Morgan says you shouldn't attempt to move for several hours. He says you've lost a great deal of blood and that you mustn't make any effort or ride a horse till tomorrow."

Dan relaxed with a sigh.

"Kate."

"Yes, honey."

Her hand travelled lightly as blown snow across his forehead. He caught it and pressed the coolness against his cheek.

"I feel as if I'd sort of been through a fire. I seem to be still seein' red."

"Dan, it makes me feel as if I never knew you! Now you must forget all that has happened. Promise me you will!"

He was silent for a moment and then he sighed again.

"Maybe I can, Kate. Which I feel, though, as if there was somethin' inside me writ—writ in red letters—I got to try to read the writin' before I can talk much."

She barely heard him. Her hand was still against his face. A deep awe and content was creeping through her, so that she began to smile and was glad that the dark covered her face. She felt abashed before him for the first time in her life, and there was a singular sense of shame. It was as if some door in her inner heart had opened so that Dan was at liberty to look down into her soul. There was terror in this feeling, but there was also gladness.

"Kate."

"Yes—honey!"

"What were you hummin'?"

She started.

"I didn't know I was humming, Dan."

"You were, all right. It sounded sort of familiar, but I couldn't figger out where I heard it."

"I know now. It's one of your own tunes."

Now she felt a tremor so strong that she feared he would notice it.

"I must go back to the house, Dan. Maybe Dad has returned. If he has, perhaps he can arrange to have you carried back tonight."

"I don't want to think of movin', Kate. I feel mighty comfortable. I'm forgettin' all about that ache in my head. Ain't that queer? Why, Kate, what in the world are you laughin' about?"

"I don't know, Dan. I'm just happy!"

"Kate."

"Yes?"

"I like you pretty much."

"I'm so glad!"

"You an' Black Bart, an' Satan——"

"Oh!" Her tone changed.

"Why are you tryin' to take your hand away, Kate?"

"Don't you care for me any more than for your horse—and your dog?"

He drew a long breath, puzzled.

"It's some different, I figger."

"Tell me!"

"If Black Bart died——"

The wolf-dog whined, hearing his name.

"Good ol' Bart! Well, if Black Bart died maybe I'd some day have another dog I'd like almost as much."

"Yes."

"An' if Satan died—even Satan!—maybe I could sometime like another hoss pretty well— if he was a pile like Satan! But if you was to die—it'd be different, a considerable pile different."

"Why?"

His pauses to consider these questions were maddening.

"I don't know," he muttered at last.

Once more she was thankful for the dark to hide her smile.

"Maybe you know the reason, Kate?"

Her laughter was rich music. His hold on her hand relaxed. He was thinking of a new theme. When he laughed in turn it startled her. She had never heard that laugh before.

"What is it, Dan?"

"He was pretty big, Kate. He was bigger'n almost any man I ever seen! It was kind of funny. After he hit me I was almost glad. I didn't hate him—— "

"Dear Dan!"

"I didn't hate him—I jest nacherally wanted to kill him—and wantin' to do that made me glad. Isn't that funny, Kate?"

He spoke of it as a chance traveller might point out a striking feature of the landscape to a companion.

"Dan, if you really care for me you must drop the thought of him."

His hand slipped away.

"How can I do that? That writin' I was tellin' you about—— "

"Yes?"

"It's about him!"

"Ah!"

"When he hit me the first time—— "

"I won't hear you tell of it!"

"The blood come down my chin—jest a little trickle of it. It was warm, Kate. That was what made me hot all through."

Her hands fell limp, cold, lifeless.

"It's as clear as the print in a book. I've got to finish him. That's the only way I can forget the taste of my own blood."

"Dan, listen to me!"

He laughed again, in the new way. She remembered that her father had dreaded the very thing that had come to Dan—this first taste of his own powers—this first taste (she shuddered) of blood!

"Dan, you've told me that you like me. You have to make a choice now, between pursuing this man, and me."

"You don't understand," he explained carefully. "I *got* to follow him. I can't help it no more'n Black Bart can help howlin' when he sees the moon."

He fell silent, listening. Far across the hills came the plaintive wail of a coyote—that shrill bodiless sound. Kate trembled.

"Dan!"

Outside, Satan whinnied softly like a call. She leaned and her lips touched his. He thrust her away almost roughly.

"They's blood on my lips, Kate! I can't kiss you till they're clean."

He turned his head.

"You must listen to me, Dan!"

"Kate, would you talk to the wind?"

"Yes, if I loved the wind!"

He turned his head.

She pleaded: "Here are my hands to cover your eyes and shut out the thoughts of this man you hate. Here are my lips, dear, to tell you that I love you unless this thirst for killing carries you away from me. Stay with me! Give me your heart to keep gentle!"

He said nothing, but even through the dark she was aware of a struggle in his face, and then, through the gloom, she began to see his eyes more clearly. They semed to be illuminated by a light from within—they changed—there was a hint of yellow in the brown. And she spoke again, blindly, passionately.

"Give me your promise! It is so easy to do. One little word will make you safe. It will save you from yourself."

Still he answered nothing. Black Bart came and crouched at his head and stared at her fixedly.

"Speak to me!"

Only the yellow light answered her. Cold

fear fought in her heart, but love still struggled against it.

"For the last time—for God's sake, Dan!"

Still that silence. She rose, shaking and weak. The changeless eyes followed her. Only fear remained now. She backed towards the door, slowly, then faster, and faster. At the threshold she whirled and plunged into the night.

Up the road she raced. Once she stumbled and fell to her knees. She cried out and glanced behind her, breathing again when she saw that nothing followed. At the house she made no pause, though she heard the voice of her father singing. She could not tell him. He should be the last in all the world to know. She went to her room and huddled into bed.

Presently a knock came at her door, and her father's voice asked if she were ill. She pleaded that she had a bad headache and wished to be alone. He asked if she had seen Dan. By a great effort she managed to reply that Dan had ridden to a neighbouring ranch. Her father left the door without further question. Afterwards she heard him in the distance singing his favourite mournful ballads. It doubled her sense of woe and brought home the clinging fear. She felt that if she could weep she might live, but otherwise her heart would burst. And after hours and hours of that torture which burns the name of "woman" in the soul of a girl, the tears came. The roosters announced the dawn before she slept.

Late the next morning old Joe Cumberland knocked again at her door. He was beginning to fear that this illness might be serious. Moreover, he had a definite purpose in rousing her.

"Yes?" she called, after the second knock.

"Look out your window, honey, down to Morgan's place. You remember I said I was goin' to clean up the landscape?"

The mention of Morgan's place cleared the sleep from Kate's mind and it brought back the horror of the night before. Shivering she slipped from her bed and went to the window. Morgan's place was a mass of towering flames!

She grasped the window-sill and stared again. It could not be. It must be merely another part of the nightmare, and no reality. Her father's voice, high with exultation, came dimly to her ears, but what she saw was Dan as he had laid there the night before, hurt, helpless, too weak to move!

"There's the end of it," Joe Cumberland was saying complacently outside her door. "There ain't goin' to be even a shadow of the saloon left nor nothin' that's in it. I jest travelled down there this mornin' and touched a match to it!''

Still she stared without moving, without making a sound. She was seeing Dan as he must have wakened from a swoonlike sleep with the smell of smoke and the heat of rising flames around him. She saw him struggle, and fail to reach his feet. She almost heard him cry out—a sound drowned easily by the roar of the fire, and the crackling of the wood. She saw him drag himself with his hands across the floor, only to be beaten back by a solid wall of flame. Black Bart crouched beside him and would not leave his doomed master. Fascinated by the raging fire the black stallion Satan would break from the shed and rush into the flames!—and so the inseparable three must have perished together!

"Why don't you speak, Kate?" called her father.

"Dan!" she screamed, and pitched forward to the floor.

CHAPTER IX

THE PHANTOM RIDER

In the daytime the willows along the wide, level river bottom seemed an unnatural growth, for they made a streak of yellow-green across the mountain-desert when all other verdure withered and died. After nightfall they became still more dreary. Even when the air was calm there was apt to be a sound as of wind, for the tenuous, trailing branches brushed lightly together, making a guarded whispering like ghosts.

In a small clearing among these willows sat Silent and his companions. A fifth member had just arrived at this rendezvous, answered the quiet greeting with a wave of his hand, and was now busy caring for his horse. Bill Kilduff, who had a natural inclination and talent for cookery, raked up the deft dying coals of the fire over which he had cooked the supper, and set about preparing bacon and coffee for the newcomer. The latter came forward, and squatted close to the cook, watching

93

the process with a careful eye. He made a sharp contrast with the rest of the group. From one side his profile showed the face of a good-natured boy, but when he turned his head the flicker of the firelight ran down a scar which gleamed in a jagged semi-circle from his right eyebrow to the corner of his mouth. This whole side of his countenance was drawn by the cut, the mouth stretching to a perpetual grimace. When he spoke it was as if he were attempting secrecy. The rest of the men waited in patience until he finished eating. Then Silent asked: "What news, Jordan?"

Jordan kept his regretful eyes a moment longer on his empty coffee cup.

"There ain't a pile to tell," he answered at last. "I suppose you heard about what happened to the chap you beat up at Morgan's place the other day?"

"Who knows that *I* beat him up?" asked Silent sharply.

"Nobody," said Jordan, "but when I heard the description of the man that hit Whistling Dan with the chair, I knew it was Jim Silent."

"What about Barry?" asked Haines, but Jordan still kept his eyes upon the chief.

"They was sayin' pretty general," he went on, "that you *needed* that chair, Jim. Is that right?"

The other three glanced covertly to each other. Silent's hand bunched into a great fist.

"He went loco. I had to slam him. Was he hurt bad?"

"The cut on his head wasn't much, but he was left lyin' in the saloon that night, an' the next mornin' old Joe Cumberland, not knowin' that Whistlin' Dan was in there, come down an' touched a match to the old joint. She went up in smoke an' took Dan along."

No one spoke for a moment. Then Silent cried out: "Then what was that whistlin' I've heard down the road behind us?"

Bill Kilduff broke into rolling bass laughter, and Hal Purvis chimed in with a squeaking tenor.

"We told you all along, Jim," said Purvis, as soon as he could control his voice, "that there wasn't any whistlin' behind us. We know you got powerful good hearin', Jim, but we all figger you been makin' somethin' out of nothin'. Am I right, boys?"

"You sure are," said Kilduff, "I ain't heard a thing."

Silent rolled his eyes angrily from face to face.

"I'm kind of sorry the lad got his in the fire. I was hopin' maybe we'd meet agin. There's nothin' I'd rather do than be alone five minutes with Whistlin' Dan."

His eyes dared any one to smile. The men merely exchanged glances. When he turned away they grinned broadly. Hal Purvis turned and caught Bill Kilduff by the shoulder.

"Bill," he said excitedly, "if Whistlin' Dan is dead there ain't any master for that dog!"

"What about him?" growled Kilduff.

"I'd like to try my hand with him," said Purvis, and he moistened his tight lips. "Did you see the black devil when he snarled at me in front of Morgan's place?"

"He sure didn't look too pleasant."

"Right. Maybe if I had him on a chain I could change his manners some, eh?"

"How?"

"A whip every day, damn him—a whip every time he showed his teeth at me. No eats till he whined and licked my hand."

"He'd die first. I know that kind of a dog—or a wolf."

"Maybe he'd die. Anyway I'd like to try my hand with him. Bill, I'm goin' to get hold of him some of these days if I have to ride a hundred miles an' swim a river!"

Kilduff grunted.

"Let the damn wolf be. You c'n have him, I say. What I'm thinkin' about is the hoss. Hal, do you remember the way he settled to his stride when he lighted out after Red Pete?"

Purvis shrugged his shoulders.

"You're a fool, Bill. Which no man but Barry could ever ride that hoss. I seen it in his eye. He'd cash in buckin'. He'd fight you like a man."

Kilduff sighed. A great yearning was in his eyes.

"Hal," he said softly, "they's some men go around for years an' huntin' for a girl whose picture is in their bean, cached away somewhere. When they see her they jest nacherally goes nutty. Hal, I don't give a damn for women folk, but I've travelled around a long time with a picture of a hoss in my brain, an' Satan is the hoss."

He closed his eyes.

"I c'n see him now. I c'n see them shoulders—an' that head—an', my God! them eyes—them fire eatin' eyes! Hal, if a man was to win the heart of that hoss he'd lay down his life for you—he'd run himself plumb to death! I won't never sleep tight till I get the feel of them satin sides of his between my knees."

Lee Haines heard them speak, but he said nothing. His heart also leaped when he heard of

7

Whistling Dan's death, but he thought neither of the horse nor the dog. He was seeing the yellow hair and the blue eyes of Kate Cumberland. He approached Jordan and took a place beside him.

"Tell me some more about it, Terry," he asked.

"Some more about what?"

"About Whistling Dan's death—about the burning of the saloon," said Haines.

"What the hell! Are you still thinkin' about that?"

"I certainly am."

"Then I'll trade you news," said Terry Jordan, lowering his voice so that it would not reach the suspicious ear of Jim Silent. "I'll tell you about the burnin' if you'll tell me something about Barry's fight with Silent!"

"It's a trade," answered Haines.

"All right. Seems old Joe Cumberland had a hunch to clean up the landscape—old fool! so he jest up in the mornin' an' without sayin' a word to any one he downs to the saloon and touches a match to it. When he come back to his house he tells his girl, Kate, what he done. With that she lets out a holler an' drops in a faint."

Haines muttered.

"What's the matter?" asked Terry, a little anxiously.

"Nothin'," said Haines. "She fainted, eh? Well, go on!"

"Yep. She fainted an' when she come to, she told Cumberland that Dan was in the saloon, an' probably too weak to get out of the fire. They started for the place on the run. When they got there all they found was a pile of red hot coals. So everyone figures that he went up in the flames. That's all I know. Now what about the fight?"

Lee Haines sat with fixed eyes.

"There isn't much to say about the fight," he said at last.

"The hell there isn't," scoffed Terry Jordan. "From what I heard, this Whistling Dan simply cut loose and raised the devil more general than a dozen mavericks corralled with a bunch of yearlings."

"Cutting loose is right," said Haines. "It wasn't a pleasant thing to watch. One moment he was about as dangerous as an eighteen-year-old girl. The next second he was like a panther that's tasted blood. That's all there was to it, Terry. After the first blow, he was all over the chief. You know Silent's a bad man with his hands?"

"I guess we all know that," said Jordan, with a significant smile.

"Well," said Haines, "he was like a baby in the hands of Barry. I don't like to talk about it—none of us do. It makes the flesh creep."

There was a loud crackling among the underbrush several hundred yards away. It drew closer and louder.

"Start up your works agin, will you, Bill?" called Silent. "Here comes Shorty Rhinehart, an' he's overdue."

In a moment Shorty swung from his horse and joined the group. He gained his nickname from his excessive length, being taller by an inch or two than Jim Silent himself, but what he gained in height he lost in width. Even his face was monstrously long, and marked with such sad lines that the favourite name of "Shorty" was affectionately varied to "Sour-face" or "Calamity." Silent went to him at once.

"You seen Hardy?" he asked.

"I sure did," said Rhinehart, "an' it's the last time I'll make that trip to him, you can lay to that."

"Did he give you the dope?"

"No."

"What do you mean?"

"I jest want you to know that this here's my last trip to Elkhead—on *any* business."

"Why?"

"I passed three marshals on the street, an' I knew them all. They was my friends, formerly. One of them was——"

"What did they do?"

"I waved my hand to them, glad an' familiar. They jest grunted. One of them, he looked up an' down the street, an' seein' that no one was in sight, he come up to me an' without shakin' hands he says: 'I'm some surprised to see you in Elkhead, Shorty.' 'Why,' says I, 'the town's all right, ain't it?' 'It's all right,' he says, 'but you'd find it a pile more healthier out on the range.'"

"What in hell did he mean by that?" growled Silent.

"He simply meant that they're beginnin' to think a lot more about us than they used to. We've been pullin' too many jobs the last six months."

"You've said all that before, Shorty. I'm runnin' this gang. Tell me about Hardy."

"I'm comin' to that. I went into the Wells Fargo office down by the railroad, an' the clerk sent me back to find Hardy in the back room, where he generally is. When he seen me he changed colour. I'd jest popped my head through the door an' sung out: 'Hello, Hardy, how's the boy?' He jumped up from the desk an' sung out so's his clerk in the outside room could hear: 'How are you, lad?' an' he pulled me quick into the room an' locked the door behind me.

"'Now what in hell have you come to Elkhead for?' says he.

"'For a drink' says I, never battin' an eye.

"'You've come a damn long ways,' says he.

"'Sure,' says I, 'that's one reason I'm so dry. Will you liquor, pal?'

"He looked like he needed a drink, all right. He begun loosening his shirt collar.

"'Thanks, but I ain't drinkin', says he. 'Look here, Shorty, are you loco to come ridin' into Elkhead this way?'

"'I'm jest beginnin' to think maybe I am,' says I.

"'Shorty,' he says in a whisper, 'they're beginnin' to get wise to the whole gang—includin' me.'

"'Take a brace,' says I. 'They ain't got a thing on you, Hardy.'

"'That don't keep 'em from thinkin' a hell of a pile,' says he, 'an' I tell you, Shorty, I'm jest about through with the whole works. It ain't worth it —not if there was a million in it. Everybody is gettin' wise to Silent, an' the rest of you. Pretty soon hell's goin' to bust loose.'

"'You've been sayin' that for two years,' says I.

"He stopped an' looked at me sort of thoughtful an' pityin'. Then he steps up close to me an' whispers in that voice: 'D'you know who's on Silent's trail now? Eh?'

"'No, an' I don't give a damn,' says I, free an' careless.

"'Tex Calder!' says he."

Silent started violently, and his hand moved instinctively to his six-gun.

"Did he say Tex Calder?"

"He said no less," answered Shorty Rhinehart, and waited to see his news take effect. Silent stood with head bowed, scowling.

"Tex Calder's a fool," he said at last. "He ought to know better'n to take'to *my* trail."

"He's fast with his gun," suggested Shorty.

"Don't I know that?" said Silent. "If Alvarez, an' Bradley, an' Hunter, an' God knows how many more could come up out of their graves, they'd tell jest how quick he *is* with a six-gun. But I'm the one man on the range that's faster."

Shorty was eloquently mute.

"I ain't askin' you to take my word for it," said Jim Silent. "Now that he's after me, I'm glad of it. It had to come some day. The mountains ain't big enough for both of us to go rangin' forever.

We had to lock horns some day. An' I say, God help Tex Calder!"

He turned abruptly to the rest of the men.

"Boys, I got somethin' to tell you that Shorty jest heard. Tex Calder is after us."

There came a fluent outburst of cursing.

Silent went on: "I know jest how slick Calder is. I'm bettin' on my draw to be jest the necessary half a hair quicker. He may die shootin'. I don't lay no bets that I c'n nail him before he gets his iron out of its leather, but I say he'll be shootin' blind when he dies. Is there any one takin' that bet?"

His eyes challenged them one after another. Their glances travelled past Silent as if they were telling over and over to themselves the stories of those many men to whom Tex Calder had played the part of Fate. The leader turned back to Shorty Rhinehart.

"Now tell me what he had to say about the coin."

"Hardy says the shipment's delayed. He don't know how long."

"How'd it come to be delayed?"

"He figures that Wells Fargo got a hunch that Silent was layin' for the train that was to carry it."

"Will he let us know when it *does* come through?"

"I asked him, an' he jest hedged.   He's quitting on us cold."

"I was a fool to send you, Shorty.   I'm goin' myself, an' if Hardy don't come through to me——"

He broke off and announced to the rest of his gang that he intended to make the journey to Elkhead.   He told Haines, who in such cases usually acted as lieutenant, to take charge of the camp.   Then he saddled his roan.

In the very act of pulling up the cinch of his saddle, Silent stopped short, turned, and raised a hand for quiet.   The rest were instantly still. Hal Purvis leaned his weazened face towards the ground.   In this manner it was sometimes possible to detect far-off sounds which to one erect would be inaudible.   In a moment, however, he straightened up, shaking his head.

"What is it?" whispered Haines.

"Shut up," muttered Silent, and the words were formed by the motion of his lips rather than through any sound.   "That damned whistling again."

Every face changed.   At a rustling in a near-by willow, Terry Jordan started and then cursed softly to himself.   That broke the spell.

"It's the whisperin' of the willows," said Purvis.

"You lie," said Silent hoarsely. "I hear the sound growing closer."

"Barry is dead," said Haines.

Silent whipped out his revolver—and then shoved it back into the holster.

"Stand by me, boys," he pleaded. "It's his ghost come to haunt me! You can't hear it, because he ain't come for you."

They stared at him with a fascinated horror.

"How do you know it's him?" asked Shorty Rhinehart.

"There ain't no sound in the whole world like it. It's a sort of cross between the singing of a bird an' the wailin' of the wind. It's the ghost of Whistlin' Dan."

The tall roan raised his head and whinnied softly. It was an unearthly effect—as if the animal heard the sound which was inaudible to all but his master. It changed big Jim Silent into a quavering coward. Here were five practised fighters who feared nothing between heaven and hell, but what could they avail him against a bodiless spirit? The whistling stopped. He breathed again, but only for a moment.

It began again, and this time much louder and nearer. Surely the others must hear it now, or else it was certainly a ghost. The men sat with dilated eyes for an instant, and then Hal Purvis cried, "I heard it, chief! If it's a ghost, it's hauntin' me too!"

Silent cursed loudly in his relief.

"It ain't a ghost. It's Whistlin' Dan himself. An' Terry Jordan has been carryin' us lies! What in hell do you mean by it?"

"I ain't been carryin' you lies," said Jordan, hotly. "I told you what I heard. I didn't never say that there was any one seen his dead body!"

The whistling began to die out. A babble of conjecture and exclamation broke out, but Jim Silent, still sickly white around the mouth, swung up into the saddle.

"That Whistlin' Dan I'm leavin' to you, Haines," he called. "I've had his blood onct, an' if I meet him agin there's goin' to be another notch filed into my shootin' iron."

CHAPTER X

THE STRENGTH OF WOMEN

HE rode swiftly into the dark of the willows, and the lack of noise told that he was picking his way carefully among the bended branches.

"It seems to me," said Terry Jordan, "which I'm not suggestin' anything—but it seems to me that the chief was in a considerable hurry to leave the camp."

"He was," said Hal Purvis, "an' if you seen that play in Morgan's place you wouldn't be wonderin' why. If I was the chief I'd do the same."

"Me speakin' personal," remarked Shorty Rhinehart, "I ain't layin' out to be no man-eater like the chief, but I ain't seen the man that'd make me take to the timbers that way. I don't noways expect there *is* such a man!"

"Shorty," said Haines calmly, "we all knows that you're quite a man, but you and Terry are the only ones of us who are surprised that Silent slid

away. The rest of us who saw this Whistling
Dan in action aren't a bit inclined to wonder.
Suppose you were to meet a black panther down
here in the willows?"

"I wouldn't give a damn if I had my Win-
chester with me."

"All right, Terry, but suppose the panther,"
broke in Hal Purvis, "could sling shootin' irons as
well as you could—maybe *that'd* make you partic'-
ler pleased."

"It ain't possible," said Terry.

"Sure it ain't," grinned Purvis amiably, "an'
this Barry ain't possible, either. Where you
going, Lee?"

Haines turned from his task of saddling his
mount.

"Private matter. Kilduff, you take my place
while I'm gone. I may be back tomorrow night.
The chief isn't apt to return so soon."

A few moments later Haines galloped out of the
willows and headed across the hills towards old
Joe Cumberland's ranch. He was remembering
his promise to Kate, to keep Dan out of danger.
He had failed from that promise once, but that
did not mean that he had forgotten. He looked
up to the yellow-bright mountain stars, and they
were like the eyes of good women smiling down

upon him. He guessed that she loved Barry and if he could bring her to Whistling Dan she might have strength enough to take the latter from Silent's trail. The lone rider knew well enough that to bring Dan and Kate together was to surrender his own shadowy hopes, but the golden eyes of the sky encouraged him. So he followed his impulse.

Haines could never walk that middle path which turns neither to the right nor the left, neither up nor down. He went through life with a free-swinging stride, and as the result of it he had crossed the rights of others. He might have lived a lawful life, for all his instincts were gentle. But an accident placed him in the shadow of the law. He waited for his legal trial, but when it came and false witness placed him behind the bars, the revolt came. Two days after his confinement, he broke away from his prison and went to the wilds. There he found Jim Silent, and the mountain-desert found another to add to its list of great outlaws.

Morning came as he drew close to the house, and now his reminiscences were cut short, for at a turn of the road he came upon Kate galloping swiftly over the hills. He drew his horse to a halt and raised his hand. She followed suit. They sat staring. If she had remembered his broken promise and started to reproach, he could have found answer, but her eyes were big with sorrow alone. He put out his hand without a word. She hesitated over it, her eyes questioning him mutely, and then with the ghost of a smile she touched his fingers.

"I want to explain," he said huskily.

"What?"

"You remember I gave you my word that no harm would come to Barry?"

"No man could have helped him."

"You don't hold it against me?"

A gust of wind moaned around them. She waved her arm towards the surrounding hills and her laugh blended with the sound of the wind, it was so faint. He watched her with a curious pang. She seemed among women what that morning was to the coming day—fresh, cool, aloof. It was hard to speak the words which would banish the sorrow from her eyes and make them brilliant with hope and shut him away from her thoughts with a barrier higher than mountains, and broader than seas.

"I have brought you news," he said at last, reluctantly.

She did not change.

"About Dan Barry."

Ay, she changed swiftly enough at that! He could not meet the fear and question of her glance. He looked away and saw the red rim of the sun pushing up above the hills. And colour poured up the throat of Kate Cumberland, up even to her forehead beneath the blowing golden hair.

Haines jerked his sombrero lower on his head. A curse tumbled up to his lips and he had to set his teeth to keep it back.

"But I have heard his whistle."

Her lips moved but made no sound.

"Five other men heard him."

She cried out as if he had hurt her, but the hurt was happiness. He knew it and winced, for she was wonderfully beautiful.

"In the willows of the river bottom, a good twenty miles south," he said at last, "and I will show you the way, if you wish."

He watched her eyes grow large with doubt.

"Can you trust me?" he asked. "I failed you once. Can you trust me now?"

Her hand went out to him.

"With all my heart," she said. "Let us start!"

"I've given my horse a hard ride. He must have some rest."

She moaned softly in her impatience, and then: "We'll go back to the house and you can stable your horse there until you're ready to start. Dad will go with us."

"Your father cannot go," he said shortly.

"Cannot?"

"Let's start back for the ranch," he said, "and I'll tell you something about it as we go."

As they turned their horses he went on: "In order that you may reach Whistling Dan, you'll have to meet first a number of men who are camping down there in the willows."

He stopped. It became desperately difficult for him to go on.

"I am one of those men," he said, "and another of them is the one whom Whistling Dan is following."

She caught her breath and turned abruptly on him.

"What are you, Mr. Lee?"

Very slowly he forced his eyes up to meet her gaze.

"In that camp," he answered indirectly, "your father wouldn't be safe!"

It was out at last!

"Then you are—— "

"Your friend."

"Forgive me.   You *are* my friend!"

"The man whom Dan is following," he went on, "is the leader.   If he gives the command four practised fighters pit themselves against Barry."

"It is murder!"

"You can prevent it," he said.   "They know Barry is on the trail, but I think they will do nothing unless he forces them into trouble.   And he *will* force them unless you stop him.   No other human being could take him off that trail."

"I know! I know!" she muttered.   "But I have already tried, and he will not listen to me!"

"But he will listen to you," insisted Haines, "when you tell him that he will be fighting not one man, but six."

"And if he doesn't listen to me?"

Haines shrugged his shoulders.

"Can't you promise that these men will not fight with him?"

"I cannot."

"But I shall plead with them myself."

He turned to her in alarm.

"No, you must not let them dream you know who they are," he warned, "for otherwise——"

Again that significant shrug of the shoulders.

He explained: "These men are in such danger that they dare not take chances.   You are a woman, but if they feel that you suspect them you will no longer be a woman in their eyes."

"Then what must I do?"

"I shall ride ahead of you when we come to the willows, after I have pointed out the position of our camp. About an hour after I have arrived, for they must not know that I have brought you, you will ride down towards the camp. When you come to it I will make sure that it is I who will bring you in. You must pretend that you have simply blundered upon our fire. Whatever you do, never ask a question while you are there—and I'll be your warrant that you will come off safely. Will you try?"

He attempted no further persuasion and contented himself with merely meeting the wistful challenge of her eyes.

"I will," she said at last, and then turning her glance away she repeated softly, "I will."

He knew that she was already rehearsing what she must say to Whistling Dan.

"You are not afraid?"

She smiled.

"Do you really trust me as far as this?"

With level-eyed tenderness that took his breath, she answered: "An absolute trust, Mr. Lee."

"My name," he said in a strange voice, "is Lee Haines."

Of one accord they stopped their horses and their hands met.

CHAPTER XI

SILENT BLUFFS

THE coming of the railroad had changed Elkhead from a mere crossing of the ways to a rather important cattle shipping point. Once a year it became a bustling town whose two streets thronged with cattlemen with pockets burdened with gold which fairly burned its way out to the open air. At other times Elkhead dropped back into a leaden-eyed sleep.

The most important citizen was Lee Hardy, the Wells Fargo agent. Office jobs are hard to find in the mountain-desert, and those who hold them win respect. The owner of a swivel-chair is more lordly than the possessor of five thousand "doggies." Lee Hardy had such a swivel-chair. Moreover, since large shipments of cash were often directed by Wells Fargo to Elkhead, Hardy's position was really more significant than the size of the village suggested. As a crowning stamp upon his dignity he had a clerk who handled the ordinary routine of work in the front room, while Hardy set himself up in state in a little rear office whose walls were decorated by two brilliant calendars and the coloured photograph of a blond beauty advertising a toilet soap.

To this sanctuary he retreated during the heat of the day, while in the morning and evening he loitered on the small porch, chatting with passers-by. Except in the hottest part of the year he affected a soft white collar with a permanent bow tie. The leanness of his features, and his crooked neck with the prominent Adam's apple which stirred when he spoke, suggested a Yankee ancestry, but the faded blue eyes, pathetically misted, could only be found in the mountain-desert.

One morning into the inner sanctum of this dignitary stepped a man built in rectangles, a square face, square, ponderous shoulders, and even square-tipped fingers. Into the smiling haze of Hardy's face his own keen black eye sparkled like an electric lantern flashed into a dark room. He was dressed in the cowboy's costume, but there was no Western languor in his make-up. Everything about him was clear cut and precise. He had a habit of clicking his teeth as he finished a sentence. In a word, when he appeared in the doorway Lee Hardy woke up, and before the stranger had spoken a dozen words the agent was leaning forward to be sure that he would not miss a syllable.

"You're Lee Hardy, aren't you?" said he, and his eyes gave the impression of a smile, though his lips did not stir after speaking.

"I am," said the agent.

"Then you're the man I want to see. If you don't mind——"

He closed the door, pulled a chair against it, and then sat down, and folded his arms. Very obviously he meant business. Hardy switched his position in his chair, sitting a little more to the right, so that the edge of the seat would not obstruct the movement of his hand towards the holster on his right thigh.

"Well," he said good naturedly, "I'm waitin'."

"Good," said the stranger, "I won't keep you here any longer than is necessary. In the first place my name is Tex Calder."

Hardy changed as if a slight layer of dust had been sifted over his face. He stretched out his hand.

"It's great to see you, Calder," he said, "of course I've heard about you. Everyone has. Here! I'll send over to the saloon for some red-eye. Are you dry?"

He rose, but Calder waved him back to the swivel-chair.

"Not dry a bit," he said cheerily. "Not five minutes ago I had a drink of—water."

"All right," said Hardy, and settled back into his chair.

"Hardy, there's been crooked work around here."

"What in hell——"

"Get your hand away from that gun, friend."

"What the devil's the meaning of all this?"

"That's very well done," said Calder. "But this isn't the stage. Are we going to talk business like friends?"

"I've got nothing agin you," said Hardy testily, and his eyes followed Calder's right hand as if fascinated. "What do you want to say? I'll listen. I'm not very busy."

"That's exactly it," smiled Tex Calder, "I want you to get busier."

"Thanks."

"In the first place I'll be straight with you. Wells Fargo hasn't sent me here."

"Who has?"

"My conscience."

"I don't get your drift."

Through a moment of pause Calder's eyes searched the face of Hardy.

"You've been pretty flush for some time."

"I ain't been starvin'."

"There are several easy ways for you to pick up extra money."

"Yes?"

"For instance, you know all about the Wells Fargo money shipments, and there are men around here who'd pay big for what you could tell them."

The prominent Adam's apple rose and fell in Hardy's throat.

"You're quite a joker, ain't you Calder? Who, for instance?"

"Jim Silent."

"This is like a story in a book," grinned Hardy. "Go on. I suppose I've been takin' Silent's money?"

The answer came like the click of a cocked revolver.

"You have!"

"By God, Calder——"

"Steady! I have some promising evidence, partner. Would you like to hear part of it?"

"This country has its share of the world's greatest liars," said Hardy, "I don't care what you've heard."

"That saves my time.   Understand me straight. I can slap you into a lock-up, if I want to, and then bring in that evidence.   I'm not going to do it. I'm going to use you as a trap and through you get some of the worst of the lone riders."

"There's nothin' like puttin' your hand on the table."

"No, there isn't.   I'll tell you what you're to do."

"Thanks."

The marshal drove straight on.

"I've got four good men in this town.   Two of them will always be hanging around your office. Maybe you can get a job for them here, eh?   I'll pay the salaries.   You simply tip them off when your visitors are riders the government wants, see? You don't have to lift a hand.   You just go to the door as the visitor leaves, and if he's all right you say: 'So long, we'll be meeting again before long.' But if he's a man I want, you say 'Good-bye.' That's all.   My boys will see that it is good-bye."

"Go on," said the agent, "and tell the rest of the story.   It starts well."

"Doesn't it?" agreed Calder, "and the way it concludes is with you reaching over and shaking hands with me and saying 'yes'!"

He leaned forward.   The twinkle was gone

from his eyes and he extended his hand to Hardy. The latter reached out with an impulsive gesture, wrung the proffered hand, and then slipping back into his chair broke into hysterical laughter.

"The real laugh," said Calder, watching his man narrowly, "will be on the long riders."

"Tex," said the agent. "I guess you have the dope. I won't say anything except that I'm glad as hell to be out of the rotten business at last. Once started I couldn't stop. I did one 'favour' for these devils, and after that they had me in their power. I haven't slept for months as I'm going to sleep tonight!"

He wiped his face with an agitated hand.

"A week ago," he went on, "I knew you were detailed on this work. I've been sweating ever since. Now that you've come—why, I'm glad of it!"

A faint sneer touched Calder's mouth and was gone.

"You're a wise man," he said. "Have you seen much of Jim Silent lately?"

Hardy hesitated. The rôle of informer was new.

"Not directly."

Calder nodded.

"Now put me right if I go off the track. The way I understand it, Jim Silent has about twenty gun fighters and long riders working in gangs under him and combining for big jobs."

"That's about it."

"The inside circle consists of Silent; Lee Haines, a man who went wrong because the law did *him* wrong; Hal Purvis, a cunning devil; and Bill Kilduff, a born fighter who loves blood for its own sake."

"Right."

"Here's something more. For Jim Silent, dead or alive, the government will pay ten thousand dollars. For each of the other three it pays five thousand. The notices aren't out yet, but they will be in a few days. Hardy, if you help me bag these men, you'll get fifty per cent. of the profits. Are you on?"

The hesitancy of Hardy changed to downright enthusiasm.

"Easy money, Tex. I'm your man, hand and glove."

"Don't get optimistic. This game isn't played yet, and unless I make the biggest mistake of my life we'll be guessing again before we land Silent. I've trailed some fast gunmen in my day, and I have an idea that Silent will be the hardest of the lot; but if you play your end of the game we may land him. I have a tip that he's lying out in the country near Elkhead. I'm riding out alone to get track of him. As I go out I'll tell my men that you're O.K. for this business."

He hesitated a moment with his hand on the door knob.

"Just one thing more, Hardy. I heard a queer tale this morning about a fight in a saloon run by a man named Morgan. Do you know anything about it?"

"No."

"I was told of a fellow who chipped four dollars thrown into the air at twenty yards."

"That's a lie."

"The man who talked to me had a nicked dollar to prove his yarn."

"The devil he did!"

"And after the shooting this chap got into a fight with a tall man twice his size and fairly mopped up the floor with him. They say it wasn't a nice thing to watch. He is a frail man, but when the fight started he turned into a tiger."

"Wish I'd seen it."

"The tall man tallies to a hair with my description of Silent."

"You're wrong. I know what Silent can do with his hands. No one could beat him up. What's the name of the other?"

"Barry. Whistling Dan Barry."

Calder hesitated.

"Right or wrong, I'd like to have this Barry with me. So long."

He was gone as he had come, with a nod and a flash of the keen, black eyes. Lee Hardy stared at the door for some moments, and then went outside. The warm light of the sun had never been more welcome to him. Under that cheering influence he began to feel that with Tex Calder behind him he could safely defy the world.

His confidence received a shock that afternoon when a heavy step crossed the outside room, and his door opening without a preliminary knock, he looked up into the solemn eyes of Jim Silent. The outlaw shook his head when Hardy offered him a chair.

"What's the main idea of them two new men out in your front room, Lee?" he asked.

"Two cowpunchers that was down on their luck. I got to stand in with the boys now and then."

"I s'pose so. Shorty Rhinehart in here to see you, Lee?"

"Yep."

"You told him that the town was gettin' pretty hot."

"It is."

"You said you had no dope on when that delayed shipment was comin' through?"

Hardy made lightning calculations. A half truth would be the best way out.

"I've just got the word you want. It come this morning."

Silent's expression changed and he leaned a little closer.

"It's the nineteenth. Train number 89. Savvy? Seven o'clock at Elkhead!"

"How much? Same bunch of coin?"

"Fifty thousand!"

"That's ten more."

"Yep. A new shipment rolled in with the old one. No objections?"

Silent grinned.

"Any other news, Lee?"

"Shorty told you about Tex Calder?"

"He did. Seen him around here?"

The slightest fraction of a second in hesitation. "No."

"Was that the straight dope you give Shorty?"

"Straighter'n hell. They're beginnin' to talk, but I guess I was jest sort of panicky when I talked with Shorty."

"This Tex Calder——"

"What about him?" This with a trace of suspicion.

"He's got a long record."

"So've you, Jim."

Once more that wolflike grin which had no mirth.

"So long, Lee. I'll be on the job. Lay to that."

He turned towards the door. Hardy followed him. A moment more, in a single word, and the job would be done. Five thousand dollars for a single word! It warmed the very heart of Lee Hardy.

Silent, as he moved away, seemed singularly thoughtful. He hesitated a moment with bowed head at the door—then whirled and shoved a six-gun under the nose of Hardy. The latter leaped back with his arms thrust above his head, straining at his hands to get them higher.

"My God, Jim!"

"You're a low-down, lyin' hound!"

Hardy's tongue clove to the roof of his mouth.

"Damn you, d'you hear me?"

"Yes! For God's sake, Jim, don't shoot!"

" Your life ain't worth a dime!"

"Give me one more chance an' I'll play square!"

A swift change came over the face of Silent, and then Hardy went hot with terror and anger.

The long rider had known nothing. The gun play had been a mere bluff, but he had played into the hands of Silent, and now his life was truly worth nothing.

"You poor fool," went on Silent, his voice purring with controlled rage. "You damn blind fool! D'you think you could double cross me an' get by with it?"

"Give me a chance, Jim. One more chance, one more chance!"

Even in his terror he remembered to keep his voice low lest those in the front room should hear.

"Out with it, if you love livin'!"

"I—I can't talk while you got that gun on me!"

Silent not only lowered his gun, but actually returned it to the holster. Nothing could more clearly indicate his contempt, and Hardy, in spite of his fear, crimsoned with shame.

"It was Tex Calder," he said at last.

Silent started a little and his eyes narrowed again.

"What of him?"

"He came here a while ago an' tried to make a deal with me."

"An' made it!" said Silent ominously.

No gun pointed at him this time, but Hardy

9

jerked his hands once more above his head and cowered against the wall.

"So help me God he didn't, Jim."

"Get your hands down."

He lowered his hands slowly.

"I told him I didn't know nothin' about you."

"What about that train? What about that shipment?"

"It's jest the way I told you, except that it's on the eighteenth instead of the nineteenth."

"I'm goin' to believe you. If you double cross me I'll have your hide. Maybe they'll get me, but there'll be enough of my boys left to get *you*. You can lay to that. How much did they offer you, Lee? How much am I worth to the little old U. S. A.?"

"I—I—it wasn't the money. I was afraid to stick with my game any longer."

The long rider had already turned towards the door, making no effort to keep his face to the agent. The latter, flushing again, moved his hand towards his hip, but stopped the movement. The last threat of Silent carried a deep conviction with it. He knew that the faith of lone riders to each other was an inviolable bond. Accordingly he followed at the heels of the other man into the outside room.

"So long, old timer," he called, slapping Silent

on the shoulder, "I'll be seein' you agin before
long."

Calder's men looked up with curious eyes.
Hardy watched Silent swing onto his horse and
gallop down the street.   Then he went hurriedly
back to his office.   Once inside he dropped into
the big swivel-chair, buried his face in his arms, and
wept like a child.

CHAPTER XII

PARTNERS

DUST powdered his hat and clothes as Tex
Calder trotted his horse north across the hills.
His face was a sickly grey, and his black hair might
have been an eighteenth century wig, so thoroughly
was it disguised. It had been a long ride. Many
a long mile wound back behind him, and still the
cattle pony, with hanging head, stuck to its task.
Now he was drawing out on a highland, and below
him stretched the light yellow-green of the willows
of the bottom land. He halted his pony and
swung a leg over the horn of his saddle. Then he
rolled a cigarette, and while he inhaled it in long
puffs he scanned the trees narrowly. Miles across,
and stretching east and west farther than his eye
could reach, extended the willows. Somewhere in
that wilderness was the gang of Jim Silent. An
army corps might have been easily concealed there.

If he was not utterly discouraged in the beginning of his search, it was merely because the rang-

ers of the hills and plains are taught patience
almost as soon as they learn to ride a horse.   He
surveyed the yellow-green forest calmly.   In the
west the low hanging sun turned crimson and
bulged at the sides into a clumsy elipse.   He
started down the slope at the same dog-trot which
the pony had kept up all day.   Just before he
reached the skirts of the trees he brought his
horse to a sudden halt and threw back his head.
It seemed to him that he heard a faint whistling.

He could not be sure.   It was so far off and
unlike any whistling he had ever heard before,
that he half guessed it to be the movement of a
breeze through the willows, but the wind was
hardly strong enough to make this sound.   For
a full five minutes he listened without moving his
horse.   Then came the thing for which he waited,
a phrase of melody undoubtedly from human lips.

What puzzled him most was the nature of the
music.   As he rode closer to the trees it grew
clearer.   It was unlike any song he had ever heard.
It was a strange improvisation with a touch of
both melancholy and savage exultation running
through it.   Calder found himself nodding in
sympathy with the irregular rhythm.

It grew so clear at last that he marked with some
accuracy the direction from which it came.   If this

was Silent's camp, it must be strongly guarded, and he should approach the place more cautiously than he could possibly do on a horse. Accordingly he dismounted, threw the reins over the pony's head, and started on through the willows. The whistling became louder and louder. He moved stealthily from tree to tree, for he had not the least idea when he would run across a guard. The whistling ceased, but the marshal was now so near that he could follow the original direction without much trouble. In a few moments he might distinguish the sound of voices. If there were two or three men in the camp he might be able to surprise them and make his arrest. If the outlaws were many, at least he could lie low near the camp and perhaps learn the plans of the gang. He worked his way forward more and more carefully. At one place he thought a shadowy figure slipped through the brush a short distance away. He poised his gun, but lowered it again after a moment's thought. It must have been a stir of shadows. No human being could move so swiftly or so noiselessly.

Nevertheless the sight gave him such a start that he proceeded with even greater caution. He was crouched close to the ground. Every inch of it he scanned carefully before he set down a foot, fearful of the cracking of a fallen twig. Like most men when they hunt, he began to feel that something followed him. He tried to argue the thought out of his brain, but it persisted, and grew stronger. Half a dozen times he whirled suddenly with his revolver poised. At last he heard a stamp which could come from nothing but the hoof of a horse. The sound dispelled his fears. In another moment he would be in sight of the camp.

"Do you figger you'll find it?" asked a quiet voice behind him.

He turned and looked into the steady muzzle of a Colt. Behind that revolver was a thin, handsome face with a lock of jet black hair falling over the forehead. Calder knew men, and now he felt a strange absence of any desire to attempt a gunplay.

"I was just taking a stroll through the willows," he said, with a mighty attempt at carelessness.

"Oh," said the other. "It appeared to me you was sort of huntin' for something. You was headed straight for my hoss."

Calder strove to find some way out. He could not. There was no waver in the hand that held that black gun. The brown eyes were decidedly discouraging to any attempt at a surprise. He felt helpless for the first time in his career.

"Go over to him, Bart," said the gentle voice of the stranger. "Stand fast!"

The last two words, directed to Calder came, with a metallic hardness, for the marshal started as a great black dog slipped from behind a tree and slunk towards him. This was the shadow which moved more swiftly and noiselessly than a human being.

"Keep back that damned wolf," he said desperately.

"He ain't goin' to hurt you," said the calm voice. "Jest toss your gun to the ground."

There was nothing else for it. Calder dropped his weapon with the butt towards Whistling Dan.

"Bring it here, Bart," said the latter.

The big animal lowered his head, still keeping his green eyes upon Calder, took up the revolver in his white fangs, and glided back to his master.

"Jest turn your back to me, an' keep your hands clear of your body," said Dan.

Calder obeyed, sweating with shame. He felt a hand pat his pockets lightly in search for a hidden weapon, and then, with his head slightly turned, he sensed the fact that Dan was dropping his revolver into its holster. He whirled and drove his clenched fist straight at Dan's face.

What happened then he would never forget to

the end of his life. Calder's weapon still hung in Dan's right hand, but the latter made no effort to use it. He dropped the gun, and as Calder's right arm shot out, it was caught at the wrist, and jerked down with a force that jarred his whole body.

"Down, Bart!" shouted Dan. The great wolf checked in the midst of his leap and dropped, whining with eagerness, at Calder's feet. At the same time the marshal's left hand was seized and whipped across his body. He wrenched away with all his force. He might as well have struggled with steel manacles. He was helpless, staring into eyes which now glinted with a yellow light that sent a cold wave tingling through his blood.

The yellow gleam died; his hands were loosed; but he made no move to spring at Dan's throat. Chill horror had taken the place of his shame, and the wolf-dog still whined at his feet with lips grinned back from the long white teeth.

"Who in the name of God are you?" he gasped, and even as he spoke the truth came to him— the whistling—the panther-like speed of hand— "Whistling Dan Barry."

The other frowned.

"If you didn't know my name why were you trailin' me?"

"I wasn't after you," said Calder.

"You was crawlin' along like that jest for fun? Friend, I figger to know you. You been sent out by the tall man to lay for me."

"What tall man?" asked Calder, his wits groping.

"The one that swung the chair in Morgan's place," said Dan. "Now you're goin' to take me to your camp. I got something to say to him."

"By the Lord!" cried the marshal, "you're trailing Silent."

Dan watched him narrowly. It was hard to accuse those keen black eyes of deceit.

"I'm trailin' the man who sent you out after me," he asserted with a little less assurance.

Calder tore open the front of his shirt and pushed back one side of it. Pinned there next to his skin was his marshal's badge.

He said: "My name's Tex Calder."

It was a word to conjure with up and down the vast expanse of the mountain-desert. Dan smiled, and the change of expression made him seem ten years younger.

"Git down, Bart. Stand behind me!" The dog obeyed sullenly. "I've heard a pile of men talk about you, Tex Calder." Their hands and their eyes met. There was a mutual respect in the glances. "An' I'm a pile sorry for this."

He picked up the gun from the ground and extended it butt first to the marshal, who restored it slowly to the holster. It was the first time it had ever been forced from his grasp.

"Who was it you talked about a while ago?" asked Dan.

"Jim Silent."

Dan instinctively dropped his hand back to his revolver.

"The tall man?"

"The one you fought with in Morgan's place."

The unpleasant gleam returned to Dan's eyes.

"I thought there was only one reason why he should die, but now I see there's a heap of 'em."

Calder was all business.

"How long have you been here?" he asked.

"About a day."

"Have you seen anything of Silent here among the willows?"

"No."

"Do you think he's still here?"

"Yes."

"Why?"

"I dunno. I'll stay here till I find him among the trees or he breaks away into the open."

"How'll you know when he leaves the willows?"

Whistling Dan was puzzled.

"I dunno," he answered. "Somethin' will tell me when he gets far away from me—he an' his men."

"It's an inner sense, eh? Like the smell of the bloodhound?" said Calder, but his eyes were strangely serious.

"This day's about done," he went on. "Have you any objections to me camping with you here?"

Not a cowpuncher within five hundred miles but would be glad of such redoubted company. They went back to Calder's horse.

"We can start for my clearing," said Dan. "Bart'll bring the hoss. Fetch him in."

The wolf took the dangling bridle reins and led on the cowpony. Calder observed his performance with starting eyes, but he was averse to asking questions. In a few moments they came out on a small open space. The ground was covered with a quantity of dried bunch grass which a glorious black stallion was cropping. Now he tossed up his head so that some of his long mane fell forward between his ears and at sight of Calder his ears dropped back and his eyes blazed, but when Dan stepped from the willows the ears came forward again with a whinny of greeting. Calder watched the beautiful animal with all the enthusiasm of an expert horseman. Satan was untethered; the saddle and bridle lay in a corner of the clearing; evidently the horse was a pet and would not leave its master. He spoke gently and stepped forward to caress the velvet shining neck, but Satan snorted and started away, trembling with excitement.

"How can you keep such a wild fellow as this without hobbling him?" asked Calder.

"He ain't wild," said Dan.

"Why, he won't let me put a hand on him."

"Yes, he will. Steady, Satan!"

The stallion stood motionless with tne veritable fires of hell in his eyes as Calder approached. The latter stopped.

"Not for me," he said. "I'd rather rub the moustache of the lion in the zoo than touch that black devil!"

Bart at that moment led in the cowpony and Calder started to remove the saddle. He had scarcely done so and hobbled his horse when he was startled by a tremendous snarling and snorting. He turned to see the stallion plunging hither and thither, striking with his fore-hooves, while around him, darting in and out under the driving feet, sprang the great black wolf, his teeth clashing like steel on steel. In another moment they might sink in the throat of the horse! Calder, with an exclamation of horror, whipped out his revolver, but checked himself at the very instant of firing. The master of the two animals stood with arms folded, actually smiling upon the fight!

"For God's sake!" cried the marshal. "Shoot the damned wolf, man, or he'll have your horse by the throat!"

"Leave 'em be," said Dan, without turning his head. "Satan an' Black Bart ain't got any other dogs an' hosses to run around with. They's jest playing a little by way of exercise."

Calder stood agape before what seemed the incarnate fury of the pair. Then he noticed that those snapping fangs, however close they came, always missed the flesh of the stallion, and the driving hoofs never actually endangered the leaping wolf.

"Stop 'em!" he cried at last. "It makes me nervous to watch that sort of play. It isn't natural!"

"All right," said Dan. "Stop it, boys."

He had not raised his voice, but they ceased their wild gambols instantly, the stallion, with head thrown high and arched tail and heaving sides, while the wolf, with lolling red tongue, strolled calmly towards his master.

The latter paid no further attention to them, but set about kindling a small fire over which to cook supper. Calder joined him. The marshal's mind was too full for speech, but now and again he turned a long glance of wonder upon the stallion or Black Bart. In the same silence they sat under the last light of the sunset and ate their supper. Calder, with head bent, pondered over the man of mystery and his two tamed animals. Tamed? Not one of the three was tamed, the man least of all.

He saw Dan pause from his eating to stare with wide, vacant eyes among the trees. The wolf-dog approached, looked up in his master's face, whined softly, and getting no response went back to his place and lay down, his eyes never moving from Dan. Still he stared among the trees. The gloom deepened, and he smiled faintly. He began to whistle, a low, melancholy strain so soft that it blended with the growing hush of the night. Calder listened, wholly overawed. That weird music seemed an interpretation of the vast spaces of the mountains, of the pitiless desert, of the limitless silences, and the whistler was an understanding part of the whole.

He became aware of a black shadow behind the musician. It was Satan, who rested his nose on the shoulder of the master. Without ceasing his whistling Dan raised a hand, touched the small muzzle, and Satan went at once to a side of the clearing and lay down. It was almost as if the two had said good-night! Calder could stand it no longer.

"Dan, I've got to talk to you," he began.

The whistling ceased; the wide brown eyes turned to him.

"Fire away—partner."

Ay, they had eaten together by the same fire— they had watched the coming of the night—they had shaken hands in friendship—they were partners. He knew deep in his heart that no human being could ever be the actual comrade of this man. This lord of the voiceless desert needed no human companionship; yet as the marshal glanced from the black shadow of Satan to the gleaming eyes of Bart, and then to the visionary face of Barry, he felt that he had been admitted by Whistling Dan into the mysterious company. The thought stirred him deeply. It was as if he had made an alliance with the wandering wind. Why he had been accepted he could not dream, but he had heard the word "partner" and he knew it was meant. After all, stranger things than this happen in the mountain-desert, where man is greater and convention less. A single word has been known to estrange lifelong comrades; a

single evening beside a camp-fire has changed foes
to partners. Calder drew his mind back to business with a great effort.

"There's one thing you don't know about Jim
Silent. A reward of ten thousand dollars lies on
his head. The notices aren't posted yet."

Whistling Dan shrugged his shoulders.

"I ain't after money," he answered.

Calder frowned. He did not appreciate a bluff.

"Look here," he said, "if we kill him, because
no power on earth will take him alive—we'll split
the money."

"If you lay a hand on him," said Dan, without
emotion, "we won't be friends no longer, I figger."

Calder stared.

"If you don't want to get him," he said, "why
in God's name are you trailing him this way?"

Dan touched his lips. "He hit me with his
fist."

He paused, and spoke again with a drawling
voice that gave his words an uncanny effect.

"My blood went down from my mouth to my
chin. I tasted it. Till I get him there ain't no
way of me forgettin' him."

His eyes lighted with that ominous gleam.

"That's why no other man c'n put a hand on
him. He's laid out all for me. Understand?"

10

The ring of the question echoed for a moment through Calder's mind.

"I certainly do," he said with profound conviction, "and I'll never forget it." He decided on a change of tactics. "But there are other men with Jim Silent and those men will fight to keep you from getting to him."

"I'm sorry for 'em," said Dan gently. "I ain't got nothin' agin any one except the big man."

Calder took a long breath.

"Don't you see," he explained carefully, "if you shoot one of these men you are simply a murderer who must be apprehended by the law and punished."

"It makes it bad for me, doesn't it?" said Dan. "An' I hope I won't have to hurt more'n one or two of 'em. You see,"—he leaned forward seriously towards Calder—"I'd only shoot for their arms or their legs. I wouldn't spoil them altogether."

Calder threw up his hands in despair. Black Bart snarled at the gesture.

"I can't listen no more," said Dan. "I got to start explorin' the willows pretty soon."

"In the dark?" exclaimed Calder.

"Sure. Black Bart'll go with me. The dark don't bother him."

"I'll go along."

"I'd rather be alone. I might meet *him*."

"Any way you want," said Calder, "but first hear my plan—it doesn't take long to tell it."

The darkness thickened around them while he talked. The fire died out—the night swallowed up their figures.

CHAPTER XIII

THE LONE RIDERS ENTERTAIN

WHEN Lee Haines rode into Silent's camp that evening no questions were asked. Questions were not popular among the long riders. He did not know more than the names of half the men who sat around the smoky fire. They were eager to forget the past, and the only allusions to former times came in chance phrases which they let fall at rare intervals. When they told an anecdote they erased all names by instinct. They would begin: "I heard about a feller over to the Circle Y outfit that was once ridin'—" etc. As a rule they themselves were "that feller over to the Circle Y outfit." Accordingly only a few grunts greeted Haines and yet he was far and away the most popular man in the group. Even solemn-eyed Jim Silent was partial to the handsome fellow.

"Heard the whistling today?" he asked.

Purvis shook his head and Terry Jordan allowed "as how it was most uncommon fortunate that this

Barry feller didn't start his noise." After this Haines ate his supper in silence, his ear ready to catch the first sound of Kate's horse as it crashed through the willows and shrubs. Nevertheless it was Shorty Rhinehart who sprang to his feet first.

"They's a hoss there comin' among the willows!" he announced.

"Maybe it's Silent," remarked Haines casually.

"The chief don't make no such a noise. He picks his goin'," answered Hal Purvis.

The sound was quite audible now.

"They's been some crooked work," said Rhinehart excitedly. "Somebody's tipped off the marshals about where we're lyin'."

"All right," said Haines quietly, "you and I will investigate."

They started through the willows. Rhinehart was cursing beneath his breath.

"Don't be too fast with your six-gun," warned Haines.

"I'd rather be too early than too late."

"Maybe it isn't a marshal. If a man were looking for us he'd be a fool to come smashing along like that."

He had scarcely spoken when Kate came into view.

"A girl, by God!" said Rhinehart, with mingled relief and disgust.

"Sure thing," agreed Haines.

"Let's beat it back to the camp."

"Not a hope. She's headed straight for the camp. We'll take her in and tell her we're a bunch from the Y Circle X outfit headed north. She'll never know the difference."

"Good idea," said Rhinehart, and he added with a chuckle, "it's been nigh three months since I've talked to a piece of calico."

"Hey, there!" called Haines, and he stepped out with Rhinehart before her horse.

"Oh!" cried Kate, reining up her horse sharply. "Who are you?"

"A beaut!" muttered Rhinehart in devout admiration.

"We're from the Y Circle X outfit," said Haines glibly, "camping over here for the night. Are you lost, lady?"

"I guess I am. I thought I could get across the willows before the night fell. I'm trying to find a man who rode in this direction."

"Come on into the camp," said Haines easily. "Maybe some of the boys can put you on his track. What sort of a looking fellow is he?"

"Rides a black horse and whistles a good deal.

His name is Barry. They call him Whistling Dan.''

''By God!'' whispered Rhinehart in the ear of Haines.

''Shut up!'' answered Haines in the same tone. ''Are you afraid of a girl?''

''I've trailed him south this far,'' went on Kate, ''and a few miles away from here I lost track of him. I think he may have gone on across the willows.''

''Haven't seen him,'' said Rhinehart amiably. ''But come on to the camp, lady. Maybe one of the boys has spotted him on the way. What's your name?''

''Kate Cumberland,'' she answered.

He removed his hat with a broad grin and reached up a hand to her.

''I'm most certainly glad to meet you, an' my name's Shorty. This here is Lee. Want to come along with us?''

''Thank you. I'm a little worried.''

'' 'S all right. Don't get worried. We'll show you the way out. Just follow us.''

They started back through the willows, Kate following half a dozen yards behind.

''Listen here, Shorty,'' said Haines in a cautious voice. ''You heard her name?''

"Sure."

"Well, that's the daughter of the man that raised Whistling Dan. I saw her at Morgan's place. She's probably been tipped off that he's following Silent, but she has no idea who we are."

"Sure she hasn't. She's a great looker, eh, Lee?"

"She'll do, I guess. Now get this: The girl is after Whistling Dan, and if she meets him she'll persuade him to come back to her father's place. She'll take him off our trail, and I guess none of us'll be sorry to know that he's gone, eh?"

"I begin to follow you, Lee. You've always had the head!"

"All right. Now we'll get Purvis to tell the girl that he's heard a peculiar whistling around here this evening. We'll advise her to stick around and go out when she hears the whistling again. That way she'll meet him and head him off, savvy?"

"Right," said Rhinehart.

"Then beat it ahead as fast as you can and wise up the boys."

"That's me—specially about their bein' Y Circle X fellers, eh?"

He chuckled and made ahead as fast as his long legs could carry him. Haines dropped back beside Kate.

"Everything goes finely," he assured her. "I told Rhinehart what to do. He's gone ahead to the camp. Now all you have to do is to keep your head. One of the boys will tell you that we've heard some whistling near the camp this evening. Then I'll ask you to stay around for a while in case the whistling should sound again, do you see? Remember, never ask a question!"

It was even more simple than Haines had hoped. Silent's men suspected nothing. After all, Kate's deception was a small affair, and her frankness, her laughter, and her beauty carried all before her.

The long riders became quickly familiar with her, but through their rough talk, the Westerners' reverence for a woman ran like a thread of gold over a dark cloth. Her fear lessened and almost passed away while she listened to their talk and watched their faces. The kindly human nature which had lain unexpressed in most of them for months together burst out torrent-like and flooded about her with a sense of security and power. These were conquerors of men, fighters by instinct and habit, but here they sat laughing and chattering with a helpless girl, and not a one of them but would have cut the others' throats rather than see her come to harm. The roughness of their past and the dread of their future they laid aside like an ugly cloak while they showed her what lies in the worst man's heart—a certain awe of woman. Their manners underwent a sudden change. Polite words, rusted by long disuse, were resurrected in her honour. Tremendous phrases came labouring forth. There was a general though covert rearranging of bandanas, and an interchange of self-conscious glances. Haines alone seemed impervious to her charm.

The red died slowly along the west. There was no light save the flicker of the fire, which played on Kate's smile and the rich gold of her hair, or caught out of the dark one of the lean, hard faces which circled her. Now and then it fell on the ghastly grin of Terry Jordan and Kate had to clench her hand to keep up her nerve.

It was deep night when Jim Silent rode into the clearing. Shorty Rhinehart and Hal Purvis went to him quickly to explain the presence of the girl and the fact that they were all members of the Y Circle X outfit. He responded with nods while his gloomy eyes held fast on Kate. When they presented him as the boss, Jim, he replied to her good-natured greeting in a voice that was half grunt and half growl.

CHAPTER XIV

DELILAH

HAINES muttered at Kate's ear: "This is the man. Now keep up your courage."

"He doesn't like this," went on Haines in the same muffled voice, "but when he understands just why you're here I think he'll be as glad as any of us."

Silent beckoned to him and he went to the chief.

"What about the girl?" asked the big fellow curtly.

"Didn't Rhinehart tell you?"

"Rhinehart's a fool and so are the rest of them. Have you gone loco too, Haines, to let a girl come here?"

"Where's the harm?"

"Why, damn it, she's marked every man here."

"I let her in because she is trying to get hold of Whistling Dan."

"Which no fool girl c'n take that feller off the trail. Nothin' but lead can do that."

"I tell you," said Haines, "the boy's in love with her. I watched them at Morgan's place. She can twist him around her finger."

A faint light broke the gloom of Silent's face.

"Yaller hair an' blue eyes. They c'n do a lot. Maybe you're right. What's that?" His voice had gone suddenly husky.

A russet moon pushed slowly up through the trees. Its uncertain light fell across the clearing. For the first time the thick pale smoke of the fire was visible, rising straight up until it cleared the tops of the willows, and then caught into swift, jagging lines as the soft wind struck it. A coyote wailed from the distant hills, and before his complaint was done another sound came through the hushing of the willows, a melancholy whistling, thin with distance.

"We'll see if that's the man you want," suggested Haines.

"I'll go along," said Shorty Rhinehart.

"And me too," said a third. The whole group would have accompanied them, but the heavy voice of Jim Silent cut in: "You'll stay here, all of you except the girl and Lee."

They turned back, muttering, and Kate followed Haines into the willows.

"Well?" growled Bill Kilduff.

"What I want to know—" broke in Terry Jordan.

"Go to hell with your questions," said Silent, "but until you go there you'll do what I say, understand?"

"Look here, Jim," said Hal Purvis, "are you a king an' we jest your slaves, maybe?"

"You're goin' it a pile too hard," said Shorty Rhinehart.

Every one of these speeches came sharply out while they glared at Jim Silent. Hands were beginning to fall to the hip and fingers were curving stiffly as if for the draw. Silent leaned his broad shoulders against the side of his roan and folded his arms. His eyes went round the circle slowly, lingering an instant on each face. Under that cold stare they grew uneasy. To Shorty Rhinehart it became necessary to push back his hat and scratch his forehead. Terry Jordan found a mysterious business with his bandana. Every one of them had occasion to raise his hand from the neighbourhood of his six-shooter. Silent smiled.

"A fine, hard crew you are," he said sarcastically, at last. "A great bunch of long riders, lettin' a slip of a yaller-haired girl make fools of you. You over there—you, Shorty Rhinehart, you'd cut the throat of a man that looked crosswise at the Cumberland girl, wouldn't you? An' you, Purvis, you're aching to get at me, ain't you? An' you're still thinkin' of them blue eyes, Jordan?"

Before any one could speak he poured in another volley between wind and water: "One slip of a girl can make fools out of five long riders? No, you ain't long riders. All you c'n handle is hobby hosses!"

"What do you want us to do?" growled swarthy Bill Kilduff.

"Keep your face shut while I'm talkin', that's what I want you to do!"

There was a devil of rage in his eyes. His folded arms tugged at each other, and if they got free there would be gun play. The four men shrank, and he was satisfied.

"Now I'll tell you what we're goin' to do," he went on. "We're goin' out after Haines an' the girl. If they come up with this Whistlin' Dan we're goin' to surround him an' fill him full of lead, while they're talkin'."

"Not for a million dollars!" burst in Hal Purvis.

"Not in a thousan' years!" echoed Terry Jordan.

Silent turned his watchful eyes from one to the other. They were ready to fight now, and he sensed it at once.

"Why?" he asked calmly.

"It ain't playin' square with the girl," announced Rhinehart.

"Purvis," said Silent, for he knew that the opposition centred in the figure of the venomous little gun fighter; "if you seen a mad dog that was runnin' straight at you, would you be kep' from shootin' it because a pretty girl hollered out an' asked you not to?"

Their eyes shifted rapidly from one to another, seeking a way out, and finding none.

"An' is there any difference between this here Whistlin' Dan an' a mad dog?"

Still they were mute.

"I tell you, boys, we got a better chance of dodgin' lightnin' an' puttin' a bloodhound off our trail than we have of gettin' rid of this Whistlin' Dan. An' when he catches up with us—well, all I'm askin' is that you remember what he done to them four dollars before they hit the dust?"

"The chief's right," growled Kilduff, staring down at the ground. "It's Whistlin' Dan or us. The mountains ain't big enough to hold him an' us!"

.   .   .   .

Before Whistling Dan the great wolf glided among the trees. For a full hour they had wan-

dered through the willows in this manner, and Dan
had made up his mind to surrender the search when
Bart, returning from one of his noiseless detours,
sprang out before his master and whined softly.
Dan turned, loosening his revolver in the holster,
and followed Bart through the soft gloom of the
tree shadows and the moonlight. His step was
almost as silent as that of the slinking animal
which went before. At last the wolf stopped and
raised his head. Almost instantly Dan saw a man
and a woman approaching through the willows.
The moonlight dropped across her face. He
recognized Kate, with Lee Haines walking a pace
before her.

"Stand where you are," he said.

Haines leaped to one side, his revolver flashing
in his hand. Dan stepped out before them while
Black Bart slunk close beside him, snarling softly.

He seemed totally regardless of the gun in
Haines's hand. His manner was that of a con-
queror who had the outlaw at his mercy.

"You," he said, "walk over there to the side of
the clearing."

"Dan!" cried Kate, as she went to him with
extended arms.

He stopped her with a gesture, his eyes upon
Haines, who had moved away.

"Watch him, Bart," said Dan.

The black wolf ran to Haines and crouched snarling at his feet. The outlaw restored his revolver to his holster and stood with his arms folded, his back turned. Dan looked to Kate. At the meeting of their eyes she shrank a little. She had expected a difficult task in persuading him, but not this hard aloofness. She felt suddenly as if she were a stranger to him.

"How do you come here—with him?"

"He is my friend!"

"You sure pick a queer place to go walkin' with him."

"Hush, Dan! He brought me here to find you!"

"*He* brought you here?"

"Don't you understand?"

"When I want a friend like him, I'll go huntin' for him myself; an' I'll pack a gun with me!"

That flickering yellow light played behind Dan's eyes.

"I looked into his face—an' he stared the other way."

She made a little imploring gesture, but his hand remained on his hips, and there was no softening of his voice.

"What fetched you here?"

Every word was like a hand that pushed her farther away.

"Are you dumb, Kate? What fetched you here?"

"I have come to bring you home, Dan."

"I'm home now."

"What do you mean?"

"There's the roof of my house," he jerked his hand towards the sky, "the mountain passes are my doors—an' the earth is my floor."

"No! no! We are waiting for you at the ranch."

He shrugged his shoulders.

"Dan, this wild trail has no end."

"Maybe, but I know that feller can show me the way to Jim Silent, an' now——"

He turned towards Haines as he spoke, but here a low, venomous snarl from Black Bart checked his words. Kate saw him stiffen—his lips parted to a faint smile—his head tilted back a little as if he listened intently, though she could hear nothing. She was not a yard from him, and yet she felt a thousand miles away. His head turned full upon her, and she would never forget the yellow light of his eyes.

"Dan!" she cried, but her voice was no louder than a whisper.

"Delilah!" he said, and leaped back into the shade of the willows.

Even as he sprang she saw the flash of the moonlight on his drawn revolver, and fire spat from it twice, answered by a yell of pain, the clang of a bullet on metal, and half a dozen shots from the woods behind her.

That word "Delilah!" rang in her brain to the exclusion of all the world. Vaguely she heard voices shouting—she turned a little and saw Haines facing her with his revolver in his hand, but prevented from moving by the wolf who crouched snarling at his feet. The order of his master kept him there even after that master was gone. Now men ran out into the clearing. A keen whistle sounded far off among the willows, and the wolf leaped away from his prisoner and into the shadows on the trail of Dan.

.   .   .   .

Tex Calder prided himself on being a light sleeper. Years spent in constant danger enabled him to keep his sense of hearing alert even when he slept. He had never been surprised. It was his boast that he never would be. Therefore when a hand dropped lightly on his shoulder he started erect from his blankets with a curse and grasped his revolver. A strong grip on his wrist paralysed his fingers.   Whistling Dan leaned above him.

"Wake up," said the latter.

"What the devil—" breathed the marshal. "You travel like a cloud shadow, Dan. You make no sound."

"Wake up and talk to me."

"I'm awake all right.   What's happened?"

There was a moment of silence while Dan seemed to be trying for speech.

Black Bart, at the other side of the clearing, pointed his nose at the yellow moon and wailed. He was very close, but the sound was so controlled that it seemed to come at a great distance from some wild spirit wandering between earth and heaven.

Instead of speaking Dan jumped to his feet and commenced pacing up and down, up and down, a rapid, tireless stride; at his heels the wolf slunk, with lowered head and tail.   The strange fellow was in some great trouble, Calder could see, and it stirred him mightily to know that the wild man had turned to him for help.   Yet he would ask no questions.

When in doubt the cattleman rolls a cigarette, and that was what Calder did.   He smoked and waited.   At last the inevitable came.

"How old are you, Tex?"

"Forty-four."

"That's a good deal. You ought to know something."

"Maybe."

"About women?"

"Ah!" said Calder.

"Bronchos is cut out chiefly after one pattern," went on Dan. "They's chiefly jest meanness. Are women the same—jest cut after one pattern?"

"What pattern, Dan?"

"The pattern of Delilah! They ain't no trust to be put in 'em?"

"A good many of us have found that out."

"I thought one woman was different from the rest."

"We all think that. Woman in particular is divine; woman in general is—hell!"

"Ay, but this one—" He stopped and set his teeth.

"What has she done?"

"She—" he hesitated, and when he spoke again his voice did not tremble; there was a deep hurt and wonder in it: "She double-crossed me!"

"When? Do you mean to say you've met a woman tonight out here among the willows?— Where—how——"

"Tex——!"

"Ay, Dan."

"It's—it's hell!"

"It is now. But you'll forget her! The mountains, the desert, and above all, time—they'll cure you, my boy."

"Not in a whole century, Tex."

Calder waited curiously for the explanation. It came.

"Jest to think of her is like hearing music. Oh, God, Tex, what c'n I do to fight agin this here cold feelin' at my heart?"

Dan slipped down beside the marshal and the latter dropped a sympathetic hand over the lean, brown fingers. They returned the pressure with a bone-crushing grip.

"Fight, Dan! It will make you forget her."

"Her skin is softer'n satin, Tex."

"Ay, but you'll never touch it again, Dan."

"Her eyes are deeper'n a pool at night an' her hair is all gold like ripe corn."

"You'll never look into her eyes again, Dan, and you'll never touch the gold of that hair."

"God!"

The word was hardly more than a whisper, but it brought Black Bart leaping to his feet.

Dan spoke again: "Tex, I'm thankin' you for

listenin' to me; I wanted to talk. Bein' silent was burnin' me up. There's one thing more."

"Fire it out, lad."

"This evenin' I told you I hated no man but Jim Silent."

"Yes."

"An' now they's another of his gang. Sometime—when she's standin' by—I'm goin' to take him by the throat till he don't breathe no more. Then I'll throw him down in front of her an' ask her if she c'n kiss the life back into his lips!"

Calder was actually shaking with excitement, but he was wise enough not to speak.

"Tex!"

"Ay, lad."

"But when I've choked his damned life away——"

"Yes?"

"Ay, lad."

"There'll be five more that seen her shamin' me. Tex—all hell is bustin' loose inside me!"

For a moment Calder watched, but that stare of cold hate mastered him. He turned his head.

CHAPTER XV

THE CROSS ROADS

As Black Bart raced away in answer to Dan's whistle, Kate recovered herself from the daze in which she stood and with a sob ran towards the willows, calling the name of Dan, but Silent sprang after her, and caught her by the arm. She cried out and struggled vainly in his grip.

"Don't follow him, boys!" called Silent. "He's a dog that can bite while he runs. Stand quiet, girl!"

Lee Haines caught him by the shoulder and jerked Silent around. His hand held the butt of his revolver, and his whole arm trembled with eagerness for the draw.

"Take your hand from her, Jim!" he said.

Silent met his eye with the same glare and while his left hand still held Kate by both her wrists his right dropped to his gun.

"Not when you tell me, Lee!"

"Damn you, I say let her go!"

"By God, Haines, I stand for too much from you!"

And still they did not draw, because each of them knew that if the crisis came it would mean death to them both. Bill Kilduff jumped between them and thrust them back.

He cried, "Ain't we got enough trouble without roundin' up work at home? Terry Jordan is shot through the arm."

Kate tugged at the restraining hand of Silent, not in an attempt to escape, but in order to get closer to Haines.

"Was this your friendship?" she said, her voice shaking with hate and sorrow, "to bring me here as a lure for Whistling Dan? Listen to me, all of you! He's escaped you now, and he'll come again. Remember him, for he shan't forget you!"

"You hear her?" said Silent to Haines. "Is this what you want me to turn loose?"

"Silent," said Haines, "it isn't the girl alone you've double crossed. You've crooked me, and you'll pay me for it sooner or later!"

"Day or night, winter or summer, I'm willing to meet you an' fight it out. Rhinehart and Purvis, take this girl back to the clearing!"

They approached, Purvis still staring at the hand from which only a moment before his gun had been knocked by the shot of Whistling Dan. It was a thing which he could not understand—he had not yet lost a most uncomfortable sense of awe. Haines made no objection when they went off, with Kate walking between them. He knew, now that his blind anger had left him, that it was folly to draw on a fight while the rest of Silent's men stood around them.

"An' the rest of you go back to the clearin'. I got somethin' to talk over with Lee," said Silent.

The others obeyed without question, and the leader turned back to his lieutenant. For a moment longer they remained staring at each other. Then Silent moved slowly forward with outstretched hand.

"Lee," he said quietly, "I'm owin' you an apology an' I'm man enough to make it."

"I can't take your hand, Jim."

Silent hesitated.

"I guess you got cause to be mad, Lee," he said. "Maybe I played too quick a hand. I didn't think about double crossin' you. I only seen a way to get Whistlin' Dan out of our path, an' I took it without rememberin' that you was the safeguard to the girl."

Haines eyed his chief narrowly.

"I wish to God I could read your mind," he said at last, "but I'll take your word that you did it without thinking."

His hand slowly met Silent's.

"An' what about the girl now, Lee?"

"I'll send her back to her father's ranch. It will be easy to put her on the right way."

"Don't you see no reason why you can't do that?"

"Are you playing with me?"

"I'm talkin' to you as I'd talk to myself. If she's loose she'll describe us all an' set the whole range on our trail."

Haines stared.

Silent went on: "If we can't turn her loose, they's only one thing left—an' that's to take her with us wherever we go."

"On your honour, do you see no other way out?"

"Do you?"

"She may promise not to speak of it."

"There ain't no way of changin' the spots of a leopard, Lee, an' there ain't no way of keepin' a woman's tongue still."

"How can we take a girl with us."

"It ain't goin' to be for long. After we pull the job that comes on the eighteenth, we'll blow farther south an' then we'll let her go."

"And no harm will come to her while she's with us?"

"Here's my hand on it, Lee."

"How can she ride with us?"

"She won't go as a woman. I've thought of that. I brought out a new outfit for Purvis from Elkhead—trousers, chaps, shirts, an' all. He's small. They'll near fit the girl."

"There isn't any other way, Jim?"

"I leave it to you. God knows *I* don't want to drag any damn calico aroun' with us."

As they went back towards their clearing they arranged the details. Silent would take the men aside and explain his purpose to them. Haines could inform the girl of what she must do. Just before they reached the camp Silent stopped short and took Haines by the shoulder.

"They's one thing I can't make out, Lee, an' that's how Whistlin' Dan made his getaway. I'd of bet a thousand bones that he would be dropped before he could touch his shootin' irons. An' then what happened? Hal Purvis jest flashed a gun—and that feller shot it out'n his hand. I never seen a draw like that. His hand jest seemed to twitch—I couldn't follow the move he made—an' the next second his gun went off."

He stared at Lee with a sort of fascinated horror.

"Silent," said Haines, "can you explain how the lightning comes down out of the sky?"

"Of course not."

"Then don't ask me to explain how Whistling Dan made his getaway. One minute I heard him talkin' with the girl. The next second there was two shots and when I whirled he was gone. But he'll come back, Jim. We're not through with him. He slipped away from you and your men like water out of a sieve, but we won't slip away from him the same way.

Silent stared on again with bowed head.

"He liked the girl, Lee?"

"Any one could see that."

"Then while she's with us he'll go pretty slow. Lee, that's another reason why she's got to stay with us. My frien'; it's time we was moving out from the willows. The next time he comes up with us he won't be numb in the head. He'll be thinkin' fast an' he'll be shootin' a damn sight faster. We got two jobs ahead of us—first to get that Wells Fargo shipment, and then to get Whistling Dan. There ain't room enough in the whole world for him and me."

CHAPTER XVI

THE THREE OF US

IN the clearing of Whistling Dan and Tex Calder the marshal had turned into his blankets once more. There was no thought of sleep in Dan's mind. When the heavy breathing of the sleeper began he rose and commenced to pace up and down on the farther side of the open space. Two pairs of glowing eyes followed him in every move. Black Bart, who trailed him up and down during the first few turns he made, now sat down and watched his master with a wistful gaze. The black stallion, who lay more like a dog than a horse on the ground, kept his ears pricked forwards, as if expecting some order. Once or twice he whinnied very softly, and finally Dan sat down beside Satan, his shoulders leaned against the satiny side and his arms flung out along the stallion's back. Several times he felt hot breath against his cheek as the horse turned a curious head towards him, but he paid no attention, even when the stallion whinnied a question in his ear. In his heart was a numb, strange feeling which made him weak. He was even blind to the fact that Black Bart at last slipped into the shadows of the willows.

Presently something cold touched his chin. He found himself staring into the yellow-green eyes of Black Bart, who panted from his run, and now dropped from his mouth something which fell into Dan's lap. It was the glove of Kate Cumberland. In the grasp of his long nervous fingers, how small it was! and yet the hand which had wrinkled the leather was strong enough to hold the heart of a man. He slipped and caught the shaggy black head of Bart between his hands. The wolf knew—in some mysterious way he knew!

The touch of sympathy unnerved him. All his sorrow and his weakness burst on his soul in a single wave. A big tear struck the shining nose of the wolf.

"Bart!" he whispered. "Did you figger on plumb bustin' my heart, pal?"

To avoid those large melancholy eyes, Bart pressed his head inside of his master's arms.

"Delilah!" whispered Dan.

After that not a sound came from the three, the

horse, the dog, or the man. Black Bart curled up at the feet of his master and seemed to sleep, but every now and then an ear raised or an eye twitched open. He was on guard aganst a danger which he did not understand. The horse, also, with a high head scanned the circling willows, alert; but the man for whom the stallion and the wolf watched gave no heed to either. There was a vacant and dreamy expression in his eye as if he was searching his own inner heart and found there the greatest enemy of all. All night they sat in this manner, silent, moveless; the animals watching against the world, the man watching against himself. Before dawn he roused himself suddenly, crossed to the sleeping marshal, and touched him on the arm.

"It's time we hit the trail," he said, as Calder sat up in the blanket.

"What's happened? Isn't it our job to comb the willows?"

"Silent ain't in the willows."

Calder started to his feet.

"How do you know?"

"They ain't close to us, that's all I know."

Tex smiled incredulously.

"I suppose," he said good humouredly, "that your *instinct* brought you this message?"

"Instinct?" repeated Dan blankly, "I dunno."
Calder grew serious.

"We'll take a chance that you may be right.
At least we can ride down the river bank and see
if there are any fresh tracks in the sand. If
Silent started this morning I have an idea he'll
head across the river and line out for the railroad."

In twenty minutes their breakfast was eaten
and they were in the saddle. The sun had not
yet risen when they came out of the willows to the
broad shallow basin of the river. In spring, when
the snow of the mountains melted, that river filled
from bank to bank with a yellow torrent; at the
dry season of the year it was a dirty little creek
meandering through the sands. Down the bank
they rode at a sharp trot for a mile and a half until
Black Bart, who scouted ahead of them at his gliding wolf-trot, came to an abrupt stop. Dan
spoke to Satan and the stallion broke into a swift
gallop which left the pony of Tex Calder labouring
in the rear. When they drew rein beside the wolf,
they found seven distinct tracks of horses which
went down the bank of the river and crossed the
basin. Calder turned with a wide-eyed amazement to Dan.

"You're right again," he said, not without a
touch of vexation in his voice; "but the dog

stopped at these tracks. How does he know we are hunting for Silent's crew?"

"I dunno," said Dan, "maybe he jest suspects."

"They can't have a long start of us," said Calder. "Let's hit the trail. We'll get them before night."

"No," said Dan, "we won't."

"Why won't we?"

"I've seen Silent's hoss, and I've ridden him. If the rest of his gang have the same kind of hoss flesh, you c'n never catch him with that cayuse of yours."

"Maybe not today," said Calder, "but in two days we'll run him down. Seven horses can't travel as two in a long chase."

They started out across the basin, keeping to the tracks of Silent's horses. It was the marshal's idea that the outlaws would head on a fairly straight line for the railroad and accordingly when they lost the track of the seven horses they kept to this direction. Twice during the day they verified their course by information received once from a range rider and once from a man in a dusty buck-board. Both of these had sighted the fast travelling band, but each had seen it pass an hour or two before Calder and Dan arrived. Such tidings encouraged the marshal to keep his horse at an increasing speed; but in the middle of the afternoon, though black Satan showed little or no signs of fatigue, the cattle-pony was nearly blown and they were forced to reduce their pace to the ordinary dog-trot.

CHAPTER XVII

THE PANTHER'S PAW

EVENING came and still they had not sighted the outlaws. As dark fell they drew near a house snuggled away among a group of cottonwoods. Here they determined to spend the night, for Calder's pony was now almost exhausted. A man of fifty came from the house in answer to their call and showed them the way to the horse-shed. While they unsaddled their horses he told them his name was Sam Daniels, yet he evinced no curiosity as to the identity of his guests, and they volunteered no information. His eyes lingered long and fondly over the exquisite lines of Satan. From behind, from the side, and in front, he viewed the stallion while Dan rubbed down the legs of his mount with a care which was most foreign to the ranges. Finally the cattleman reached out a hand toward the smoothly muscled shoulders.

It was Calder who stood nearest and he managed to strike up Daniels's extended arm and jerk him back from the region of danger.

"What'n hell is that for?" exclaimed Daniels.

"That horse is called Satan," said Calder, "and when any one save his owner touches him he lives up to his name and raises hell."

Before Daniels could answer, the light of his lantern fell upon Black Bart, hitherto half hidden by the deepening shadows of the night, but standing now at the entrance of the shed. The cattleman's teeth clicked together and he slapped his hand against his thigh in a reach for the gun which was not there.

"Look behind you," he said to Calder. "A wolf!"

He made a grab for the marshal's gun, but the latter forestalled him.

"Go easy, partner," he said, grinning, "that's only the running mate of the horse. He's not a wolf, at least not according to his owner—and as for being wild—look at that!"

Bart had stalked calmly into the shed and now lay curled up exactly beneath the feet of the stallion.

The two guests received a warmer welcome from Sam Daniels' wife when they reached the house. Their son, Buck, had been expected home for supper, but it was too late for them to delay the meal longer. Accordingly they sat down at once and the dinner was nearly over when Buck, having announced himself with a whoop as he rode up, entered, banging the door loudly behind him. He greeted the strangers with a careless wave of the hand and sat down at the table. His mother placed food silently before him. No explanations of his tardiness were asked and none were offered. The attitude of his father indicated clearly that the boy represented the earning power of the family. He was a big fellow with broad, thick wrists, and a straight black eye. When he had eaten, he broke into breezy conversation, and especially of a vicious mustang he had ridden on a bet the day before.

"Speakin' of hosses, Buck," said his father, "they's a black out in the shed right now that'd make your eyes jest nacherally pop out'n their sockets. No more'n fifteen hands, but a reg'lar picture. Must be greased lightnin'."

"I've heard talk of these streaks of greased lightnin'," said Buck, with a touch of scorn, "but I'll stack old Mike agin the best of them."

"An' there's a dog along with the hoss—a dog that's the nearest to a wolf of any I ever seen."

There was a sudden change in Buck—a change to be sensed rather than definitely noted with the eye. It was a stiffening of his body—an alertness of which he was at pains to make no show. For almost immediately he began to whistle softly, idly, his eyes roving carelessly across the wall while he tilted back in his chair. Dan dropped his hand close to the butt of his gun. Instantly, the eyes of Buck flashed down and centred on Dan for an instant of keen scrutiny. Certainly Buck had connected that mention of the black horse and the wolf-dog with a disturbing idea.

When they went to their room—a room in which there was no bed and they had to roll down their blankets on the floor—Dan opened the window and commenced to whistle one of his own wild tunes. It seemed to Calder that there was a break in that music here and there, and a few notes grouped together like a call. In a moment a shadowy figure leaped through the window, and Black Bart landed on the floor with soft padding feet.

Recovering from his start Calder cursed softly.

"What's the main idea?" he asked.

Dan made a signal for a lower tone.

"There ain't no idea," he answered, "but these Daniels people—do you know anything about them?"

"No. Why?"

"They interest me, that's all."

"Anything wrong?"

"I guess not."

"Why did you whistle for this infernal wolf? It makes me nervous to have him around. Get out, Bart."

The wolf turned a languid eye upon the marshal.

"Let him be," said Dan. "I don't feel no ways nacheral without havin' Bart around."

The marshal made no farther objections, and having rolled himself in his blankets was almost immediately asleep and breathing heavily. The moment Dan heard his companion draw breath with a telltale regularity, he sat up again in his blankets. Bart was instantly at his side. He patted the shaggy head lightly, and pointed towards the door.

"Guard!" he whispered.

Then he lay down and was immediately asleep. Bart crouched at his feet with his head pointed directly at the door.

In other rooms there was the sound of the Daniels family going to bed—noises distinctly heard throughout the flimsy frame of the house. After that a deep silence fell which lasted many hours, but in that darkest moment which just precedes the dawn, a light creaking came up the hall. It was very faint and it occurred only at long intervals, but at the first sound Black Bart raised his head from his paws and stared at the door with those glowing eyes which see in the dark.

Now another sound came, still soft, regular. There was a movement of the door. In the pitch dark a man could never have noticed it, but it was plainly visible to the wolf. Still more visible, when the door finally stood wide, was the form of the man who stood in the opening. In one hand he carried a lantern thoroughly hooded, but not so well wrapped that it kept back a single ray which flashed on a revolver. The intruder made a step forward, a step as light as the fall of feathers, but it was not half so stealthy as the movement of Black Bart as he slunk towards the door. He had been warned to watch that door, but it did not need a warning to tell him that a danger was approaching the sleeping master. In the crouched form of the man, in the cautious step, he recognized the unmistakable stalking of one who hunts. Another soft step the man made forward.

Then, with appalling suddenness, a blacker shadow shot up from the deep night of the floor, and white teeth gleamed before the stranger's face. He threw up his hand to save his throat. The teeth sank into his arm—a driving weight hurled him against the wall and then to the floor—the revolver and the lantern dropped clattering, and the latter, rolling from its wrapping, flooded the room with light. But neither man nor wolf uttered a sound.

Calder was standing, gun in hand, but too bewildered to act, while Dan, as if he were playing a part long rehearsed, stood covering the fallen form of Buck Daniels.

"Stand back from him, Bart!" he commanded.

The wolf slipped off a pace, whining with horrible eagerness, for he had tasted blood. Far away a shout came from Sam Daniels. Dan lowered his gun.

"Stand up," he ordered.

The big fellow picked himself up and stood against the wall with the blood streaming down his right arm. Still he said nothing and his keen eyes darted from Calder to Whistling Dan.

"Give me a strip of that old shirt over there, will you, Tex?" said Dan, "an' keep him covered while I tie up his arm."

Before Calder could move, old Daniels appeared at the door, a heavy Colt in his hand. For a moment he stood dumbfounded, but then, with a cry, jerked up his gun—a quick movement, but a fraction of a second too slow, for the hand of Dan darted out and his knuckles struck the wrist of the old cattleman. The Colt rattled on the floor.

He lunged after his weapon, but the voice of Buck stopped him short.

"The game's up, Dad," he growled, "that older feller is Tex Calder."

The name, like a blow in the face, straightened old Daniels and left him white and blinking. Whistling Dan turned his back on the father and deftly bound up the lacerated arm of Buck.

"In the name o' God, Buck," moaned Sam, "what you been tryin' to do in here?"

"What you'd do if you had the guts for it. That's Tex Calder an' this is Dan Barry. They're on the trail of big Jim. I wanted to put 'em off that trail."

"Look here," said Calder, "how'd you know us?"

"I've said my little say," said Buck sullenly, "an' you'll get no more out of me between here an' any hell you can take me to."

"He knew us when his father talked about Satan an' Black Bart," said Dan to Tex. "Maybe he's one of Silent's."

"Buck, for God's sake tell 'em you know nothin' of Silent," cried old Daniels. "Boy, boy, it's hangin' for you if they get you to Elkhead an' charge you with that!"

"Dad, you're a fool," said Buck. "I ain't goin' down on my knees to 'em. Not me."

Calder, still keeping Buck covered with his gun, drew Dan a little to one side.

"What can we do with this fellow, Dan?" he said. "Shall we give up the trail and take him over to Elkhead?"

"An' break the heart of the ol' man?"

"Buck is one of the gang, that's certain."

"Get Silent an' there won't be no gang left."

"But we caught this chap in red blood——"

"He ain't very old, Tex. Maybe he could change. I think he ain't been playin' Silent's game any too long."

"We can't let him go. It isn't in reason to do that."

"I ain't thinkin' of reason. I'm thinkin' of old Sam an' his wife."

"And if we turn him loose?"

"He'll be your man till he dies."

Calder scowled.

"The whole range is filled with these silent partners of the outlaws—but maybe you're right, Dan. Look at them now!"

The father was standing close to his son and pouring out a torrent of appeal—evidently begging him in a low voice to disavow any knowledge of

Silent and his crew, but Buck shook his head sullenly. He had given up hope. Calder approached them.

"Buck," he said, "I suppose you know that you could be hung for what you've tried to do tonight. If the law wouldn't hang you a lynching party would. No jail would be strong enough to keep them away from you."

Buck was silent, dogged.

"But suppose we were to let you go scot free?"

Buck started. A great flush covered his face.

"I'm taking the advice of Dan Barry in doing this," said Calder. "Barry thinks you could go straight. Tell me man to man, if I give you the chance will you break loose from Silent and his gang?"

A moment before, Buck had been steeled for the worst, but this sudden change loosened all the bonds of his pride. He stammered and choked. Calder turned abruptly away.

"Dan," he said, "here's the dawn, and it's time for us to hit the trail."

They rolled their blankets hastily and broke away from the gratitude which poured like water from the heart of old Sam. They were in their saddles when Buck came beside Dan. His pride, his shame, and his gratitude broke his voice.

"I ain't much on words," he said, "but it's *you* I'm thankin'!"

His hand reached up hesitatingly, and Dan caught it in a firm grip.

"Why," he said gently, "even Satan here stumbles now an' then, but that ain't no reason I should get rid of him. Good luck—partner!"

He shook the reins and the stallion leaped off after Calder's trotting pony. Buck Daniels stood motionless looking after them, and his eyes were very dim.

For an hour Dan and Tex were on the road before the sun looked over the hills. Calder halted his horse to watch.

"Dan," he said at last, "I used to think there were only two ways of handling men—one with the velvet touch and one with the touch of steel. Mine has been the way of steel, but I begin to see there's a third possibility—the touch of the panther's paw—the velvet with the steel claws hid beneath. That's your way, and I wonder if it isn't the best. I think Buck Daniels would be glad to die for you!"

He turned directly to Dan.

"But all this is aside from the point, which is that the whole country is full of these silent partners of the outlaws. The law plays a lone hand in the mountain-desert."

"You've played the lone hand and won twenty times," said Dan.

"Ay, but the twenty-first time I may fail. The difference between success and failure in this country is just the length of time it takes to pull a trigger—and Silent is fast with a gun. He's the root of the outlaw power. We may kill a hundred men, but till he's gone we've only mowed the weeds, not pulled them. But what's the use of talking? One second will tell the tale when I stand face to face with Jim Silent and we go for our six-guns. And somewhere between that rising sun and those mountains I'll find Jim Silent and the end of things for one of us."

He started his cattle-pony into a sudden gallop, and they drove on into the bright morning.

CHAPTER XVIII

CAIN

HARDLY a score of miles away, Jim Silent and his six companions topped a hill. He raised his hand and the others drew rein beside him. Kate Cumberland shifted her weight a little to one side of the saddle to rest and looked down from the crest on the sweep of country below. A mile away the railroad made a streak of silver light across the brown range and directly before them stood the squat station-house with red-tiled roof. Just before the house, a slightly broader streak of that gleaming light showed the position of the siding rails. She turned her head towards the outlaws. They were listening to the final directions of their chief, and the darkly intent faces told their own story. She knew, from what she had gathered of their casual hints, that this was to be the scene of the train hold-up.

It seemed impossible that this little group of men could hold the great fabric of a train with all

its scores of passengers at their mercy. In spite
of herself, half her heart wished them success.
There was Terry Jordan forgetful of the wound
in his arm; Shorty Rhinehart, his saturnine face
longer and more calamitous than ever; Hal Purvis,
grinning and nodding his head; Bill Kilduff with
his heavy jaw set like a bull dog's; Lee Haines,
with a lock of tawny hair blowing over his forehead, smiling faintly as he listened to Silent as if
he heard a girl tell a story of love; and finally
Jim Silent himself, huge, solemn, confident. She
began to feel that these six men were worth six
hundred.

She hated them for some reasons; she feared
them for others; but the brave blood of Joe Cumberland was thick in her and she loved the danger
of the coming moment. Their plans were finally
agreed upon, their masks arranged, and after
Haines had tied a similar visor over Kate's face,
they started down the hill at a swinging gallop.

In front of the house of the station-agent they
drew up, and while the others were at their horses,
Lee Haines dismounted and rapped loudly at
the door. It was opened by a grey-bearded man
smoking a pipe. Haines covered him. He tossed
up his hands and the pipe dropped from his
mouth.

"Who's in the house here with you?" asked Haines.

"Not a soul!" stammered the man. "If you're lookin' for money you c'n run through the house. You won't find a thing worth takin'."

"I don't want money. I want you," said Haines; and immediately explained, "you're perfectly safe. All you have to do is to be obliging. As for the money, you just throw open that switch and flag the train when she rolls along in a few moments. We'll take care of the rest. You don't have to keep your hands up."

The hands came down slowly. For a brief instant the agent surveyed Haines and the group of masked men who sat their horses a few paces away, and then without a word he picked up his flag from behind the door and walked out of the house. Throughout the affair he never uttered a syllable. Haines walked up to the head of the siding with him while he opened the switch and accompanied him back to the point opposite the station-house to see that he gave the "stop" signal correctly. In the meantime two of the other outlaws entered the little station, bound the telegrapher hand and foot, and shattered his instrument. That would prevent the sending of any call for help after the hold-up. Purvis and Jordan (since Terry could shoot with his left hand in case of need) went to the other side of the track and lay down against the grade. It was their business to open fire on the tops of the windows as the train drew to a stop. That would keep the passengers inside. The other four were distributed along the side nearest to the station-house. Shorty Rhine-hart and Bill Kilduff were to see that no passengers broke out from the train and attempted a flank attack. Haines would attend to having the fire box of the engine flooded. For the cracking of the safe, Silent carried the stick of dynamite.

Now the long wait began. There is a dreamlike quality about bright mornings in the open country, and everything seemed unreal to Kate. It was impossible that tragedy should come on such a day. The moments stole on. She saw Silent glance twice at his watch and scowl. Evidently the train was late and possibly they would give up the attempt. Then a light humming caught her ear.

She held her breath and listened again. It was unmistakable—a slight thing—a tremor to be felt rather than heard. She saw Haines peering un-der shaded eyes far down the track, and following the direction of his gaze she saw a tiny spot of haze on the horizon. The tiny puff of smoke developed to a deeper, louder note.   The station-agent took his place on the track.

Now the train bulked big, the engine wavering slightly to the unevenness of the road bed.   The flag of the station-agent moved.   Kate closed her eyes and set her teeth.   There was a rumbling and puffing and a mighty grinding—a shout somewhere—the rattle of a score of pistol shots—she opened her eyes to see the train rolling to a stop on the siding directly before her.

Kilduff and Shorty Rhinehart, crouching against the grade, were splintering the windows one by one with nicely placed shots.   The baggage-cars were farther up the siding than Silent calculated.   He and Haines now ran towards the head of the train.

The fireman and engineer jumped from their cab, holding their arms stiffly above their heads; and Haines approached with poised revolver to make them flood the fire box.   In this way the train would be delayed for some time and before it could send out the alarm the bandits would be far from pursuit.   Haines had already reached the locomotive and Silent was running towards the first baggage-car when the door of that car slid open and at the entrance appeared two men with rifles at their shoulders.   As they opened fire

Silent pitched to the ground. Kate set her teeth and forced her eyes to stay open.

Even as the outlaw fell his revolver spoke and one of the men threw up his hands with a yell and pitched out of the open door. His companion still kept his post, pumping shots at the prone figure. Twice more the muzzle of Silent's gun jerked up and the second man crumpled on the floor of the car.

A great hissing and a jetting cloud of steam announced that Haines had succeeded in flooding the fire box. Silent climbed into the first baggage-car, stepping, as he did so, on the limp body of the Wells Fargo agent, who lay on the road bed. A moment later he flung out the body of the second messenger. The man flopped on the ground heavily, face downwards, and then—greatest horror of all!—dragged himself to his hands and knees and began to crawl laboriously. Kate ran and dropped to her knees beside him.

"Are you hurt badly?" she pleaded. "Where? Where?"

He sagged to the ground and lay on his left side, breathing heavily.

"Where is the wound?" she repeated.

He attempted to speak, but only a bloody froth came to his lips. That was sufficient to tell her that he had been shot through the lungs.

She tore open his shirt and found two purple spots high on the chest, one to the right, and one to the left. From that on the left ran a tiny trickle of blood, but that on the right was only a small puncture in the midst of a bruise. He was far past all help.

"Speak to me!" she pleaded.

His eyes rolled and then checked on her face.

"Done for," he said in a horrible whisper, "that devil done me. Kid—cut out—this life. I've played this game—myself—an' now—I'm goin'—to hell for it!"

A great convulsion twisted his face.

"What can I do?" cried Kate.

"Tell the world—I died—game!"

His body writhed, and in the last agony his hand closed hard over hers. It was like a silent farewell, that strong clasp.

A great hand caught her by the shoulder and jerked her to her feet.

"The charge is goin' off! Jump for it!" shouted Silent in her ear.

She sprang up and at the same time there was a great boom from within the car. The side bulged out—a section of the top lifted and fell back with a crash—and Silent ran back into the smoke. Haines, Purvis, and Kilduff were instantly at the car, taking the ponderous little canvas sacks of coin as their chief handed them out.

Within two minutes after the explosion ten small sacks were deposited in the saddlebags on the horses which stood before the station-house. Silent's whistle called in Terry Jordan and Shorty Rhinehart—a sharp order forced Kate to climb into her saddle—and the train robbers struck up the hillside at a racing pace. A confused shouting rose behind them. Rifles commenced to crack where some of the passengers had taken up the weapons of the dead guards, but the bullets flew wide, and the little troop was soon safely out of range.

On the other side of the hill-top they changed their course to the right. For half an hour the killing pace continued, and then, as there was not a sign of immediate chase, the lone riders drew down to a soberer pace. Silent called: "Keep bunched behind me. We're headed for the old Salton place—an' a long rest."

CHAPTER XIX

REAL MEN

SOME people pointed out that Sheriff Gus
Morris had never made a single important arrest
in the ten years during which he had held office,
and there were a few slanderers who spoke insinu-
atingly of the manner in which the lone riders
flourished in Morris's domain. These "knockers,"
however, were voted down by the vast majority,
who swore that the sheriff was the finest fellow who
ever threw leg over saddle. They liked him for
his inexhaustible good-nature, the mellow baritone
in which he sang the range songs at any one's
request, and perhaps more than all, for the very
laxness with which he conducted his work. They
had had enough of the old school of sheriffs who
lived a few months gun in hand and died fighting
from the saddle. The office had never seemed
desirable until Gus Morris ran for it and smiled
his way to a triumphant election.

Before his career as an office-holder began, he

ran a combined general merchandise store, saloon, and hotel. That is to say, he ran the hostelry in name. The real executive head, general manager, clerk, bookkeeper, and cook, and sometimes even bar-tender was his daughter, Jacqueline. She found the place only a saloon, and a poorly patronized one at that. Her unaided energy gradually made it into a hotel, restaurant, and store. Even while her father was in office he spent most of his time around the hotel; but no matter how important he might be elsewhere, in his own house he had no voice. There the only law was the will of Jacqueline.

Out of the stable behind this hostelry Dan and Tex Calder walked on the evening of the train robbery. They had reached the place of the hold-up a full two hours after Silent's crew departed; and the fireman and engineer had been working frantically during the interim to clean out the soaked fire box and get up steam again. Tex looked at the two dead bodies, spoke to the conductor, and then cut short the voluble explanations of a score of passengers by turning his horse and riding away, followed by Dan. All that day he was gloomily silent. It was a shrewd blow at his reputation, for the outlaws had actually carried out the robbery while he was on their trail. Not

till they came out of the horse-shed after stabling
their horses did he speak freely.

"Dan," he said, "do you know anything about
Sheriff Gus Morris?"

"No"

"Then listen to this and salt every word away.
I'm an officer of the law, but I won't tell that to
Morris. I hope he doesn't know me. If he does
it will spoil our game. I am almost certain he is
playing a close hand with the lone riders. I'll
wager he'd rather see a stick of dynamite than a
marshal. Remember when we get in that place
that we're not after Jim Silent or any one else.
We're simply travelling cowboys. No questions.
I expect to learn something about the location of
Silent's gang while we're here, but we'll never find
out except by hints and chance remarks. We
have to watch Morris like hawks. If he suspects
us he'll find a way to let Silent know we're here and
then the hunters will be hunted."

In the house they found a dozen cattlemen
sitting down at the table in the dining-room. As
they entered the room the sheriff, who sat at the
head of the table, waved his hand to them.

"H'ware ye, boys?" he called. "You'll find a
couple of chairs right in the next room. Got two
extra plates, Jac?"

As Dan followed Tex after the chairs he noticed the sheriff beckon to one of the men who sat near him. As they returned with the chairs someone was leaving the room by another door.

"Tex," he said, as they sat down side by side, "when we left the dining-room for the chairs, the sheriff spoke to one of the boys and as we came back one of them was leavin' through another door. D'you think Morris knew you when you came in?"

Calder frowned thoughtfully and then shook his head.

"No," he said in a low voice. "I watched him like a hawk when we entered. He didn't bat an eye when he saw me. If he recognized me he's the greatest actor in the world, bar none! No, Dan, he doesn't know us from Adam and Abel."

"All right," said Dan, "but I don't like somethin' about this place—maybe it's the smell of the air. Tex, take my advice an' keep your gun ready for the fastest draw you ever made."

"Don't worry about me," smiled Calder. "How about yourself?"

"Hello," broke in Jacqueline from the end of the table. "Look who we've picked in the draw!"

Her voice was musical, but her accent and manner were those of a girl who has lived all her

life among men and has caught their ways—with
an exaggeration of that self-confidence which a
woman always feels among Western men. Her
blue eyes were upon Dan.

"Ain't you a long ways from home?" she went
on.

The rest of the table, perceiving the drift of her
badgering, broke into a rumbling bass chuckle.

"Quite a ways," said Dan, and his wide brown
eyes looked seriously back at her.

A yell of delight came from the men at this naïve
rejoinder. Dan looked about him with a sort of
childish wonder. Calder's anxious whisper came
at his side: "Don't let them get you mad, Dan!"
Jacqueline, having scored so heavily with her first
shot, was by no means willing to give up her
sport.

"With them big eyes, for a starter," she said,
"all you need is long hair to be perfect. Do your
folks generally let you run around like this?"

Every man canted his ear to get the answer and
already they were grinning expectantly.

"I don't go out much," returned the soft voice
of Dan, "an' when I do, I go with my friend, here.
He takes care of me."

Another thunder of laughter broke out. Jacqueline had apparently uncovered a tenderfoot,

and a rare one even for that absurd species. A sandy-haired cattle puncher who sat close to Jacqueline now took the cue from the mistress of the house.

"Ain't you a bit scared when you get around among real men?" he asked, leering up the table towards Dan.

The latter smiled gently upon him.

"I reckon maybe I am," he said amiably.

"Then you must be shakin' in your boots right now," said the other over the sound of the laughter.

"No, said Dan," "I feel sort of comfortable."

The other replied with a frown that would have intimidated a balky horse.

"What d'you mean? Ain't you jest said men made you sort of—nervous?"

He imitated the soft drawl of Dan with his last words and raised another yell of delight from the crowd. Whistling Dan turned his gentle eyes upon Jacqueline.

"Pardon me, ma'am," he began.

An instant hush fell on the men. They would not miss one syllable of the delightful remarks of this rarest of all tenderfoots, and the prelude of this coming utterance promised something that would eclipse all that had gone before.

"Talk right out, Brown-eyes," said Jacqueline,

wiping the tears of delight from her eyes. "Talk right out as if you was a man. *I* won't hurt you."

"I jest wanted to ask," said Dan, "if these are real men?"

The ready laughter started, checked, and died suddenly away. The cattlemen looked at each other in puzzled surprise.

"Don't they look like it to you, honey?" asked Jacqueline curiously.

Dan allowed his eyes to pass lingeringly around the table from face to face.

"I dunno," he said at last, "they look sort of queer to me."

"For God's sake cut this short, Dan," pleaded Tex Calder in an undertone. "Let them have all the rope they want. Don't trip up our party before we get started."

"Queer?" echoed Jacqueline, and there was a deep murmur from the men.

"Sure," said Dan, smiling upon her again, "they all wear their guns so awful high."

Out of the dead silence broke the roar of the sandy-haired man: "What'n hell d'you mean by that?"

Dan leaned forward on one elbow, his right hand free and resting on the edge of the table, but still his smile was almost a caress.

"Why," he said, "maybe you c'n explain it to me. Seems to me that all these guns is wore so high they's more for ornament than use."

"You damned pup——" began Sandy.

He stopped short and stared with a peculiar fascination at Dan, who started to speak again. His voice had changed—not greatly, for its pitch was the same and the drawl was the same—but there was a purr in it that made every man stiffen in his chair and make sure that his right hand was free. The ghost of his former smile was still on his lips, but it was his eyes that seemed to fascinate Sandy.

"Maybe I'm wrong, partner," he was saying, "an' maybe you c'n prove that *your* gun ain't jest ornamental hardware?"

What followed was very strange. Sandy was a brave man and everyone at that table knew it. They waited for the inevitable to happen. They waited for Sandy's lightning move for his gun. They waited for the flash and the crack of the revolver. It did not come. There followed a still more stunning wonder.

"You c'n see," went on that caressing voice of Dan, "that everyone is waitin' for you to demonstrate—which the lady is most special interested."

And still Sandy did not move that significant

right hand.   It remained fixed in air a few inches
above the table, the fingers stiffly spread.   He
moistened his white lips.   Then—most strange of
all!—his eyes shifted and wandered away from
the face of Whistling Dan.   The others exchanged
incredulous glances.   The impossible had happened—Sandy had taken water!   The sheriff
was the first to recover, though his forehead was
shining with perspiration.

"What's all this stuff about?" he called.   "Hey,
Sandy, quit pickin' trouble with the stranger!"

Sandy seized the loophole through which to
escape with his honour.   He settled back in his
chair.

"All right, gov'nor," he said, "I won't go
spoilin' your furniture.   I won't hurt him."

CHAPTER XX

BUT this deceived no one. They had seen him palpably take water. A moment of silence followed, while Sandy stared whitefaced down at the table, avoiding all eyes; but all the elements of good breeding exist under all the roughness of the West. It was Jacqueline who began with a joke which was rather old, but everyone appreciated it —at that moment—and the laughter lasted long enough to restore some of the colour to Sandy's face. A general rapid fire of talk followed.

"How did you do it?" queried Calder. "I was all prepared for a gun-play."

"Why, you seen I didn't do nothin'."

"Then what in the world made Sandy freeze while his hand was on the way to his gun?"

"I dunno," sighed Dan, "but when I see his hand start movin' I sort of wanted his blood—I *wanted* him to keep right on till he got hold of his gun—and maybe he seen it in my eyes an' that sort of changed his mind."

"I haven't the least doubt that it did," said Calder grimly.

At the foot of the table Jacqueline's right-hand neighbour was saying: ' What happened, Jac?"

"Don't ask me," she replied. "All I know is that I don't think any less of Sandy because he backed down. I saw that stranger's face myself an' I'm still sort of weak inside."

"How did he look?"

"I dunno. Jest—jest *hungry*. Understand?"

She was silent for a time, but she was evidently thinking hard. At last she turned to the same man.

"Did you hear Brown-eyes say that the broad-shouldered feller next to him was his friend?"

"Sure. I seen them ride in together. That other one looks like a hard nut, eh?"

She returned no answer, but after a time her eyes raised slowly and rested for a long moment on Dan's face. It was towards the end of the meal when she rose and went towards the kitchen. At the door she turned, and Dan, though he was looking down at his plate, was conscious that someone was observing him. He glanced up and the moment his eyes met hers she made a significant backward gesture with her hand. He hesitated a moment and then shoved back his chair. Calder was busy talking to a table mate, so he walked out of the house without speaking to his companion. He went to the rear of the house and as he had expected she was waiting for him.

"Brown-eyes," she said swiftly, "that feller who sat beside you—is he your partner?"

"I dunno," said Dan evasively, "why are you askin'?"

Her breath was coming audibly as if from excitement.

"Have you got a fast hoss?"

"There ain't no faster."

"Believe me, he can't go none too fast with you tonight. Maybe they're after you, too."

"Who?"

"I can't tell you. Listen to me, Brown-eyes. Go get your hoss an' feed him the spur till you're a hundred miles away, an' even then don't stop runnin'."

He merely stared at her curiously.

She stamped.

"Don't stop to talk. If they're after him and you're his partner, they probably want you, too."

"I'll stay aroun'. If they're curious about me, I'll tell 'em my name—I'll even spell it for 'em. Who are they?"

"They are—hell—that's all."

"I'd like to see 'em. Maybe *they're* real men."

"They're devils. If I told you their names you'd turn stiff."

"I'll take one chance. Tell me who they are."

"I don't dare tell you."

She hesitated.

"I *will* tell you! You've made a fool out of me with them big baby eyes. Jim Silent is in that house!"

He turned and ran, but not for the horse-shed; he headed straight for the open door of the house.

.   .   .   .

In the dining-room two more had left the table, but the rest, lingering over their fresh filled coffee cups, sat around telling tales, and Tex Calder was among them. He was about to push back his chair when the hum of talk ceased as if at a command. The men on the opposite side of the table were staring with fascinated eyes at the door, and then a big voice boomed behind him: "Tex Calder, stan' up. You've come to the end of the trail!"

He whirled as he rose, kicking down the chair behind him, and stood face to face with Jim Silent. The great outlaw was scowling; but his gun was in its holster and his hands rested lightly on his hips. It was plain for all eyes to see that he had come not to murder but to fight a fair duel. Behind him loomed the figure of Lee Haines scarcely less imposing.

All eternity seemed poised and waiting for the second when one of the men would make the move for his gun. Not a breath was drawn in the room. Hands remained frozen in air in the midst of a gesture. Lips which had parted to speak did not close. The steady voice of the clock broke into the silence—a dying space between every tick. For the second time in his life Tex Calder knew fear.

He saw no mere man before him, but his own destiny. And he knew that if he stood before those glaring eyes another minute he would become like poor Sandy a few minutes before—a white-faced, palsied coward. The shame of the thought gave him power.

"Silent," he said, "there's a quick end to the longest trail, because——"

His hand darted down. No eye could follow the lightning speed with which he whipped out his revolver and fanned it, but by a mortal fraction of a second the convulsive jerk of Silent's hand was faster still. Two shots followed—they were rather like one drawn-out report. The woodwork splintered above the outlaw's head; Tex Calder seemed to laugh, but his lips made no sound. He pitched forward on his face.

"He fired that bullet," said Silent, "after mine hit him."

Then he leaped back through the door.

"Keep 'em back one minute, Lee, an' then after me!" he said as he ran. Haines stood in the door with folded arms. He knew that no one would dare to move a hand.

Two doors slammed at the same moment—the front door as Silent leaped into the safety of the night, and the rear door as Whistling Dan rushed into the house. He stood at the entrance from the kitchen to the dining-room half crouched, and swaying from the suddenness with which he had checked his run. He saw the sprawled form of Tex Calder on the floor and the erect figure of Lee Haines just opposite him.

"For God's sake!" screamed Gus Morris, "don't shoot, Haines! He's done nothin'. Let him go!"

"My life—or his!" said Haines savagely. "He's not a man—he's a devil!"

Dan was laughing low—a sound like a croon.

"Tex," he said, "I'm goin' to take him alive for you!"

As if in answer the dying man stirred on the floor. Haines went for his gun, a move almost as lightning swift as that of Jim Silent, but now far, far too late. The revolver was hardly clear of its holster when Whistling Dan's weapon spoke. Haines, with a curse, clapped his left hand over his wounded right forearm, and then reached after his weapon as it clattered to the floor. Once more he was too late. Dan tossed his gun away with a snarl like the growl of a wolf; cleared the table at a leap, and was at Haines's throat. The bandit fought back desperately, vainly. One instant they struggled erect, swaying, the next Haines was lifted bodily, and hurled to the floor. He writhed, but under those prisoning hands he was helpless.

The sheriff headed the rush for the scene of the struggle, but Dan stopped them.

"All you c'n do," he said, "is to bring me a piece of rope."

Jacqueline came running with a stout piece of twine which he twisted around the wrists of Haines. Then he jerked the outlaw to his feet, and stood close, his face inhumanly pale.

"If he dies," he said, pointing with a stiff arm back at the prostrate figure of Tex Calder, "you —you'll burn alive for it!"

The sheriff and two of the other men turned the body of Calder on his back. They tore open his shirt, and Jacqueline leaned over him with a basin of water trying to wipe away the ever recurrent blood which trickled down his breast. Dan brushed them away and caught the head of his companion in his arms.

"Tex!" he moaned, "Tex! Open your eyes, partner, I got him for you. I got him alive for you to look at him! Wake up!"

As if in obedience to the summons the eyes of Calder opened wide. The lids fluttered as if to clear his vision, but even then his gaze was filmed with a telltale shadow.

"Dan—Whistling Dan," he said, "I'm seeing you a long, long ways off. Partner, I'm done for."

The whole body of Dan stiffened.

"Done? Tex, you can't be! Five minutes ago you sat at that there table, smilin' an' talkin'!"

"It doesn't take five minutes. Half a second can take a man all the way to hell!"

"If you're goin', pal, if you goin', Tex, take one comfort along with you! I got the man who killed you! Come here!"

He pulled the outlaw to his knees beside the dying marshal whose face had lighted wonderfully. He strained his eyes painfully to make out the face of his slayer. Then he turned his head.

He said: "The man who killed me was Jim Silent."

Dan groaned and leaned close to Calder.

"Then I'll follow him to the end—" he began.

The feeble accent of Calder interrupted him.

"Not that way. Come close to me. I can't hear my own voice, hardly."

Dan bowed his head. A whisper murmured on for a moment, broken here and there as Dan nodded his head and said, "Yes!"

"Then hold up your hand, your right hand," said Calder at last, audibly.

Dan obeyed.

"You swear it?"

"So help me God!"

"Then here's the pledge of it!"

Calder fumbled inside his shirt for a moment, and then withdrawing his hand placed it palm down in that of Dan. The breath of the marshal was coming in a rattling gasp.

He said very faintly: "I've stopped the trails of twenty men. It took the greatest of them all to get me. He got me fair. He beat me to the draw!"

He stopped as if in awe.

"He played square—he's a better man than I. Dan, when you get him, do it the same way—face to face—with time for him to think of hell before he gets there. Partner, I'm going. Wish me luck."

"Tex—partner—good luck!"

It seemed as if that parting wish was granted, for Calder died with a smile.

When Dan rose slowly Gus Morris stepped up and laid a hand on his arm: "Look here, there ain't no use of bein' sad for Tex Calder. His business was killin' men, an' his own time was overdue."

Dan turned a face that made Morris wince.

"What's the matter?" he asked, with an attempt at bluff good nature. "Do you hate everyone because one man is dead? I'll tell you what I'll do. I'll loan you a buckboard an' a pair of hosses to take Tex back to Elkhead. As for this feller Haines, I'll take care of him."

"I sure need a buckboard," said Dan slowly, "but I'll get the loan from a—white man!"

He turned his back sharply on the sheriff and asked if any one else had a wagon they could lend him. One of the men had stopped at Morris's place on his way to Elkhead. He immediately proposed that they make the trip together.

"All right," said Morris carelessly. "I won't pick trouble with a crazy man. Come with me, Haines."

He turned to leave the room.

"Wait!" said Dan.

Haines stopped as though someone had seized him by the shoulder.

"What the devil is this now?" asked Morris furiously. "Stranger, d'you think you c'n run the world? Come on with me, Haines!"

"He stays with me," said Dan.

"By God," began Morris, "if I thought——"

"This ain't no place for you to begin thinkin'," said the man who had offered his buckboard to Dan. "This feller made the capture an' he's got the right to take him into Elkhead if he wants. They's a reward on the head of Lee Haines."

"The arrest is made in my county," said Morris stoutly, "an' I've got the say as to what's to be done with a prisoner."

"Morris," said Haines earnestly, "if I'm taken to Elkhead it'll be simply a matter of lynching. You know the crowd in that town."

"Right—right," said Morris, eagerly picking up the word. "It'd be plain lynchin'—murder——"

Dan broke in: "Haines, step over here behind me!"

For one instant Haines hesitated, and then obeyed silently.

"This is contempt of the law and an officer of the law," said Morris. "An' I'll see that you get fined so that——"

"Better cut it short there, sheriff," said one of

the men. "I wouldn't go callin' the attention of folks to the way Jim Silent walked into your own house an' made his getaway without you tryin' to raise a hand. Law or no law, I'm with this stranger."

"Me too," said another; "any man who can fan a gun like him don't need no law."

The sheriff saw that the tide of opinion had set strongly against him and abandoned his position with speed if not with grace. Dan ordered Haines to walk before him outside the house. They faced each other in the dim moonlight.

"I've got one question to ask you," he said.

"Make it short," said Haines calmly. "I've got to do my talking before the lynching crowd."

"You can answer it in one word. Does Kate Cumberland—what is she to you?"

Lee Haines set his teeth.

"All the world," he said.

Even in the dim light he saw the yellow glow of Dan's eyes and he felt as if a wolf stood there trembling with eagerness to leap at his throat.

"An' what are you to her?"

"No more than the dirt under her feet!"

"Haines, you lie!"

"I tell you that if she cared for me as much as she does for the horse she rides on, I'd let the whole world know if I had to die for it the next moment."

Truth has a ring of its own.

"Haines, if I could hear that from her own lips, I'd let you go free. If you'll show me the way to Kate, I'll set you loose the minute I see her."

"I can't do it. I've given my faith to Silent and his men. Where she is, they are."

"Haines, that means death for you."

"I know it."

Another plan had come to Dan as they talked. He took Haines inside again and coming out once more, whistled for Bart. The wolf appeared as if by magic through the dark. He took out Kate's glove, which the wolf had brought to him in the willows, and allowed him to smell it. Bart whined eagerly. If he had that glove he would range the hills until he found its owner, directed to her by that strange instinct of the wild things. If Kate still loved him the glove would be more eloquent than a thousand messages. And if she managed to escape, the wolf would guide her back to his master.

He sat on his heels, caught the wolf on either side of the shaggy head, and stared into the glow of the yellow green eyes. It was as if the man were speaking to the wolf.

At last, as if satisfied, he drew a deep breath, rose, and dropped the glove. It was caught in the flashing teeth. For another moment Bart stood whining and staring up to the face of his master Then he whirled and fled out into the night.

CHAPTER XXI

ONE WAY OUT

IN a room of the Salton place, on the evening of the next day after Calder's death, sat Silent, with Kilduff, Rhinehart, and Jordan about him. Purvis was out scouting for the news of Haines, whose long absence commenced to worry the gang. Several times they tried to induce Kate to come out and talk with them, but she was resolute in staying alone in the room which they had assigned to her. Consequently, to while away the time, Bill Kilduff produced his mouth organ and commenced a dolorous ballad. He broke short in the midst of it and stared at the door. The others followed the direction of his eyes and saw Black Bart standing framed against the fading daylight. They started up with curses; Rhinehart drew his gun.

"Wait a minute," ordered Silent.

"Damn it!" exclaimed Jordan, "don't you see Whistling Dan's wolf? If the wolf's here, Dan isn't far behind."

Silent shook his head.

"If there's goin' to be any shootin' of that wolf leave it to Hal Purvis. He's jest nacherally set his heart on it. An' Whistlin' Dan ain't with the wolf. Look! there's a woman's glove hangin' out of his mouth. He picked that up in the willows, maybe, an' followed the girl here. Watch him!"

The wolf slunk across the room to the door which opened on Kate's apartment. Kate threw the door open—cried out at the sight of Bart— and then snatched up the glove he let drop at her feet.

"No cause for gettin' excited," said Silent. "Whistlin' Dan ain't comin' here after the wolf."

For answer she slammed the door.

At the same moment Hal Purvis entered. He stepped directly to Silent, and stood facing him with his hands resting on his hips. His smile was marvellously unpleasant.

"Well," said the chief, "what's the news? You got eloquent eyes, Hal, but I want words."

"The news is plain hell," said Purvis, "Haines——"

"What of him?"

"He's in Elkhead!"

"Elkhead?"

"Whistling Dan got him at Morris's place and took him in along with the body of Tex Calder. Jim, you got to answer for it to all of us. You went to Morris's with Lee. You come away without him and let him stay behind to be nabbed by that devil Whistlin' Dan."

"Right," said Kilduff, and his teeth clicked. "Is that playin' fair?"

"Boys," said Silent solemnly, "if I had knowed that Whistlin' Dan was there, I'd of never left Haines to stay behind. Morris said nothin' about Calder havin' a runnin' mate. Me an' Haines was in the upstairs room an' about supper-time up came a feller an' told us that Tex Calder had jest come into the dinin'-room. That was all. Did Whistlin' Dan get Lee from behind?"

"He got him from the front. He beat Lee to the draw so bad that Haines hardly got his gun out of its leather!"

"The feller that told you that lied," said Silent. "Haines is as fast with his shootin' iron as I am—almost!"

The rest of the outlaws nodded to each other significantly.

Purvis went on without heeding the interruption. "After I found out about the fight I swung

15

towards Elkhead. About five miles out of town I met up with Rogers, the deputy sheriff at Elkhead. I thought you had him fixed for us, Jim?''

"Damn his hide, I did. Is he playing us dirt now?''

"A frosty mornin' in December was nothin' to the way he talked.''

"Cut all that short," said Rhinehart, "an' let's know if Rogers is goin' to be able to keep the lynching party away from Haines!''

"He says he thinks it c'n be done for a couple of days," said Purvis, "but the whole range is risin'. All the punchers are ridin' into Elkhead an' wantin' to take a look at the famous Lee Haines. Rogers says that when enough of 'em get together they'll take the law in their own hands an' nothin' can stop 'em then.''

"Why don't the rotten dog give Haines a chance to make a getaway?" asked Silent. "Ain't we paid him his share ever since we started workin' these parts?''

"He don't dare take the chance," said Purvis. "He says the boys are talkin' mighty strong. They want action. They've put up a guard all around the jail an' they say that if Haines gets loose they'll string up Rogers. Everyone's wild about the killin' of Calder. Jim, ol' Saunderson, he's put up five thousand out of his own pocket to raise the price on your head!"

"An' this Whistlin' Dan," said Silent. "I s'pose they're makin' a hero out of him?"

"Rogers says every man within ten miles is talkin' about him. The whole range'll know of him in two days. He made a nice play when he got in. You know they's five thousand out on Haines's head. It was offered to him by Rogers as soon as Dan brought Lee in. What d'you think he done? Pocketed the cheque? No, he grabbed it, an' tore it up small: 'I ain't after no blood money,' he says."

"No," said Silent. "He ain't after no money—he's after me!"

"Tomorrow they bury Calder. The next day Whistlin' Dan'll be on our trail again—an' he'll be playin' the same lone hand. Rogers offered him a posse. He wouldn't take it."

"They's one pint that ain't no nearer bein' solved," said Bill Kilduff in a growl, "an' that's how you're goin' to get Haines loose. Silent, it's up to you. Which you rode away leavin' him behind."

Silent took one glance around that waiting circle. Then he nodded.

"It's up to me. Gimme a chance to think."

He started walking up and down the room, muttering. At last he stopped short.

"Boys, it can be done! They's nothin' like talkin' of a woman to make a man turn himself into a plumb fool, an' I'm goin' to make a fool out of Whistlin' Dan with this girl Kate!"

"But how in the name of God c'n you make her go out an' talk to him?" said Rhinehart.

"Son," answered Silent, "they's jest one main trouble with you—you talk a hell of a pile too much. When I've done this I'll tell you how it was figgered out!"

CHAPTER XXII

THE WOMAN'S WAY

IT was a day later, in the morning, that a hand knocked at Kate's door and she opened it to Jim Silent. He entered, brushing off the dust of a long journey.

"Good-mornin', Miss Cumberland."

He extended a hand which she overlooked.

"You still busy hatin' me?"

"I'm simply—surprised that you have come in here to talk to me."

"You look as if you seen somethin' in my face?" he said suspiciously. "What is it? Dirt?"

He brushed a hand across his forehead.

"Whatever it is," she answered, "you can't *rub* it away."

"I'm thinkin' of givin' you a leave of absence— if you'll promise to come back."

"Would you trust my honour?"

"In a pinch like this," he said amiably, "I would. But here's my business. Lee Haines is jailed in Elkhead. The man that put him behind the bars an' the only one that can take him out agin is Whistlin' Dan. An' the one person who can make Dan set Lee loose is you. Savvy? Will you go an' talk with Dan? This wolf of his would find him for you."

She shook her head.

"Why not?" cried Silent in a rising voice.

"The last time he saw me," she said, "he had reason to think that I tried to betray him because of Lee Haines. If I went to him now to plead for Haines he'd be sure that I was what he called me —Delilah!"

"Is that final?"

"Absolutely!"

"Now get me straight. They's a crowd of cow-punchers gatherin' in Elkhead, an' today or to-morrow they'll be strong enough to take the law into their own hands and organize a little lynchin' bee, savvy?"

She shuddered.

"It ain't pleasant, is it, the picture of big, good-lookin' Lee danglin' from the end of a rope with the crowd aroun' takin' pot-shots at him? No, it ain't, an' you're goin' to stop it. You're goin' to start from here in fifteen minutes with your hoss an' this wolf, after givin' me your promise to come back when you've seen Whistlin' Dan. You're goin' to make Dan go an' set Lee loose."

She smiled in derision.

"If Dan did that he'd be outlawed."

"You won't stir?"

"Not a step!"

"Well, kid, for everything that happens to Lee somethin' worse will happen to someone in the next room.   Maybe you'd like to see him?"

He opened the door and she stepped into the entrance.   Almost opposite her sat old Joe Cumberland with his hands tied securely behind his back.   At sight of her he rose with a low cry. She turned on big Silent and whipped the six-gun from his hip.   He barely managed to grasp her wrist and swing the heavy revolver out of line with his body.

"You little fiend," he snarled, "drop the gun, or I'll wring your neck."

"I don't fear you," she said, never wincing under the crushing grip on her wrists, "you murderer!"

He said, calmly repossessing himself of his gun, "Now take a long look at your father an' repeat all the things you was just saying' to me."

She stared miserably at her father.   When Silent

caught Kate's hand Cumberland had started forward, but Kilduff and Rhinehart held him.

"What is it, Kate," he cried. "What does it mean?"

She explained it briefly: "This is Jim Silent!"

He remained staring at her with open mouth as if his brain refused to admit what his ear heard.

"There ain't no use askin' questions how an' why she's here," said Silent. "This is the pint. Lee Haines is behind the bars in Elkhead. Whistlin' Dan put him there an' maybe the girl c'n persuade Dan to bring him out again. If she don't—then everything the lynchin' gang does to Haines we're goin' to do to you. Git down on your ol' knees, Cumberland, an' beg your daughter to save your hide!"

The head of Kate dropped down.

"Untie his hands," she said. "I'll talk with Dan."

"I knew you'd see reason," grinned Silent.

"Jest one minute," said Cumberland. "Kate, is Lee Haines one of Silent's gang?"

"He is."

"An' Dan put him behind the bars?"

"Yes."

" If Dan takes him out again the boy'll be outlawed, Kate."

"Cumberland," broke in Kilduff savagely, "here's your call to stop thinkin' about Whistlin' Dan an' begin figgerin' for yourself."

"Don't you see?" said Kate, "it's your death these cowards mean."

Cumberland seemed to grow taller, he stood so stiffly erect with his chin high like a soldier.

"You shan't make no single step to talk with Dan!"

"Can't you understand that it's *you* they threaten?" she cried.

"I understan' it all," he said evenly. "I'm too old to have a young man damned for my sake."

"Shut him up!" ordered Silent. "The old fool!"

The heavy hand of Terry Jordan clapped over Joe's mouth effectually silenced him. He struggled vainly to speak again and Kate turned to Silent to shut out the sight.

"Tell your man to let him go," she said, "I will do what you wish."

"That's talkin' sense," said Silent. "Come out with me an' I'll saddle your hoss. Call the wolf."

He opened the door and in response to her whistle Black Bart trotted out and followed them out to the horse shed. There the outlaw quickly saddled Kate's pony.

He said: "Whistlin' Dan is sure headin' back in this direction because he's got an idea I'm somewhere near. Bart will find him on the way."

Silent was right. That morning Dan had started back towards Gus Morris's place, for he was sure that the outlaws were camped in that neighbourhood. A little before noon he veered half a mile to the right towards a spring which welled out from a hillside, surrounded by a small grove of willows. Having found it, he drank, and watered Satan, then took off the saddle to ease the stallion, and lay down at a little distance for a ten-minute siesta, one of those half wakeful sleeps the habit of which he had learned from his wolf.

He was roused from the doze by a tremendous snorting and snarling and found Black Bart playing with Satan. It was their greeting after an absence, and they dashed about among the willows like creatures possessed. Dan brought horse and dog to a motionless stand with a single whistle, and then ran out to the edge of the willows. Down the side of the hill rode Kate at a brisk gallop. In a moment she saw him and called his name, with a welcoming wave of her arm. Now she was off her horse and running to him. He caught her hands and held her for an instant far from him like one striving to draw out the note of happiness into a song. They could not speak.

At last: "I knew you'd find a way to come."

"They let me go, Dan."

He frowned, and her eyes faltered from his.

"They sent me to you to ask you—to free Lee Haines!"

He dropped her hands, and she stood trying to find words to explain, and finding none.

"To free Haines?" he repeated heavily.

"It is Dad," she cried. "They have captured him, and they are holding him. They keep him in exchange for Haines."

"If I free Haines they'll outlaw me. You know that, Kate?"

She made a pace towards him, but he retreated.

"What can I do?" she pleaded desperately. "It is for my father——"

His face brightened as he caught at a new hope.

"Show me the way to Silent's hiding place and I'll free your father an' reach the end of this trail at the same time, Kate!"

She blenched pitifully. It was hopeless to explain.

"Dan—honey—I can't!"

She watched him miserably.

"I've given them my word **to** come **back alone.**"

His head bowed.   Out of the willows came Satan and Black Bart and stood beside him, the stallion nosing his shoulder affectionately.

"Dan, dear, won't you speak to me?   Won't you tell me that you try to understand?"

He said at last: "Yes.   I'll free Lee Haines."

The fingers of his right hand trailed slowly across the head of Black Bart.   His eyes raised and looked past her far across the running curves of the hills, far away to the misty horizon.

"Kate——"

"Dan, you *do* understand?"

"I didn't know a woman could love a man the way you do Lee Haines.   When I send him back to you tell him to watch himself.   I'm playin' your game now, but if I meet him afterwards, I'll play my own."

All she could say was: "Will you listen to me no more, Dan?"

"Here's where we say good-bye."

He took her hand and his eyes were as unfathomable as a midnight sky.   She turned to her horse and he helped her to the saddle with a steady hand.

That was all.   He went back to the willows, his right arm resting on the withers of Black Satan as if upon the shoulder of a friend.   As she reached the top of the hill she heard a whistling from the willows, a haunting complaint which brought the tears to her eyes. She spurred her tired horse to escape the sound.

CHAPTER XXIII

HELL STARTS

BETWEEN twilight and dark Whistling Dan entered Elkhead. He rose in the stirrups, on his toes, stretching the muscles of his legs. He was sensing his strength. So the pianist before he plays runs his fingers up and down the keys and sees that all is in tune and the touch perfect.

Two rival saloons faced each other at the end of the single street. At the other extremity of the lane stood the house of deputy sheriff Rogers, and a little farther was the jail. A crowd of horses stood in front of each saloon, but from the throngs within there came hardly a sound. The hush was prophetic of action; it was the lull before the storm. Dan slowed his horse as he went farther down the street.

The shadowy figure of a rider showed near the jail. He narrowed his eyes and looked more closely. Another, another, another horseman showed—four in sight on his side of the jail and probably as many more out of his vision. Eight cattlemen guarded the place from which he must take Lee Haines, and every one of the eight, he had no doubt, was a picked man. Dan pulled up Satan to a walk and commenced to whistle softly. It was like one of those sounds of the wind, a thing to guess at rather than to know, but the effect upon Satan and Black Bart was startling.

The ears of the stallion dropped flat on his neck. He began to slink along with a gliding step which was very like the stealthy pace of Black Bart, stealing ahead. His footfall was as silent as if he had been shod with felt. Meantime Dan ran over a plan of action. He saw very clearly that he had little time for action. Those motionless guards around the jail made his task difficult enough, but there was a still greater danger. The crowds in the two saloons would be starting up the street for Haines before long. Their silence told him that.

A clatter of hoofs came behind him. He did not turn his head, but his hand dropped down to his revolver butt. The fast riding horseman swept and shot on down the street, leaving a pungent though invisible cloud of dust behind him. He stopped in front of Rogers's house and darted up the steps and through the door. Acting upon a premonition, Dan dismounted a short distance

from Rogers's house and ran to the door. He
opened it softly and found himself in a narrow hall
dimly lighted by a smoking lamp. Voices came
from the room to his right.

"What d'you mean, Hardy?" the deputy sheriff
was saying.

"Hell's startin'!"

"There's a good many kinds of hell. Come out
with it, Lee. I ain't no mind reader."

"They're gettin' ready for the big bust!"

"What big bust?"

"It ain't no use bluffin'. Ain't Silent told you
that I'm on the inside of the game?"

"You fool!" cried Rogers. "Don't use that
name!"

Dan slipped a couple of paces down the hall and
flattened himself against the wall just as the door
opened. Rogers looked out, drew a great breath
of relief, and went back into the room. Dan resumed his former position.

"Now talk fast!" said Rogers.

"About time for you to drop that rotten bluff.
Why, man, I could even tell you jest how much
you've cost Jim Silent."

Rogers growled: "Tell me what's up."

"The boys are goin' for the jail tonight. They'll
get out Haines an' string him up."

"It's comin' to him. He's played a hard game for a long time."

"An' so have you, Rogers, for a damn long time!"

Rogers swallowed the insult, apparently.

"What can I do?" he asked plaintively. "I'm willin' to give Silent and his gang a square deal."

"You should of done something while they was only a half-dozen cowpunchers in town. Now the town's full of riders an' they're all after blood."

"An' my blood if they don't get Haines!" broke in the deputy sheriff.

Hardy grunted.

"They sure are," he said. "I've heard 'em talk, an' they mean business. All of 'em. But how'd you answer to Jim Silent, Rogers? If you let 'em get Haines—well, Haines is Silent's partner an' Jim'll bust everything wide to get even with you."

"I c'n explain," said Rogers huskily. "I c'n show Silent how I'm helpless."

Footsteps went up and down the room.

"If they start anything," said Rogers, "I'll mark down the names of the ringleaders and I'll give 'em hell afterwards. That'll soothe Jim some."

"You won't know 'em. They'll wear masks."

Dan opened the door and stepped into the room.

Rogers started up with a curse and gripped his revolver.

"I never knew you was so fond of gun play," said Dan. "Maybe that gun of yours would be catchin' cold if you was to leave it out of the leather long?"

The sheriff restored his revolver slowly to the holster, glowering.

"An' Rogers won't be needin' you for a minute or two," went on Dan to Hardy.

They seemed to fear even his voice. The Wells Fargo agent vanished through the door and clattered down the steps.

"How long you been standin' at that door?" said Rogers, gnawing his lips.

"Jest for a breathin' space," said Dan.

Rogers squinted his eyes to make up for the dimness of the lamplight.

"By God!" he cried suddenly. "You're Whistlin' Dan Barry!"

He dropped into his chair and passed a trembling hand across his forehead.

He stammered: "Maybe you've changed your mind an' come back for that five thousand?"

"No, I've come for a man, not for money."

"A man?"

"I want Lee Haines before the crowd gets him."

"Would you really try to take Haines out?" asked Rogers with a touch of awe.

"Are there any guards in the jail?"

"Two. Lewis an' Patterson."

"Give me a written order for Haines."

The deputy wavered.

"If I do that I'm done for in this town!"

"Maybe. I want the key for Haines's handcuffs."

"Go over an' put your hoss up in the shed behind the jail," said Rogers, fighting for time, "an' when you come back I'll have the order written out an' give it to you with the key."

"Why not come over with me now?"

"I got some other business."

"In five minutes I'll be back," said Dan, and left the house.

Outside he whistled to Satan, and the stallion trotted up to him. He swung into the saddle and rode to the jail. There was not a guard in sight. He rode around to the other side of the building to reach the stable. Still he could not sight one of those shadowy horsemen who had surrounded the place a few minutes before. Perhaps the crowd had called in the guards to join the attack.

He put Satan away in the stable and as he led him into a stall he heard a roar of many voices far away. Then came the crack of half a dozen revolvers. Dan set his teeth and glanced quickly over the half-dozen horses in the little shed. He recognized the tall bay of Lee Haines at once and threw on its back the saddle which hung on a peg directly behind it. As he drew up the cinch another shout came from the street, but this time very close.

When he raced around the jail he saw the crowd pouring into the house of the deputy sheriff. He ran on till he came to the outskirts of the mob. Every man was masked, but in the excitement no one noticed that Dan's face was bare. Squirming his way through the press, Dan reached the deputy's office. It was almost filled. Rogers stood on a chair trying to argue with the cattlemen.

"No more talk, sheriff," thundered one among the cowpunchers, "we've had enough of your line of talk. Now we want some action of our own brand. For the last time: Are you goin' to order Lewis an' Patterson to give up Haines, or are you goin' to let two good men die fightin' for a damn lone rider?"

"What about the feller who's goin' to take Lee Haines out of Elkhead?" cried another.

The crowd yelled with delight.

"Yes, where is he? What about him?"

Rogers, glancing down from his position on the chair, stared into the brown eyes of Whistling Dan. He stretched out an arm that shook with excitement.

"That feller there!" he cried, "that one without a mask! Whistlin' Dan Barry is the man!"

CHAPTER XXIV

THE RESCUE

THE throng gave back from Dan, as if from the vicinity of a panther. Dan faced the circle of scowling faces, smiling gently upon them.

"Look here, Barry," called a voice from the rear of the crowd, "why do you want to take Haines away? Throw in your cards with us. We need you."

"If it's fightin' you want," cried a joker, "maybe Lewis an' Patterson will give us all enough of it at the jail."

"I ain't never huntin' for trouble," said Dan.

"Make your play quick," said another. "We got no time to waste even on Dan Barry. Speak out, Dan. Here's a lot of good fellers aimin' to take out Haines an' give him what's due him— no more. Are you with us?"

"I'm not."

"Is that final?"

"It is."

"All right. Tie him up, boys. There ain't no other way!"

"Look out!" shouted a score of voices, for a gun flashed in Dan's hand.

He aimed at no human target. The bullet shattered the glass lamp into a thousand shivering and tinkling splinters. Thick darkness blotted the room. Instantly thereafter a blow, a groan, and the fall of a body; then a confused clamour.

"He's here!"

"Give up that gun, damn you!"

"You got the wrong man!"

"I'm Bill Flynn!"

"Guard the door!"

"Lights, for God's sake!"

"Help!"

A slender figure leaped up against the window and was dimly outlined by the starlight outside. There was a crash of falling glass, and as two or three guns exploded the figure leaped down outside the house.

"Follow him!"

"Who was that?"

"Get a light! Who's got a match?"

Half the men rushed out of the room to pursue that fleeing figure. The other half remained to see what had happened. It seemed impossible that

Whistling Dan had escaped from their midst. Half a dozen sulphur matches spurted little jets of blue flame and discovered four men lying prone on the floor, most of them with the wind trampled from their bodies, but otherwise unhurt. One of them was the sheriff.

He lay with his shoulders propped against the wall. His mouth was a mass of blood.

"Who got you, Rogers?"

"Where's Barry?"

"The jail, the jail!" groaned Rogers. "Barry has gone for the jail!"

Revolvers rattled outside.

"He's gone for Haines," screamed the deputy. "Go get him, boys!"

"How can he get Haines? He ain't got the keys."

"He has, you fools! When he shot the lights out he jumped for me and knocked me off the chair. Then he went through my pockets and got the keys. Get on your way! Quick!"

The lynchers, yelling with rage, were already stamping from the room.

With the jangling bunch of keys in one hand and his revolver in the other, Dan started full speed for the jail as soon as he leaped down from the window. By the time he had covered half the intervening

distance the first pursuers burst out of Rogers's
house and opened fire after the shadowy fugitive.
He whirled and fired three shots high in the air.
No matter how impetuous, those warning shots
would make the mob approach the jail with some
caution.

On the door of the jail he beat furiously with
the bunch of keys.

"What's up? Who's there?" cried a voice
within.

"Message from Rogers. Hell's started! He's
sent me with the keys!"

The door jerked open and a tall man, with a
rifle slung across one arm, blocked the entrance.

"What's the message?" he asked.

"This!" said Dan, and drove his fist squarely
into the other's face.

He fell without a cry and floundered on the floor,
gasping. Dan picked him up and shoved him
through the door, bolting it behind him. A narrow hall opened before him and ran the length of
the small building. He glanced into the room on
one side. It was the kitchen and eating-room in
one. He rushed into the one on the other side.
Two men were there. One was Haines, sitting
with his hands manacled. The other was the
second guard, who ran for Dan, whipping his rifle

to his shoulder. As flame spurted from the mouth of the gun, Dan dived at the man's knees and brought him to the floor with a crash. He rose quickly and leaned over the fallen man, who lay without moving, his arms spread wide. He had struck on his forehead when he dropped. He was stunned for the moment, but not seriously hurt. Dan ran to Haines, who stood with his hands high above his head. Far away was the shout of the coming crowd.

"Shoot and be damned!" said Haines sullenly.

For answer Dan jerked down the hands of the lone rider and commenced to try the keys on the handcuffs. There were four keys. The fourth turned the lock. Haines shouted as his hands fell free.

"After me!" cried Dan, and raced for the stable.

As they swung into their saddles outside the shed, the lynchers raced their horses around the jail.

"Straightaway!" called Dan. "Through the cottonwoods and down the lane. After me. Satan!"

The stallion leaped into a full gallop, heading straight for a tall group of cottonwoods beyond which was a lane fenced in with barbed wire. Half a dozen of the pursuers were in a position to cut them off, and now rushed for the cottonwoods, yelling to their comrades to join them. A score of lights flashed like giant fireflies as the lynchers opened fire.

"They've blocked the way!" groaned Haines.

Three men had brought their horses to a sliding stop in front of the cottonwoods and their revolvers cracked straight in the faces of Dan and Haines. There was no other way for escape. Dan raised his revolver and fired twice, aiming low. Two of the horses reared and pitched to the ground. The third rider had a rifle at his shoulder. He was holding his fire until he had drawn a careful bead. Now his gun spurted and Dan bowed far over his saddle as if he had been struck from behind.

Before the rifleman could fire again Black Bart leaped high in the air. His teeth closed on the shoulder of the lyncher and the man catapulted from his saddle to the ground. With his yell in their ears, Dan and Haines galloped through the cottonwoods, and swept down the lane.

CHAPTER XXV

A CHEER of triumph came from the lynchers. In fifty yards the fugitives learned the reason, for they glimpsed a high set of bars blocking the lane. Dan pulled back beside Haines.

"Can the bay make it?" he called.

"No. I'm done for."

For answer Dan caught the bridle of Lee's horse close to the bit. They were almost to the bars. A dark shadow slid up and over them. It was Black Bart, with his head turned to look back even as he jumped, as if he were setting an example which he bid them follow. Appallingly high the bars rose directly in front of them.

"Now!" called Dan to the tall bay, and jerked up on the bit.

Satan rose like a swallow to the leap. The bay followed in gallant imitation. For an instant they hung poised in air. Then Satan pitched to the ground, landing safely and lightly on four cat-like feet. A click and a rattle behind them—the bay was also over, but his hind hoofs had knocked down the top bar. He staggered, reeled far to one side, but recovering, swept on after Satan and Dan. A yell of disappointment rang far behind.

Glancing back Haines saw the foremost of the pursuers try to imitate the feat of the fugitives, but even with the top bar down he failed. Man and horse pitched to the ground.

For almost a mile the lane held straight on, and beyond stretched the open country. They were in that free sweep of hills before the pursuers remounted beyond the bars. In daytime a mile would have been a small handicap, but with the night and the hills to cover their flight, and with such mounts as Satan and the tall bay, they were safe. In half an hour all sound of them died out, and Haines, following Dan's example, slowed his horse to an easy gallop.

The long rider was puzzled by his companion's horsemanship, for Dan rode leaning far to the right of his saddle, with his head bowed. Several times Haines was on the verge of speaking, but he refrained. He commenced to sing in the exultation of freedom. An hour before he had been in the "rat-trap" with a circle of lynchers around him, and only two terror-stricken guards to save him from the most horrible of deaths. Then came Fate and tore him away and gave him to the liberty of the boundless hills. Fate in the person of this slender, sombre man. He stared at Dan with awe.

At the top of a hill his companion drew rein, reeling in the saddle with the suddenness of the halt. However, in such a horseman, this could not be. It must be merely a freak feature of his riding.

"Move," said Dan, his breath coming in pants. "Line out and get to her."

"To who?" said Haines, utterly bewildered.

"Delilah!"

"What?"

"Damn you, she's waitin' for you."

"In the name of God, Barry, why do you talk like this after you've saved me from hell?"

He stretched out his hand eagerly, but Dan reined Satan back.

"Keep your hand. I hate you worse'n hell. There ain't room enough in the world for us both. If you want to thank me do it by keepin' out of my path. Because the next time we meet you're goin' to die, Haines. It's writ in a book. Now feed your hoss the spur and run for Kate Cumberland. But remember—I'm goin' to get you again if I can."

"Kate—" began Haines. "She sent you for me?"

Only the yellow blazing eyes made answer and the wail of a coyote far away on the shadowy hill.

"Kate!" cried Haines again, but now there was a world of new meaning in his voice. He swung his horse and spurred down the slope.

At the next hill-crest he turned in the saddle, saw the motionless rider still outlined against the sky, and brought the bay to a halt. He was greatly troubled. For a reason mysterious and far beyond the horizon of his knowledge, Dan was surrendering Kate Cumberland to him.

"He's doing it while he still loves her," muttered Haines, "and am I cur enough to take her from him after he has saved me from God knows what?"

He turned his horse to ride back, but at that moment he caught the weird, the unearthly note of Dan's whistling. There was both melancholy and gladness in it. The storm wind running on the hills and exulting in the blind terror of the night had such a song as this to sing.

"If he was a man," Haines argued briefly with himself, "I'd do it. But he isn't a man. He's a devil. He has no more heart than the wolf which owns him as master. Shall I give a girl like Kate

Cumberland to that wild panther? She's mine—
all mine!"

Once more he turned his horse and this time
galloped steadily on into the night.

When Haines dropped out of sight, Dan's
whistling stopped. He looked up to the pitiless
glitter of the stars. He looked down to the sombre sweep of black hills. The wind was like a
voice saying over and over again: "Failure."
Everything was lost.

He slipped from the saddle and took off his coat.
From his left shoulder the blood welled slowly,
steadily. He tore a strip from his shirt and attempted to make a bandage, but he could not
manage it with one hand.

The world thronged with hostile forces eager
to hunt him to the death. He needed all his
strength, and now that was ebbing from a wound
which a child could have staunched for him, but
where could he find even a friendly child? Truly
all was lost! The satyr or the black panther
once had less need of man's help than had Dan,
but now he was hurt in body and soul. That
matchless co-ordination of eye with hand and foot
was gone. He saw Kate smiling into the eyes of
Haines; he imagined Bill Kilduff sitting on the
back of Satan, controlling all that glorious force

and speed; he saw Hal Purvis fighting venomously with Bart for the mastery which eventually must belong to the man.

He turned to the wild pair. Vaguely they sensed a danger threatening their master, and their eyes mourned for his hurt. He buried his face on the strong, smooth shoulder of Satan, and groaned. There came the answering whinny and the hot breath of the horse against the side of his face. There was the whine of Black Bart behind him, then the rough tongue of the wolf touched the dripping fingers. Then he felt a hot gust of the wolf's breath against his hand.

Too late he realized what that meant. He whirled with a cry of command, but the snarl of Black Bart cut it short. The wolf stood bristling, trembling with eagerness for the kill, his great white fangs gleaming, his snarl shrill and guttural with the frenzy of his desire, for he had tasted blood. Dan understood as he stared into the yellow green fury of the wolf's eyes, yet he felt no fear, only a glory in the fierce, silent conflict. He could not move the fingers of his left hand, but those of his right curved, stiffened. He desired nothing more in the world than the contact with that great, bristling black body, to leap aside from those ominous teeth, to set his fingers in the wolf's

17

throat. Reason might have told him the folly of such a strife, but all that remained in his mind was the love of combat—a blind passion. His eyes glowed like those of the wolf, yellow fire against the green. Black Bart crouched still lower, gathering himself for the spring, but he was held by the man's yellow gleaming eyes. They invited the battle. Fear set its icy hand on the soul of the wolf.

The man seemed to tower up thrice his normal height. His voice rang, harsh, sudden, unlike the utterance of man or beast: *"Down!"*

Fear conquered Black Bart. The fire died from his eyes. His body sank as if from exhaustion. He crawled on his belly to the feet of his master and whined an unutterable submission.

And then that hand, warm and wet with the thing whose taste set the wolf's heart on fire with the lust to kill, was thrust against his nose. He leaped back with bared teeth, growling horribly. The eyes commanded him back, commanded him relentlessly. He howled dismally to the senseless stars, yet he came; and once more that hand was thrust against his nose. He licked the fingers.

That blood-lust came hotter than before, but his fear was greater. He licked the strange hand again, whining. Then the master kneeled. Another hand, clean, and free from that horrible warm, wet sign of death, fell upon his shaggy back. The voice which he knew of old came to him, blew away the red mist from his soul, comforted him.

"Poor Bart!" said the voice, and the hand went slowly over his head. "It weren't your fault."

The stallion whinnied softly. A deep growl formed in the throat of the wolf, a mighty effort at speech. And now, like a gleam of light in a dark room, Dan remembered the house of Buck Daniels. There, at least, they could not refuse him aid. He drew on his coat, though the effort set him sweating with agony, got his foot in the stirrup with difficulty, and dragged himself to the saddle. Satan started at a swift gallop.

"Faster, Satan! Faster, partner!"

What a response! The strong body settled a little closer to the earth as the stride increased. The rhythm of the pace grew quicker, smoother. There was no adequate phrase to describe the matchless motion. And in front—always just a little in front with the plunging forefeet of the horse seeming to threaten him at every stride, ran Black Bart with his head turned as if he were the guard and guide of the fugitive.

Dan called and Black Bart yelped in answer. Satan tossed up his head and neighed as he raced along. The two replies were like human assurances that there was still a fighting chance.

The steady loss of blood was telling rapidly now. He clutched the pommel, set his teeth, and felt oblivion settle slowly and surely upon him. As his senses left him he noted the black outlines of the next high range of hills, a full ten miles away.

He only knew the pace of Satan never slackened. There seemed no effort in it. He was like one of those fabled horses, the offspring of the wind, and like the wind, tireless, eternal of motion.

A longer oblivion fell upon Dan. As he roused from it he found himself slipping in the saddle. He struggled desperately to grasp the saddle-horn and managed to draw himself up again; but the warning was sufficient to make him hunt about for some means of making himself more secure in the saddle. It was a difficult task to do anything with only one hand, but he managed to tie his left arm to the bucking-strap. If the end came, at least he was sure to die in the saddle. Vaguely he was aware as he looked around that the black hills were no longer in the distance. He was among them.

On went Satan. His breath was coming more and more laboured. It seemed to Dan's dim consciousness that some of the spring was gone from that glorious stride which swept on and on with the slightest undulation, like a swallow skimming before the wind; but so long as strength remained he knew that Satan would never falter in his pace. As the delirium swept once more shadow-like on his brain, he allowed himself to fall forward, and wound his fingers as closely as possible in the thick mane. His left arm jerked horribly against the bonds. Black night swallowed him once more.

Only his invincible heart kept Satan going throughout that last stretch. His ears lay flat on his neck, lifting only when the master muttered and raved in his fever. Foam flew back against his throat and breast. His breath came shorter, harder, with a rasp; but the gibbering voice of his rider urged him on, faster, and faster. They topped a small hill, and a little to the left and a mile away, rose a group of cottonwoods, and Dan, recovering consciousness, knew the house of Buck. He also knew that his last moment of consciousness was come. Surges of sleepy weakness swept over his brain. He could never guide Satan to the house.

"Bart!" he called feebly.

The wolf whining, dropped back beside him. Dan pointed his right arm straight ahead. Black

Bart leaped high into the air and his shrill yelp told that he had seen the cottonwoods and the house.

Dan summoned the last of his power and threw the reins over the head of Satan.

"Take us in, Bart," he said, and twisting his fingers into Satan's mane fell across the saddle-horn.

Satan, understanding the throwing of the reins as an order to halt, came to a sharp stop, and the body of the senseless rider sagged to one side. Black Bart caught the reins. They were bitter and salt with blood of the master.

He tugged hard. Satan whinnied his doubt, and the growl of Black Bart answered, half a threat. In a moment more they were picking their way through the brush towards the house of Buck Daniels.

Satan was far gone with exhaustion. His head drooped; his legs sprawled with every step; his eyes were glazed. Yet he staggered on with the great black wolf pulling at the reins. There was the salt taste of blood in the mouth of Black Bart; so he stalked on, saliva dripping from his mouth, and his eyes glazed with the lust to kill. His furious snarling was the threat which urged on the stallion.

CHAPTER XXVI

BLACK BART TURNS NURSE

IT was old Mrs. Daniels who woke first at the sound of scratching and growling. She roused her husband and son, and all three went to the door, Buck in the lead with his six-gun in his hand. At sight of the wolf he started back and raised the gun, but Black Bart fawned about his feet.

"Don't shoot—it's a dog, an' there's his master!" cried Sam. "By the Lord, they's a dead man tied on that there hoss!"

Dan lay on Satan, half fallen from the saddle, with his head hanging far down, only sustained by the strength of the rein. The stallion, wholly spent, stood with his legs braced, his head low, and his breath coming in great gasps. The family ran to the rescue. Sam cut the rein and Buck lowered the limp body in his arms.

"Buck, is he dead?" whispered Mrs. Daniels.

"I don't feel no heart beat," said Buck. "Help me fetch him into the house, Dad!"

"Look out for the hoss!" cried Sam.

Buck started back with his burden just in time, for Satan, surrendering to his exhaustion, pitched to the ground, and lay with sprawling legs like a spent dog rather than a horse.

"Let the hoss be," said Buck. "Help me with the man. He's hurt bad."

Mrs. Daniels ran ahead and lighted a lamp. They laid the body carefully upon a bed. It made a ghastly sight, the bloodless face with the black hair fallen wildly across the forehead, the mouth loosely open, and the lips black with dust.

"Dad!" said Buck. "I think I've seen this feller. God knows if he's livin' or dead."

He dropped to his knees and pressed his ear over Dan's heart.

"I can't feel no motion. Ma, get that hand mirror——"

She had it already and now held it close to the lips of the wounded man. When she drew it away their three heads drew close together.

"They's a mist on it! He's livin'!" cried Buck.

"It ain't nothing," said Sam. "The glass ain't quite clear, that's all."

Mrs. Daniels removed the last doubt by running her finger across the surface of the glass. It left an unmistakable mark.

They wasted no moment then. They brought hot and cold water, washed out his wound, cleansed away the blood; and while Mrs. Daniels and her husband fixed the bandage, Buck pounded and rubbed the limp body to restore the circulation. In a few minutes his efforts were rewarded by a great sigh from Dan.

He shouted in triumph, and then: "By God, it's Whistlin' Dan Barry."

"It is!" said Sam. "Buck, they's been devils workin' tonight. It sure took more'n one man to nail him this way."

They fell to work frantically. There was a perceptible pulse, the breathing was faint but steady, and a touch of colour came in the face.

"His arm will be all right in a few days," said Mrs. Daniels, "but he may fall into a fever. He's turnin' his head from side to side and talkin'. What's he sayin', Buck?"

"He's sayin': 'Faster, Satan.'"

"That's the hoss," interpreted Sam.

"'Hold us straight, Bart!' That's what he's sayin' now."

"That's the wolf."

"'An' it's all for Delilah!' Who's Delilah, Dad?"

"Maybe it's some feller Dan knows."

"Some feller?" repeated Mrs. Daniels with scorn. "It's some worthless girl who got Whistlin' Dan into this trouble."

Dan's eyes opened but there was no understanding in them.

"Haines, I hate you worse'n hell!"

"It's Lee Haines who done this!" cried Sam.

"If it is, I'll cut out his heart!"

"It can't be Haines," broke in Mrs. Daniels. "Old man Perkins, didn't he tell us that Haines was the man that Whistlin' Dan Barry had brought down into Elkhead? How could Haines do this shootin' while he was in jail?"

"Ma," said Sam, "you watch Whistlin' Dan. Buck an' me'll take care of the hoss—that black stallion. He's pretty near all gone, but he's worth savin'. What I don't see is how he found his way to us. It's certain Dan didn't guide him all the way."

"How does the wind find its way?" said Buck. "It was the wolf that brought Dan here, but standin' here talkin' won't tell us how. Let's go out an' fix up Satan."

It was by no means an easy task. As they approached the horse he heaved himself up, snorting, and stood with legs braced, and pendant head. Even his eyes were glazed with exhaustion, but behind them it was easy to guess the dauntless anger which raged against these intruders. Yet he would have been helpless against them. It was Black Bart who interfered at this point. He stood before them, his hair bristling and his teeth bared.

Sam suggested: "Leave the door of the house open an' let him hear Whistlin' Dan's voice."

It was done. At once the delirious voice of Dan stole out to them faintly. The wolf turned his head to Satan with a plaintive whine, as if asking why the stallion remained there when that voice was audible. Then he raced for the open door and disappeared into the house.

"Hurry in, Buck!" called Sam. "Maybe the wolf'll scare Ma!"

They ran inside and found Black Bart on the bed straddling the body of Whistling Dan, and growling at poor Mrs. Daniels, who crouched in a corner of the room. It required patient work before he was convinced that they actually meant no harm to his master.

"What's the reason of it?" queried Sam helplessly. "The damn wolf let us take Dan off the hoss without makin' any fuss."

"Sure he did," assented Buck, "but he ain't sure of me yet, an' every time he comes near me he sends the cold chills up my back."

Having decided that he might safely trust them
to touch Dan's body, the great wolf went the round
and sniffed them carefully, his hair bristling and
the forbidding growl lingering in his throat. In
the end he apparently decided that they might be
tolerated, though he must keep an eye upon their
actions. So he sat down beside the bed and followed with an anxious eye every movement of
Mrs. Daniels. The men went back to the stallion.
He still stood with legs braced far apart, and head
hanging low. Another mile of that long race and
he would have dropped dead beneath his rider.

Nevertheless at the coming of the strangers he
reared up his head a little and tried to run away.
Buck caught the dangling reins near the bit.
Satan attempted to strike out with his forehoof.
It was a movement as clumsy and slow as the blow
of a child, and Buck easily avoided it. Realizing
his helplessness Satan whinnied a heart-breaking
appeal for help to his unfailing friend, Black Bart.
The wail of the wolf answered dolefully from the
house.

"Good Lord," groaned Buck. "Now we'll have
that black devil on our hands again."

"No, we won't," chuckled Sam, "the wolf won't
leave Dan. Come on along, old hoss."

Nevertheless it required hard labour to urge and

drag the stallion to the stable. At the end of that time they had the saddle off and a manger full of fodder before him. They went back to the house with the impression of having done a day's work.

"Which it shows the fool nature of a hoss," moralized Sam. "That stallion would be willin' to lay right down and die for the man that's jest rode him up to the front door of death, but he wishes everlastingly that he had the strength to kick the daylight out of you an' me that's been tryin' to take care of him. You jest write this down inside your brain, Buck: a hoss is like a woman. They jest nacherally ain't no reason in 'em!"

They found Dan in a heavy sleep, his breath coming irregularly. Mrs. Daniels stated that it was the fever which she had feared and she offered to sit up with the sick man through the rest of that night. Buck lifted her from the chair and took her place beside the bed.

"No one but me is goin' to take care of Whistlin' Dan," he stated.

So the vigil began, with Buck watching Dan, and Black Bart alert, suspicious, ready at the first wrong move to leap at the throat of Buck.

CHAPTER XXVII

THAT night the power which had sent Dan into Elkhead, Jim Silent, stood his turn at watch in the narrow canyon below the old Salton place. In the house above him sat Terry Jordan, Rhinehart, and Hal Purvis playing poker, while Bill Kilduff drew a drowsy series of airs from his mouth-organ. His music was getting on the nerves of the other three, particularly Jordan and Rhinehart, for Purvis was winning steadily.

"Let up!" broke out Jordan at last, pounding on the table with his fist. "Your damn tunes are gettin' my goat. Nobody can think while you're hittin' it up like that. This ain't no prayer meetin', Bill."

For answer Kilduff removed the mouth-organ to take a deep breath, blinked his small eyes, and began again in a still higher key.

"Go slow, Terry," advised Rhinehart in a soft tone. "Kilduff ain't feelin' none too well tonight."

"What's the matter with him?" growled the

scar-faced man, none too anxious to start an open quarrel with the formidable Kilduff.

Rhinehart jerked his thumb over his shoulder.

"The gal in there. He don't like the game the chief has been workin' with her."

"Neither do I," said Purvis, "but I'd do worse than the chief done to get Lee Haines back."

"Get Haines back?" said Kilduff, his voice ominously deep. "There ain't no chance of that. If there was I wouldn't have no kick against the chief for what he's done to Kate."

"Maybe there's *some* chance," suggested Rhinehart.

"Chance, hell!" cried Kilduff. "One man agin a whole town full? I say all that Jim has done is to get Whistlin' Dan plugged full of lead."

"Well," said Purvis, "if that's done, ain't the game worth while?"

The rest of the men chuckled and even Kilduff smiled.

"Old Joe Cumberland is sure takin' it hard," said "Calamity" Rhinehart. "All day he's been lightin' into the girl."

"The funny part," mused Purvis, "is that the old boy really means it. I think he'd of sawed off his right hand to keep her from goin' to Whistlin' Dan."

"An' her sittin' white-faced an' starin' at nothin' an' tryin' to comfort *him!*" rumbled Kilduff, standing up under the stress of his unwonted emotion. "My God, she was apologizin' for what she done, an' tryin' to cheer him up, an' all the time her heart was bustin'."

He pulled out a violently coloured bandana and wiped his forehead.

"When we all get down to hell," he said, "they'll be quite a little talkin' done about this play of Jim's—you c'n lay to that."

"Who's that singin' down the canyon?" asked Jordan. "It sounds like——"

He would not finish his sentence as if he feared to prove a false prophet. They rose as one man and stared stupidly at one another.

"Haines!" broke out Rhinehart at last.

"It ain't no ways possible!" said Kilduff. "And yet—by God, it is!"

They rushed for the door and made out two figures approaching, one on horseback, and the other on foot.

"Haines!" called Purvis, his shrill voice rising to a squeak with his excitement.

"Here I am!" rang back the mellow tones of the big lone rider, and in a moment he and Jim Silent entered the room.

Glad faces surrounded him. There was infinite wringing of his hand and much pounding on the back. Kilduff and Rhinehart pushed him back into a chair. Jordan ran for a flask of whisky, but Haines pushed the bottle away.

"I don't want anything on my breath," he said, "because I have to talk to a woman. Where's Kate?"

The men glanced at each other uneasily.

"She's here, all right," said Silent hastily. "Now tell us how you got away."

"Afterwards," said Haines. "But first Kate."

"What's your hurry to see her?" said Kilduff.

Haines laughed exultantly.

"You're jealous, Bill! Why, man, she sent for me! Sent Whistling Dan himself for me."

"Maybe she did," said Kilduff, "but that ain't no partic'lar sign I'm jealous. Tell us about the row in Elkhead."

"That's it," said Jordan. "We can't wait, Lee."

"Just one word explains it," said Haines. "Barry!"

"What did he do?" This from every throat at once.

"Broke into the jail with all Elkhead at his heels flashing their six-guns—knocked down the two guards—unlocked my bracelets (God knows where he got the key!)—shoved me onto the bay—drove away with me—shot down two men while his wolf pulled down a third—made my horse jump a set of bars as high as my head—and here I am!"

There was a general loosening of bandanas. The eyes of Jim Silent gleamed.

"And all Elkhead knows that he's the man who took you out of jail?" he asked eagerly.

"Right. He's put his mark on them," responded Haines, "but the girl, Jim!"

"By God!" said Silent. "I've got him! The whole world is agin him—the law an' the outlaws. He's done for!"

He stopped short.

"Unless you're feelin' uncommon grateful to him for what he done for you, Lee?"

"He told me he hated me like hell," said Haines. "I'm grateful to him as I'd be to a mountain lion that happened to do me a good turn. Now for Kate!"

"Let him see her," said Silent. "That's the quickest way. Call her out, Haines. We'll take a little walk while you're with her."

The moment they were gone Haines rushed to the door and knocked loudly. It was opened at once and Kate stood before him. She winced at sight of him.

"It's I, Kate!" he cried joyously. "I've come back from the dead."

She stepped from the room and closed the door behind her.

"What of Dan? Tell me! Was—was he hurt?"

"Dan?" he repeated with an impatient smile. "No, he isn't hurt. He pulled me through—got me out of jail and safe into the country. He had to drop two or three of the boys to do it."

Her head fell back a little and in the dim light, for the first time, he saw her face with some degree of clearness, and started at its pallor.

"What's the matter, Kate—dear?" he said anxiously.

"What of Dan?" she asked faintly.

"I don't know. He's outlawed. He's done for. The whole range will be against him. But why are you so worried about him, Kate?—when he told me that you loved me——"

She straightened.

"Love? *You?*"

His face lengthened almost ludicrously.

"But why—Dan came for me—he said you sent him—he——" he broke down, stammering, utterly confused.

"This is why I sent him!" she answered, and throwing open the door gestured to him to enter.

He followed her and saw the lean figure of old Joe Cumberland lying on a blanket close to the wall.

"That's why!" she whispered.

"How does he come here?"

"Ask the devil in his human form! Ask your friend, Jim Silent!"

He walked into the outer room with his head low. He found the others already returned. Their carefully controlled grins spoke volumes.

"Where's Silent?" he asked heavily.

"He's gone," said Jordan.

Hal Purvis took Haines to one side.

"Take a brace," he urged.

"She hates me, Hal," said the big fellow sadly. "For God's sake, was there no other way of getting me out?"

"Not one! Pull yourself together, Lee. There ain't no one for you to hold a spite agin. Would you rather be back in Elkhead dangling from the end of a rope?"

"It seems to have been a sort of—joke," said Haines.

"Exactly. But at that sort of a joke nobody laughs!"

"And Whistling Dan Barry?"

"He's done for. We're all agin him, an' now

even the rangers will help us hunt him down. Think it over careful, Haines. You're agin him because you want the girl. I want that damned wolf of his, Black Bart. Kilduff would rather get into the saddle of Satan than ride to heaven. An' Jim Silent won't never rest till he sees Dan lyin' on the ground with a bullet through his heart. Here's four of us. Each of us want something that belongs to him, from his life to his dog. Haines, I'm askin' you man to man, was there any one ever born who could get away from four men like us?''

CHAPTER XXVIII

WHISTLING DAN, DESPERADO

IT was an urgent business which sent Silent galloping over the hills before dawn. When the first light came he was close to the place of Gus Morris. He slowed his horse to a trot, but after a careful reconnoitring, seeing no one stirring around the sheriff's house, he drew closer and commenced to whistle a range song, broken here and there with a significant phrase which sounded like a signal. Finally a cloth was waved from a window, and Silent, content, turned his back on the house, and rode away at a walk.

Within half an hour the pounding of a horse approached from behind. The plump sheriff came to a halt beside him, jouncing in the saddle with the suddenness of the stop.

"What's up?" he called eagerly.

"Whistlin' Dan."

"What's new about him? I know they're talkin' about that play he made agin Haines. They's some says he's a faster man than you, Jim!"

"They say too damned much!" snarled Silent. "This is what's new. Whistlin' Dan Barry—no less—has busted open the jail at Elkhead an' set Lee Haines free."

The sheriff could not speak.

"I fixed it, Gus. I staged the whole little game."

"*You* fixed it with Whistlin' Dan?"

"Don't ask me how I worked it. The pint is that he did the job. He got into the jail while the lynchers was guardin' it, gettin' ready for a rush. They opened fire. It was after dark last night. Haines an' Dan made a rush for it from the stable on their hosses. They was lynchers everywhere. Haines didn't have no gun. Dan wouldn't trust him with one. He did the shootin' himself. He dropped two of them with two shots. His devil of a wolf-dog brung down another."

"Shootin' at night?"

"Shootin' at night," nodded Silent. "An' now, Gus, they's only one thing left to complete my little game—an' that's to get Whistlin' Dan Barry proclaimed an outlaw an' put a price on his head, savvy?"

"Why d'you hate him so?" asked Morris curiously.

"Morris, why d'you hate smallpox?"

"Because a man's got no chance fightin' agin it."

"Gus, that's why I hate Whistlin' Dan, but I ain't here to argue. I want you to get Dan proclaimed an outlaw."

The sheriff scowled and bit his lip.

"I can't do it, Jim."

"Why the hell can't you?"

"Don't go jumpin' down my throat. It ain't human to double cross nobody the way you're double crossin' that kid. He's clean. He fights square. He's jest done you a good turn. I can't do it, Jim."

There was an ominous silence.

"Gus," said the outlaw, "how many thousand have I given you?"

The sheriff winced.

"I dunno," he said, "a good many, Jim."

"An' now you're goin' to lay down on me?"

Another pause.

"People are gettin' pretty excited nowadays," went on Silent carelessly. "Maybe they'd get a lot more excited if they was to know jest how much I've paid you, Gus."

The sheriff struck his forehead with a pudgy hand.

"When a man's sold his soul to the devil they ain't no way of buyin' it back."

"When you're all waked up," said Silent soothingly, "they ain't no more reasonable man than you, Gus. But sometimes you get to seein' things cross-eyed. Here's my game. What do you think they'd do in Elkhead if a letter came for Dan Barry along about now?"

" The boys must be pretty hot," said the sheriff. "I suppose the letter'd be opened."

"It would," said the outlaw. "You're sure a clever feller, Gus. You c'n see a white hoss in the sunlight. Now what d'you suppose they'd think if they opened a letter addressed to Dan Barry and read something like this:

" 'DEAR DAN: You made great play for L. H. None of us is going to forget it. Maybe the thing for you to do is to lay low for a while. Then join us any time you want to. We all think nobody could of worked that stunt any smoother than you done. The rest of the boys say that two thousand ain't enough for the work you've done. They vote that you get an extra thousand for it. I'm agreeable about that, and when you get short of cash just drop up and see us—you know where..

" ' That's a great bluff you've made about being on my trail. Keep it up. It'll fool everybody for a while. They'll think, maybe, that what you did for L. H. was because he was your personal friend. They won't suspect that you're now one of us. Adios,

" 'J. S.' "

Silent waited for the effect of this missive to show in Morris's face.

"Supposin' they was to read a letter like that, Gus. D'you think maybe it'd sort of peeve them?"

"He'd be outlawed inside of two days!"

"Right. Here's the letter. An' you're goin' to see that it's delivered in Elkhead, Morris."

The sheriff looked sombrely on the little square of white.

"I sort of think," he said at last, "that this here's the death warrant for Whistlin' Dan Barry."

"So do I," grinned Silent, considerably thirsty for action. "That's your chance to make one of your rarin', tarin' speeches. Then you hop into the telegraph office an' send a wire to the Governor askin' that a price be put on the head of the blood-thirsty desperado, Dan Barry, commonly known as Whistlin' Dan."

"It's like something out of a book," said the sheriff slowly. "It's like some damned horror story."

"The minute you get the reply to that telegram swear in forty deputies and announce that they's a price on Barry's head. So long, Gus. This little play'll make the boys figger you're the most efficient sheriff that never pulled a gun."

He turned his horse, laughing loudly, and the sheriff, with that laughter in his ears, rode back towards his hotel with a downward head.

.   .   .   .

All day at the Daniels's house the fever grew perceptibly, and that night the family held a long consultation.

"They's got to be somethin' done," said Buck. "I'm goin' to ride into town tomorrow an' get ahold of Doc Geary."

"There ain't no use of gettin' that fraud Geary," said Mrs. Daniels scornfully. "I think that if the boy c'n be saved I c'n do it as well as that doctor. But there ain't no doctor c'n help him. The trouble with Dan ain't his wound—it's his mind that's keepin' him low."

"His mind?" queried old Sam.

"Listen to him now. What's all that talkin' about Delilah?"

"If it ain't Delilah it's Kate," said Buck. "Always one of the two he's talkin' about. An' when he talks of them his fever gets worse. Who's Delilah, an' who's Kate?"

"They's one an' the same person," said Mrs. Daniels. "It do beat all how blind men are!"

"Are we now?" said her husband with some

heat. "An' what good would it do even if we knowed that they was the same?"

"Because if we could locate the girl they's a big chance she'd bring him back to reason. She'd make his brain quiet, an' then his body'll take care of itself, savvy?"

"But they's a hundred Kates in the range," said Sam. "Has he said her last name, Buck, or has he given you any way of findin' out where she lives?"

"There ain't no way," brooded Buck, "except that when he talks about her sometimes he speaks of Lee Haines like he wanted to kill him. Sometimes he's dreamin' of havin' Lee by the throat. D'you honest think that havin' the girl here would do any good, ma?"

"Of course it would," she answered. "He's in love, that poor boy is, an' love is worse than bullets for some men. I don't mean you or Sam. Lord knows *you* wouldn't bother yourselves none about a woman."

Her eyes challenged them.

"He talks about Lee havin' the girl?" asked Sam.

"He sure does," said Buck, "which shows that he's jest ravin'. How could Lee have the girl, him bein' in jail at Elkhead?"

"But maybe Lee had her before Whistlin' Dan got him at Morris's place. Maybe she's up to Silent's camp now."

"A girl in Jim Silent's camp?" repeated Buck scornfully. "Jim'd as soon have a ton of lead hangin' on his shoulders."

"Would he though?" broke in Mrs. Daniels. "You're considerable young, Buck, to be sayin' what men'll do where they's women concerned. Where is this camp?"

"I dunno," said Buck evasively. "Maybe up in the hills. Maybe at the old Salton place. If I thought she was there, I'd risk goin' up and gettin' her—with her leave or without it!"

"Don't be talkin' fool stuff like that," said his mother anxiously. "You ain't goin' near Jim Silent agin, Buck!"

He shrugged his shoulders, with a scowl, and turned away to go back to the bedside of Whistling Dan.

In the morning Buck was hardly less haggard than Dan. His mother, with clasped hands and an anxious face, stood at the foot of the bed, but her trouble was more for her son than for Dan. Old Sam was out saddling Buck's horse, for they had decided that the doctor must be brought from Elkhead at once.

"I don't like to leave him," growled Buck. "I misdoubt what may be happenin' while I'm gone."

"Don't look at me like that," said his mother. "Why, Buck, a body would think that if he dies while you're gone you'll accuse your father an' mother of murder."

"Don't be no minute away from him," urged Buck, "that's all I ask."

"Cure his brain," said his mother monotonously, "an' his body'll take care of itself. Who's that talkin' with your dad outside?"

Very faintly they caught the sound of voices, and after a moment the departing clatter of a galloping horse. Old Sam ran into the house breathless.

"Who was it? What's the matter, pa?" asked his wife, for the old cowpuncher's face was pale even through his tan.

"Young Seaton was jest here. He an' a hundred other fellers is combin' the range an' warnin' everyone agin that Dan Barry. The bullet in his shoulder—he got it while he was breaking jail with Lee Haines. An' he shot down the hosses of two men an' his dog pulled down a third one."

"Busted jail with Lee Haines!" breathed Buck. "It ain't no ways nacheral. Which Dan hates Lee Haines!"

"He was bought off by Jim Silent," said old Sam. "They opened a letter in Elkhead, an' the letter told everything. It was signed "J. S." an' it thanked Dan for gettin' "L. H. free.""

"It's a lie!" said Buck doggedly.

"Buck! Sam!" cried Mrs. Daniels, seeing the two men of her family glaring at each other with something like hate in their eyes. "Sam, have you forgot that this lad has eat your food in your house?"

Sam turned as crimson as he had been pale before.

"I forgot," he muttered. "I was scared an' forgot!"

'An' maybe you've forgot that I'd be swingin' on the end of a rope in Elkhead if it wasn't for Dan Barry?" suggested Buck.

"Buck," said his father huskily, "I'm askin' your pardon. I got sort of panicky for a minute, that's all. But what are we goin' to do with him? If he don't get help he'll be a dead man quick. An' you can't go to Elkhead for the doctor. They'd doctor Dan with six-guns, that's what they'd do."

"What could of made him do it?" said Mrs. Daniels, wiping a sudden burst of tears from her eyes.

"Oh, God," said Buck. "How'd I know why he

done it? How'd I know why he turned me loose when he should of took me to Elkhead to be lynched by the mob there? The girl's the only thing to help him outside of a doctor. I'm goin' to get the girl."

"Where?"

"I dunno. Maybe I'll try the old Salton place."

"And take her away from Jim Silent?" broke in his father. "You might jest as well go an' shoot yourse'f before startin'. That'll save your hoss the long ride, an' it'll bring you to jest the same end."

"Listen!" said Buck, "they's the wolf mournin'!"

"Buck, you're loco!"

"Hush, pa!" whispered Mrs. Daniels.

She caught the hand of her brawny son.

"Buck, I'm no end proud of you, lad. If you die, it's a good death! Tell me, Buck dear, have you got a plan?"

He ground his big hand across his forehead, scowling.

"I dunno," he said, drawing a long breath. "I jest know that I got to get the girl. Words don't say what I mean. All I know is that I've got to go up there an' get that girl, and bring her back so's she can save Dan, not from the people that's huntin' him, but from himself."

"There ain't no way of changin' you?" said his father.

"Pa," said Mrs. Daniels, "sometimes you're a plumb fool!"

Buck was already in the saddle. He waved farewell, but after he set his face towards the far-away hills he never turned his head. Behind him lay the untamed three. Before him, somewhere among those naked, sunburned hills, was the woman whose love could reclaim the wild.

A dimness came before his eyes. He attempted to curse at this weakness, but in place of the blasphemy something swelled in his throat, and a still, small music filled his heart. And when at last he was able to speak his lips framed a vow like that of the old crusaders.

19

CHAPTER XXIX

"WEREWOLF"

BUCK's cattle pony broke from the lope into a steady dog-trot. Now and then Buck's horse tossed his head high and jerked his ears quickly back and forth as if he were trying to shake off a fly. As a matter of fact he was bothered by his master's whistling. The only sound which he was accustomed to hear from the lips of his rider was a grunted curse now and then. This whistling made the mustang uneasy.

Buck himself did not know what the music meant, but it brought into his mind a thought of strong living and of glorious death. He had heard it whistled several times by Dan Barry when the latter lay delirious. It seemed to Buck, while he whistled this air, that the spirit of Dan travelled beside him, nerving him to the work which lay ahead, filling the messenger with his own wild strength.

As Buck dropped into a level tract of country he

caught sight of a rider coming from the opposite direction. As they drew closer the other man swung his mount far to one side. Buck chuckled softly, seeing that the other evidently desired to pass without being recognized. The chuckle died when the stranger changed direction and rode straight for Buck. The latter pulled his horse to a quick stop and turned to face the on-comer. He made sure that his six-gun was loose in the holster, for it was always well to be prepared for the unusual in these chance meetings in the mountain-desert.

"Hey, Buck!" called the galloping horseman.

The hand of Daniels dropped away from his revolver, for he recognized the voice of Hal Purvis, who swiftly ranged alongside.

"What's the dope?" asked Buck, producing his tobacco and the inevitable brown papers.

"Jest lookin' the landscape over an' scoutin' around for news," answered Purvis.

"Pick up anything?"

"Yeh. Ran across some tenderfoot squatters jest out of Elkhead."

Buck grunted and lighted his cigarette.

"Which you've been sort of scarce around the outfit lately," went on Purvis.

"I'm headin' for the bunch now," said Buck.

"D'you bring along that gun of mine I left at your house?"

"Didn't think of it."

"Let's drop back to your house an' get it. Then I'll ride up to the camp with you."

Buck drew a long puff on his cigarette. He drew a quick mental picture of Purvis entering the house, finding Dan, and then——"

"Sure," he said, "you c'n go back to the house an' ask pa for the gun, if you want to. I'll keep on for the hills."

"What's your hurry? It ain't more'n three miles back to your house. You won't lose no time to speak of."

"It ain't time I'm afraid of losin'," said Buck significantly.

"Then what the devil is it? I can't afford to leave that gun."

"All right," said Buck, forcing a grin of derision, "so long, Hal."

Purvis frowned at him with narrowing eyes.

"Spit it out, Buck. What's the matter with me goin' back for that gun? Ain't I apt to find it?"

"Sure. That's the point. You're apt to find *lots* of guns. Here's what I mean, Hal. Some of the cowpunchers are beginnin' to think I'm a little partial to Jim Silent's crowd. An' they're watchin' my house."

"The hell!"

"You're right. It is. That's one of the reasons I'm beatin' it for the hills."

He started his horse to a walk. "But of course if you're bound to have that gun, Hal——"

Purvis grinned mirthlessly, his lean face wrinkling to the eyes, and he swung his horse in beside Buck.

"Anyway," said Buck, "I'm glad to see you ain't a fool. How's things at the camp?"

"Rotten. They's a girl up there——"

"A girl?"

"You look sort of pleased. Sure they's a girl. Kate Cumberland, she's the one. She seen us hold up the train, an' now we don't dare let her go. She's got enough evidence to hang us all if it came to a show-down."

"Kate! Delilah."

"What you sayin'?"

"I say it's damn queer that Jim'll let a girl stay at the camp."

"Can't be helped. She's makin' us more miserable than a whole army of men. We had her in the house for a while, an' then Silent rigged up the little shack that stands a short ways——"

"I know the one you mean."

"She an' her dad is in that. We have to guard 'em at night. She ain't had no good word for any of us since she's been up there. Every time she looks at a feller she makes you feel like you was somethin' low-down—a snake, or somethin'."

"D'you mean to say none of the boys please her?" asked Buck curiously. He understood from Dan's delirious ravings that the girl was in love with Lee Haines and had deserted Barry for the outlaw. "Say, ain't Haines goodlookin' enough to please her?"

Purvis laughed unpleasantly.

"He'd like to be, but he don't quite fit her idea of a man. We'd all like to be, for that matter. She's a ravin' beauty, Buck. One of these blue-eyed, yaller-haired kind, see, with a voice like silk. Speakin' personal, I'm free to admit she's got me stopped."

Buck drew so hard on the diminishing butt of his cigarette that he burned his fingers.

"Can't do nothin' with her?" he queried.

"What you grinnin' about?" said Purvis hotly. "D'you think *you'd* have any better luck with her?"

Buck chuckled.

"The trouble with you fellers," he said complacently, "is that you're all too damned afraid of a girl. You all treat 'em like they was queens an' you was their slaves. They like a master."

The thin lips of Purvis curled.

"You're quite a man, ain't you?"

"Man enough to handle any woman that ever walked."

Purvis broke into loud laughter.

"That's what a lot of us thought," he said at last, "but she breaks all the rules. She's got her heart set on another man, an' she's that funny sort that don't never love twice. Maybe you'll guess who the man is?"

Buck frowned thoughtfully to cover his growing excitement.

"Give it up, Buck," advised Purvis. "The feller she loves is Whistlin' Dan Barry. You wouldn't think no woman would look without shiverin' at that hell-raiser. But she's goin' on a hunger strike on account of him. Since yesterday she wouldn't eat none. She says she'll starve herself to death unless we turn her loose. The hell of it is that she will. I know it an' so does the rest of the boys."

"Starve herself to death?" said Buck exuberantly. "Wait till I get hold of her!"

"*You?*"

"Me!"

Purvis viewed him with compassion.

"Me bein' your friend, Buck," he said, "take my tip an' don't try no fool stunts around that girl. Which she once belongs to Whistlin' Dan Barry an' therefore she's got the taboo mark on her for any other man. Everything he's ever owned is different, damned different!"

His voice lowered to a tone which was almost awe.

"Speakin' for myself, I don't hanker after his hoss like Bill Kilduff; or his girl, like Lee Haines; or his life, like the chief. All I want is a shot at that wolf-dog, that Black Bart!"

"You look sort of het up, Hal."

"He come near puttin' his teeth into my leg down at Morgan's place the day Barry cleaned up the chief."

"Why, any dog is apt to take a snap at a feller."

"This ain't a dog. It's a wolf. An' Whistlin' Dan—" he stopped.

"You look sort of queer, Hal. What's up?"

"You won't think I'm loco?"

"No."

"They's some folks away up north that thinks a man now an' then turns into a wolf."

Buck nodded and shrugged his shoulders. A little chill went up and down his back.

"Here's my idea, Buck. I've been thinkin'—
no, it's more like dreamin' than thinkin'—that
Dan Barry is a wolf turned into a man, an' Black
Bart is a man turned into a wolf."

"Hal, you been drinkin'."

"Maybe."

"What made you think—" began Buck, but the
long rider put spurs to his horse and once more
broke into a fast gallop.

CHAPTER XXX

" THE MANHANDLING "

IT was close to sunset time when they reached
the old Salton place, where they found Silent
sitting on the porch with Haines, Kilduff, Jordan,
and Rhinehart. They stood up at sight of the
newcomers and shouted a welcome. Buck waved
his hand, but his thoughts were not for them.
The music he had heard Dan whistle formed in his
throat. It reached his lips not in sound but as a
smile.

At the house he swung from the saddle and shook
hands with Jim Silent. The big outlaw retained
Buck's fingers.

"You're comin' in mighty late," he growled,
"Didn't you get the signal?"

Buck managed to meet the searching eyes.

"I was doin' better work for you by stayin'
around the house," he said.

"How d'you mean?"

"I stayed there to pick up things you might

want to know. It wasn't easy. The boys are beginnin' to suspect me."

"The cowpunchers is gettin' so thick around those parts," broke in Purvis, "that Buck wouldn't even let me go back to his house with him to get my gun."

The keen eyes of Silent never left the face of Daniels.

"Don't you know that Gus Morris gives us all the news we need, Buck?"

Rhinehart and Jordan, who were chatting together, stopped to listen. Buck smiled easily.

"I don't no ways doubt that Morris tells you all he knows," he said, "but the pint is that he don't know everything."

"How's that?"

"The rangers is beginnin' to look sidewise an' whisper when Morris is around. He's played his game with us too long, an' the boys are startin' to think. Thinkin' is always dangerous."

"You seem to have been doin' some tall thinkin' yourself," said Silent drily; "you guess the cowpunchers are goin' on our trail on their own hook?"

"There ain't no doubt of it."

"Where'd you hear it?"

"Young Seaton."

"He's one of them?"

"Yes."

"I'll remember him. By the way, I see you got a little token of Whistlin' Dan on your arm."

He pointed to the bandage on Buck's right forearm.

"It ain't nothin'," said Buck, shrugging his shoulders. "The cuts are all healin' up. The arm's as good as ever now."

"Anyway," said Silent, "you got somethin' comin' to you for the play you made agin that devil."

He reached into his pocket, drew out several twenty dollar gold pieces (money was never scarce with a lone rider) and passed them to Buck. The latter received the coin gingerly, hesitated, and then returned it to the hand of the chief.

"What the hell's the matter?" snarled the big outlaw. "Ain't it enough?"

"I don't want no money till I earn it," said Buck.

"Life's gettin' too peaceful for you, eh?" grinned Silent.

"Speakin' of peace," chimed in Purvis, with a liberal wink at the rest of the gang, "Buck allows he's the boy who c'n bring the dove o' the same into this camp. He says he knows the way to bring the girl over there to see reason."

Buck followed the direction of Purvis's eyes and saw Kate sitting on a rock at a little distance from the shanty in which she lived with her father. She made a pitiful figure, her chin cupped in her hand, and her eyes staring fixedly down the valley. He was recalled from her by the general laughter of the outlaws.

"You fellers laugh," he said complacently, "because you don't know no more about women than a cow knows about pictures."

"What do you think we should do with her, Solomon?" Buck met the cold blue eye of Haines.

"Maybe I ain't Solomon," he admitted genially, "but I don't need no million wives to learn all there is to know about women."

"Don't make a fool of yourself, Buck," said Silent. "There ain't no way of movin' that damn girl. She's gone on a hunger strike an' she'll die in it. We can't send her out of the valley. It's hell to have her dyin' on our hands here. But there ain't no way to make her change her mind. I've tried pleadin' with her—I've even offered her money. It don't do no good. Think of that!"

"Sure it don't," sneered Buck. "Why, you poor bunch of yearlin' calves, she don't need no coaxin'. What she needs is a manhandlin'. She wants a master, that's what she wants."

"I suppose," said Haines, "you think you're man enough to change her?"

"None of that!" broke in Silent. "D'you really think you could do somethin' with her, Buck?"

"Can I do somethin' with her?" repeated Buck scornfully. "Why, boys, there ain't nothin' I can't do with a woman."

"Is it because of your pretty face or your winnin' smile?" growled the deep bass of Bill Kilduff.

"Both!" said Buck, promptly. "The wilder they are the harder they fall for me. I've had a thirty-year old maverick eatin' out of my hand like she'd been trained for it all her life. The edyoucated ones say I'm 'different'; the old maids allow that I'm 'naïve'; the pretty ones jest say I'm a 'man,' but they spell the word with capital letters."

"Daniels, you're drunk," said Haines.

"Am I? It'll take a better man than you to make me sober, Haines!"

The intervening men jumped back, but the deep voice of Silent rang out like a pistol shot: "Don't move for your six-guns, or you'll be playin' agin me!"

Haines transferred his glare to Silent, but his hand dropped from his gun. Daniels laughed.

"I ain't no mile post with a hand pointin' to

trouble," he said gently. "All I say is that the girl needs excitement. Life's so damned dull for her that she ain't got no interest in livin'."

"If you're fool enough to try," said Silent, "go ahead. What are you plannin' to do?"

"You'll learn by watchin'," grinned Buck, taking the reins of his horse. "I'm goin' to ask the lady soft an' polite to step up to her cabin an' pile into some ham an' eggs. If she don't want to, I'll rough her up a little, an' she'll love me for it afterwards!"

"The way she loves a snake!" growled Kilduff.

"By God, Silent," said Haines, his face white with emotion, "if Buck puts a hand on her I'll——"

"Act like a man an' not like a damn fool boy," said Silent, dropping a heavy hand on the shoulder of his lieutenant. "He won't hurt her none, Lee. I'll answer for that. Come on, Buck. Speakin' personal, I wish that calico was in hell."

Leading his horse, Buck followed Silent towards the girl. She did not move when they approached. Her eyes still held far down the valley. The steps of the big outlaw were shorter and shorter as they drew close to the girl. Finally he stopped and turned to Buck with a gesture of resignation.

"Look at her! This is what she's been doin'

ever since yesterday. Buck, it's up to you to make good. There she is!"

"All right," said Buck, "it's about time for you amachoors to exit an' leave the stage clear for the big star. Now jest step back an' take notes on the way I do it. In fifteen minutes by the clock she'll be eatin' out of my hand."

Silent, expectant but baffled, retired a little. Buck removed his hat and bowed as if he were in a drawing-room.

"Ma'am," he said, "I got the honour of askin' you to side-step up to the shanty with me an' tackle a plate of ham an' eggs. Are you on?"

To this Chesterfieldian outpouring of the heart, she responded with a slow glance which started at Buck's feet, travelled up to his face, and then returned to the purple distance down the canyon. In spite of himself the tell-tale crimson flooded Buck's face. Far away he caught the muffled laughter of the outlaws. He replaced his hat.

"Don't make no mistake," he went on, his gesture including the bandits in the background, and Silent particularly, "I ain't the same sort as these other fellers. I c'n understand the way you feel after bein' herded around with a lot of tin horns like these. I'm suggestin' that you take a long look at me an' notice the difference between an imitation an' a real man."

She did look at him. She even smiled faintly, and the smile made Buck's face once more grow very hot. His voice went hard.

"For the last time, I'm askin' if you'll go up to the cabin."

There was both wonder and contempt in her smile.

In an instant he was in his saddle. He swung far to one side and caught her in his arms. Vaguely he heard the yell of excitement from the outlaws. All he was vividly conscious of was the white horror of her face. She fought like a wild-cat. She did not cry out. She struck him full in the face with the strength of a man, almost. He prisoned her with a stronger grip, and in so doing nearly toppled from the saddle, for his horse reared up, snorting.

A gun cracked twice and two bullets hummed close to his head. From the corner of his eye he was aware of Silent and Rhinehart flinging them-selves upon Lee Haines, who struggled furiously to fire again. He drove his spurs deep and the cattle pony started a bucking course for the shanty.

"Dan!" he muttered at her ear.

The yells of the men drowned his voice. She

20

managed to jerk her right arm free and struck him in the face. He shook her furiously.

"For Whistling Dan!" he said more loudly. "He's dying!"

She went rigid in his arms.

"Don't speak!" he panted. "Don't let them know!"

The outlaws were running after them, laughing and waving their hats.

"Dan!"

"*Faint, you fool!*"

Her eyes widened with instant comprehension. Every muscle of her body relaxed; her head fell back; she was a lifeless burden in his arms. Buck dismounted from the saddle before the shanty. He was white, shaking, but triumphant. Rhinehart and Purvis and Jordan ran up to him. Silent and Kilduff were still struggling with Haines in the distance.

Rhinehart dropped his head to listen at her breast for the heartbeat.

"She's dead!" cried Jordan.

"You're a fool," said Buck calmly. "She's jest fainted, an' when she comes to, she'll begin tellin' me what a wonderful man I am."

"She ain't dead," said Rhinehart, raising his

head from her heart, "but Haines'll kill you for this, Buck!"

"Kate!" cried an agonized voice from the shanty, and old white-haired Joe Cumberland ran towards them.

"Jest a little accident happened to your daughter," explained Buck. "Never mind. I c'n carry her in all right. You fellers stay back. A crowd ain't no help. Ain't no cause to worry, Mr. Cumberland. She ain't hurt!"

He hastened on into the shanty and laid her on the bunk within. Her father hurried about to bathe her face and throat. Buck pushed the other three men out of the room.

"She ain't hurt," he said calmly, "she's jest a little fussed up. Remember I said in fifteen minutes I'd have her eatin' out of my hand. I've still got ten minutes of that time. When the ten minutes is up you all come an' take a look through that window. If you don't see the girl eatin' at that table, I'll chaw up my hat."

He crowded them through the door and shut it behind them. A cry of joy came from old Joe Cumberland and Buck turned to see Kate sitting up on the bunk.

CHAPTER XXXI

"LAUGH, DAMN IT!"

She brushed her father's anxious arms aside and ran to Buck.

"Shut up!" said Buck. "Talk soft. Better still, don't say nothin'!"

"Kate," stammered her father, "what has happened?"

"Listen an' you'll learn," said Buck. "But get busy first. I got to get you out of here to-night. You'll need strength for the work ahead of you. You got to eat. Get me some eggs. Eggs and ham. Got 'em? Good. You, there!" (This to Joe.) "Rake down them ashes. On the jump, Kate. Some wood here. I got only ten minutes!"

In three minutes the fire was going, and the eggs in the pan, while Joe set out some tin dishes on the rickety table, under orders from Buck, making as much noise as possible. While they worked Buck talked. By the time Kate's plate was ready his tale was done. He expected hysterics. She was merely white and steady-eyed.

"You're ready?" he concluded.

"Yes."

"Then begin by doin' what I say an' ask no questions. Silent an' his crew'll be lookin' through the window over there pretty soon. You got to be eatin' an' appearin' to enjoy talkin' to me. Get that an' don't forget it. Mix in plenty of smiles. Cumberland, you get back into the shadow an' stay there. Don't never come out into the light. Your face tells more'n a whole book, an' believe me, Jim Silent is a quick reader."

Joe retreated to a corner of the room into which the light of the lamp did not penetrate.

"Sit down at that table!" ordered Buck, and he placed a generous portion of fried eggs and ham before her.

"I can't eat. Is Dan——"

"I hear 'em at the window!"

He slipped onto a box on the opposite side of the table and leaned towards her, supporting his chin in his hands. Kate began to eat hurriedly.

"No! no!" advised Buck. "You eat as if you was scared. You want to be slow an' deliberate. Watch out! They've moved the board that covers the window!"

For he saw a group of astonished faces 'outside.

"Smile at me!"

Her response made even Buck forget her pallor. Outside the house there was a faint buzz of whispers.

"Keep it up!"

"I'll do my best," she said faintly.

Buck leaned back and burst into uproarious laughter.

"That's a good one!" he cried, slamming the broad palm of his hand against the table so that the tin dishes jumped. "I never heard the beat of it!" And in a whispered tone aside: "*Laugh, damn it!*"

Her laughter rang true enough, but it quavered perilously close to a sob towards the close.

"I always granted Jim Silent a lot of sense," he said, "an' has he really left you alone all this time? Damn near died of homesickness, didn't you?"

She laughed again, more confidently this time. The board was suddenly replaced at the window.

"Now I got to go out to them," he said. "After what Silent has seen he'll trust me with you. He'll let me come back."

She dropped her soft hands over his clenched fist.

"It will be soon? Minutes are greater than hours."

"I ain't forgot. Tonight's the time."

Before he reached the door she ran to him. Two arms went round his neck, two warm lips fluttered against his.

"God bless you!" she whispered.

Buck ran for the door. Outside he stood bareheaded, breathing deeply. His face was hot with shame and delight, and he had to walk up and down for a moment before he could trust himself to enter the ranch house. When he finally did so he received a greeting which made him think himself a curiosity rather than a man. Even Jim Silent regarded him with awe.

"Buck," said Jordan, "you don't never need to work no more. All you got to do is to walk into a town, pick out the swellest heiress, an' marry her."

"The trouble with girls in town," said Buck, "is that there ain't no room for a man to operate. You jest nacherally can't ride a hoss into a parlour."

Lee Haines drew Buck a little to one side.

"What message did you bring to her, Buck?" he said.

"What d'you mean?"

"Look here, friend, these other boys are too thick-headed to understand Kate Cumberland, but I know her kind."

"You're a little peeved, ain't you Lee?" grinned Buck. "It ain't my fault that she don't like you."

Haines ground his teeth.

"It was a very clever little act that you did with her, but it couldn't quite deceive me. She was too pale when she laughed."

"A jealous feller sees two things for every one that really happens, Lee."

"Who was the message from?"

"Did she ever smile at you like she done at me?"

"Was it from Dan Barry that you brought word?"

"Did she ever let her eyes go big an' soft when she looked at you?"

"Damn you."

"Did she ever lean close to you, so's you got the scent of her hair, Lee?"

"I'll kill you for this, Daniels!"

"When I left she kissed me good-bye, Lee."

In spite of his bravado, Buck was deeply anxious. He watched Haines narrowly. Only two men in the mountain-desert would have had a chance against this man in a fight, and Buck knew perfectly well that he was not one of the two.

"Watch yourself, Daniels," said Haines. "I know you're lying and I'm going to keep an eye on you."

"Thanks," grinned Buck. "I like to have a friend watchin' out for me."

Haines turned on his heel and went back to the card table, where Buck immediately joined the circle.

"Wait a minute, Lee," said Silent. "Ain't it your turn to stand guard on the Cumberlands tonight?"

"Right—O," answered Haines cheerfully, and rose from the table.

"Hold on," said Buck. "Are you goin' to spoil all the work I done today with that girl?"

"What's the matter?" asked Silent.

"Everything's the matter! Are you goin' to put a man she hates out there watchin' her."

"Damn you, Daniels," said Haines fiercely, "you're rolling up a long account, but it only takes a bullet to collect that sort of a bill!"

"If it hadn't been for Haines, would the girl's father be here?" asked Buck. "Besides, she don't like blonds."

"What type does she like?" asked Silent, enjoying the quarrel between his lieutenant and the recruit.

"Likes 'em with dark hair an' eyes," said Buck calmly. "Look at me, for instance!"

Even Haines smiled, though his lips were white with anger.

"D'you want to stand guard over her yourself?" said the chief.

"Sure," grinned Buck, "maybe she'd come out an' pass the time o' night with me."

"Go ahead and take the job," nodded Silent. "I got an idea maybe she will."

"Silent," warned Haines, "hasn't it occurred to you that there's something damned queer about the ease with which Buck slid into the favour of the girl?"

"Well?"

"All his talk about manhandling her is bunk. He had some message for her. I saw him speak to her when she was struggling in his arms. Then she conveniently fainted."

Silent turned on Buck.

"Is that straight?"

"It is," said Daniels easily.

The outlaws started and their expectant grins died out.

"By God, Buck!" roared Silent, "if you're double crossin' me—but I ain't goin' to be hasty now. What happened? Tell it yourself! What did you say to her?"

"While she was fightin' with me," said Buck, "she hollered: 'Let me go!' I says: 'I'll see you in hell first!' Then she fainted."

The roar of laughter drowned Haines's further protest.

"You win, Buck," said Silent. "Take the job."

As Buck started for the door Haines called to him:

"Hold on, Buck, if you're aboveboard you won't mind giving your word to see that no one comes up the valley and that you'll be here in the morning?"

The words set a swirling blackness before Buck's eyes. He turned slowly.

"That's reasonable," said Silent. "Speak up, Daniels."

"All right," said Buck, his voice very low. "I'll be here in the morning, and I'll see that no one comes up the valley."

There was the slightest possible emphasis on the word "up."

On a rock directly in front of the shanty Buck took up his watch. The little house behind him was black. Presently he heard the soft call of Kate: "Is it time?"

His eyes wandered to the ranch house. He

could catch the drone of many voices. He made no reply.

"Is it time?" she repeated.

Still he would not venture a reply, however guarded. She called a third time, and when he made no response he heard her voice break to a moan of hopelessness. And yet he waited, waited, until the light in the ranch house went out, and there was not a sound.

"Kate!" he said, gauging his voice carefully so that it could not possibly travel to the ranch house, which all the while he carefully scanned.

For answer the front door of the shanty squeaked.

"Back!" he called. "Go back!"

The door squeaked again.

"They're asleep in the ranch house," she said. "Aren't we safe?"

"S—sh!" he warned. "Talk low! They aren't all asleep. There's one in the ranch house who'll never take his eyes off me till morning."

"What can we do?"

"Go out the back way. You won't be seen if you're careful. Haines has his eyes on me, not you. Go for the stable. Saddle your horses. Then lead them out and take the path on the other side of the house. Don't mount them until you're

far below the house. Go slow all the way.
Sounds travel far up this canyon."

"Aren't you coming with us?"

"No."

"But when they find us gone?"

"Think of Dan—not me!"

"God be merciful to you!"

In a moment the back door of the shanty creaked.
They must be opening it by inches. When it was
wide they would run for the stable. He wished
now that he had warned Kate to walk, for a slow
moving object catches the eye more seldom than
one which travels fast. If Lee Haines was watching at that moment his attention must be held to
Buck for one all important minute. He stood up,
rolled a cigarette swiftly, and lighted it. The
spurt and flare of the match would hold even the
most suspicious eye for a short time, and in those
few seconds Kate and her father might pass out
of view behind the stable.

He sat down again. A muffled sneeze came
from the ranch house and Buck felt his blood run
cold. The forgotten cigarette between his fingers
burned to a dull red and then went out. In the
stable a horse stamped. He leaned back, locked
his hands idly behind his head, and commenced
to whistle. Now there was a snort, as of a horse

when it leaves the shelter of a barn and takes the first breath of open air.

All these sounds were faint, but to Buck, straining his ears in an agony of suspense, each one came like the blast of a trumpet. Next there was a click like that of iron striking against rock. Evidently they were leading the horses around on the far side of the house. With a trembling hand he relighted his cigarette and waited, waited, waited. Then he saw them pass below the house! They were dimly stalking figures in the night, but to Buck it seemed as though they walked in the blaze of ten thousand searchlights. He held his breath in expectancy of that mocking laugh from the house—that sharp command to halt—that crack of the revolver.

Yet nothing happened. Now he caught the click of the horses' iron shoes against the rocks farther and farther down the valley. Still no sound from the ranch house. They were safe!

It was then that the great temptation seized on Buck.

It would be simple enough for him to break away. He could walk to the stable, saddle his horse, and tear past the ranch house as fast as his pony could gallop. By the time the outlaws were ready for the pursuit, he would be a mile or more away, and in the hills such a handicap was enough. One thing held him. It was frail and subtle like the invisible net of the enchanter—that word he had passed to Jim Silent, to see that nothing came up the valley and to appear in the ranch house at sunrise.

In the midst of his struggle, strangely enough, he began to whistle the music he had learned from Dan Barry, the song of The Untamed, those who hunt for ever, and are for ever hunted. When his whistling died away he touched his hand to his lips where Kate had kissed him, and then smiled. The sun pushed up over the eastern hills.

When he entered the ranch house the big room was a scene of much arm stretching and yawning as the outlaws dressed. Lee Haines was already dressed. Buck smiled ironically.

"I say, Lee," he said, "you look sort of used up this mornin', eh?"

The long rider scowled.

"I'd make a guess you've not had much sleep, Haines," went on Buck. "Your eyes is sort of hollow."

"Not as hollow as your damned lying heart!"

"Drop that!" commanded Silent. "You hold a grudge like a woman, Lee! How was the watch, Buck? Are you all in?"

"Nothin' come up the valley, an' here I am at sunrise," said Buck. "I reckon that speaks for itself."

"It sure does," said Silent, "but the gal and her father are kind of slow this mornin'. The old man generally has a fire goin' before dawn is fairly come. There ain't no sign of smoke now."

"Maybe he's sleepin' late after the excitement of yesterday," said Bill Kilduff. "You must of thrown some sensation into the family, Buck."

The eyes of Haines had not moved from the face of Buck.

"I think I'll go over and see what's keeping them so late in bed," he said, and left the house.

"He takes it pretty hard," said Jordan, his scarred face twisted with Satanic mirth, "but don't go rubbin' it into him, Buck, or you'll be havin' a man-sized fight on your hands. I'd jest about as soon mix with the chief as cross Haines. When he starts the undertaker does the finishin'!"

"Thanks for remindin' me," said Buck drily. Through the window he saw Haines throw open the door of the shanty.

The outcry which Buck expected did not follow. For a long moment the long rider stood there without moving. Then he turned and walked slowly

back to the house, his head bent, his forehead
gathered in a puzzled frown.

"What's the matter, Lee?" called Silent as his
lieutenant entered the room again. "You look
sort of sick. Didn't she have a bright mornin'
smile for you?"

Haines raised his head slowly. The frown was
not yet gone.

"They aren't there," he announced.

His eyes shifted to Buck. Everyone followed
his example, Silent cursing softly.

"As a joker, Lee," said Buck coldly, "you're
some Little Eva. I s'pose they jest nacherally
evaporated durin' the night, maybe?"

"Haines," said Silent sharply, "are you serious?"

The latter nodded.

"Then by God, Buck, you'll have to say a lot
in a few words. Lee, you suspected him all the
time, but I was a fool!"

Daniels felt the colour leaving his face, but help
came from the quarter from which he least expected
it.

"Jim, don't draw!" cried Haines.

The eyes of the chief glittered like the hawk's
who sees the field-mouse scurrying over the ground
far below.

"He ain't your meat, Lee," he said. "It's me he's double crossed."

"Chief," said Haines, "last night while he watched the shanty, I watched *him!*"

"Well?"

"I saw him keep his post in front of the cabin all night without moving. And he was wide-awake all the time."

"Then how in hell——"

"The back door of the cabin!" said Kilduff suddenly.

"By God, that's it! They sneaked out there and then went down on the other side of the house."

"If I had let them go," interposed Buck, "do you suppose I'd be here?"

The keen glance of Silent moved from Buck to Haines, and then back again. He turned his back on them.

The quiet which had fallen on the room was now broken by the usual clatter of voices, cursing, and laughter. In the midst of it Haines stepped close to Buck and spoke in a guarded voice.

"Buck," he said, "I don't know how you did it, but I have an idea——"

"Did what?"

The eyes of Haines were sad.

"I was a clean man, once," he said quietly, "and you've done a clean man's work!"

He put out his hand and that of Buck's advanced slowly to meet it.

"Was it for Dan or Kate that you did it?"

The glance of Buck roamed far away.

"I dunno," he said softly. "I think it was to save my own rotten soul!"

On the other side of the room Silent beckoned to Purvis.

"What is it?" asked Hal, coming close.

"Speak low," said Silent. "I'm talking to you, not to the crowd. I think Buck is crooked as hell. I want you to ride down to the neighbourhood of his house. Scout around it day and night. You may see something worth while."

Meanwhile, in that utter blackness which precedes the dawn, Kate and her father reached the mouth of the canyon.

"Kate," said old Joe in a tremulous voice, "if I was a prayin' man I'd git down on my knees an' thank God for deliverin' you tonight."

"Thank Buck Daniels, who's left his life in pawn for us. I'll go straight for Buck's house. You must ride to Sheriff Morris and tell him that an honest man is up there in the power of Silent's gang."

"But——" he began.

She waved her hand to him, and spurring her horse to a furious gallop raced off into the night. Her father stared after her for a few moments, but then, as she had advised, rode for Gus Morris.

CHAPTER XXXII

THOSE WHO SEE IN THE DARK

IT was still early morning when Kate swung from her horse before the house of Buck Daniels. Instinct seemed to lead her to the sick-room, and when she reached it she paid not the slightest attention to the old man and his wife, who sat nodding beside the bed. They started up when they heard the challenging growl of Black Bart, which relapsed into an eager whine of welcome as he recognized Kate.

She saw nothing but the drawn white face of Dan and his blue pencilled eyelids. She ran to him. Old Sam, hardly awake, reached out to stop her. His wife held him back.

"It's Delilah!" she whispered. "I seen her face!"

Kate was murmuring soft, formless sounds which made the old man and his wife look to each other with awe. They retreated towards the door as if they had been found intruding where they had no right.

They saw the fever-bright eyes of Dan open. They heard him murmur petulantly, his glance wandering. Her hand passed across his forehead, and then her touch lingered on the bandage which surrounded his left shoulder. She cried out at that, and Dan's glance checked in its wandering and fixed upon the face which leaned above him. They saw his eyes brighten, widen, and a frown gradually contract his forehead. Then his hand went up slowly and found hers.

He whispered something.

"What did he say?" murmured Sam.

"I dunno," she answered. "I think it was 'Delilah!' See her shrink!"

"Shut up!" cautioned Sam. "Ma, he's comin' to his senses!"

There was no doubt of it now, for a meaning had come into his eyes.

"Shall I take her away?" queried Sam in a hasty whisper. "He may do the girl harm. Look at the yaller in his eyes!"

"No," said his wife softly, "it's time for us to leave 'em alone."

"But look at him now!" he muttered. "He's makin' a sound back in his throat like the growl of a wolf! I'm afeard for the gal, ma!"

"Sam, you're an old fool!"

He followed her reluctantly from the room.

"Now," said his wife, "we c'n leave the door a little open—jest a crack—an' you c'n look through and tell when she's in any reel danger."

Sam obeyed.

"Dan ain't sayin' a word," he said. "He's jest glarin' at her."

"An' what's she doin'?" asked Mrs. Daniels.

"She's got her arm around his shoulders. I never knew they could be such a pile of music in a gal's voice, ma!"

"Sam, you was always a fool!"

"He's pushin' her away to the length of his arm."

"An' she? An' she?" whispered Mrs. Daniels.

"She's talkin' quick. The big wolf is standin' close to them an' turnin' his head from one face to the other like he was wonderin' which was right in the argyment."

"The ways of lovers is as queer as the ways of the Lord, Sam!"

"Dan has caught an arm up before his face, an' he's sayin' one word over an' over. She's dropped on her knees beside the bed. She's talkin'. Why does she talk so low, ma?"

"She don't dare speak loud for fear her silly heart would bust. Oh, I know, I know! What fools all men be! What fools! She's askin' him to forgive her."

"An' he's tryin' all his might not to," whispered Mrs. Daniels in an awe-stricken voice.

"Black Bart has put his head on the lap of the gal. You c'n hear him whine! Dan looks at the wolf an' then at the girl. He seems sort of dumb-founded. She's got her one hand on the head of Bart. She's got the other hand to her face, and she's weepin' into that hand. Martha, she's give up tryin' to persuade him."

There was a moment of silence.

"He's reachin' out his hand for Black Bart. His fingers is on those of the girl. They's both starin'."

"Ay, ay!" she said. "An' what now?"

But Sam closed the door and set his back to it, facing his wife.

"I reckon the rest of it's jest like the endin' of a book, ma," he said.

"Men is all fools!" whispered Mrs. Daniels, but there were tears in her eyes.

Sam went out to put up Kate's horse in the stable. Mrs. Daniels sat in the dining-room, her hands clasped in her lap while she watched the grey dawn come up the east. When Sam entered and spoke to her, she returned no answer. He shook his head as if her mood completely baffled him, and then, worn out by the long watching, he went to bed.

For a long time Mrs. Daniels sat without moving, with the same strange smile transfiguring her. Then she heard a soft step pause at the entrance to the room, and turning saw Kate. There was something in their faces which made them strangely alike. A marvellous grace and dignity came to Mrs. Daniels as she rose.

"My dear!" she said.

"I'm so happy!" whispered Kate.

"Yes, dear! And Dan?"

"He's sleeping like a child! Will you look at him? I think the fever's gone!"

They went hand in hand—like two girls, and they leaned above the bed where Whistling Dan lay smiling as he slept. On the floor Black Bart growled faintly, opened one eye on them, and then relapsed into slumber. There was no longer anything to guard against in that house.

.   .   .   .

It was several days later that Hal Purvis, returning from his scouting expedition, met no less a person that Sheriff Gus Morris at the mouth of the canyon leading to the old Salton place.

"Lucky I met you, Hal," said the genial sheriff. "I've saved you from a wild-goose chase."

"How's that?"

"Silent has jest moved."

"Where?"

"He's taken the trail up the canyon an' cut across over the hills to that old shanty on Bald-eagle Creek. It stands——"

"I know where it is," said Purvis. "Why'd he move?"

"Things was gettin' too hot. I rode over to tell him that the boys was talkin' of huntin' up the canyon to see if they could get any clue of him. They knowed from Joe Cumberland that the gang was once here."

"Cumberland went to you when he got out of the valley?" queried Purvis with a grin.

"Straight."

"And then where did Cumberland go?"

"I s'pose he went home an' joined his gal."

"He didn't," said Purvis drily.

"Then where is he? An' who the hell cares where he is?"

"They're both at Buck Daniels's house."

"Look here, Purvis, ain't Buck one of your own men? Why, I seen him up at the camp jest a while ago!"

"Maybe you did, but the next time you call around he's apt to be missin'."

"D'you think——"

"He's double crossed us. I not only seen the girl an' her father at Buck's house, but I also seen a big dog hangin' around the house. Gus, it was Black Bart, an' where that wolf is you c'n lay to it that Whistlin' Dan ain't far away!"

The sheriff stared at him in dumb amazement, his mouth open.

"They's a price of ten thousand on the head of Whistlin' Dan," suggested Purvis.

The sheriff still seemed too astonished to understand.

"I s'pose," said Purvis, "that you wouldn't care special for an easy lump sum of ten thousand, what?"

"In Buck Daniels's house!" burst out the sheriff.

"Yep," nodded Purvis, "that's where the money is if you c'n get enough men together to gather in Whistlin' Dan Barry."

"D'you really think I'd get some boys together to round up Whistlin' Dan? Why, Hal, you know there ain't no real reason for that price on his head!"

"D'you always wait for 'real reasons' before you set your fat hands on a wad of money?"

The sheriff moistened his lips.

"Ten thousand dollars!"

"Ten thousand dollars!" echoed Purvis.

"By God, I'll do it! If I got him, the boys would forget all about Silent. They're afraid of Jim, but jest the thought of Barry paralyzes them! I'll start roundin' up the boys I need today. Tonight we'll do our plannin'. Tomorrer mornin' bright an' early we'll hit the trail."

"Why not go after him tonight?"

"Because he'd have an edge on us. I got a hunch that devil c'n see in the dark."

He grinned apologetically for this strange idea, but Purvis nodded with perfect sympathy, and then turned his horse up the canyon. The sheriff rode home whistling. On ten thousand dollars more he would be able to retire from this strenuous life.

CHAPTER XXXIII

THE SONG OF THE UNTAMED

BUCK and his father were learning of a thousand crimes charged against Dan. Wherever a man riding a black horse committed an outrage it was laid to the account of this new and most terrible of long riders. Two cowpunchers were found dead on the plains. Their half-emptied revolvers lay close to their hands, and their horses were not far off. In ordinary times it would have been accepted that they had killed each other, for they were known enemies, but now men had room for one thought only. And why should not a man with the courage to take an outlaw from the centre of Elkhead be charged with every crime on the range? Jim Silent had been a grim plague, but at least he was human. This devil defied death.

These were both sad and happy days for Kate. The chief cause of her sadness, strangely enough, was the rapidly returning strength of Dan. While he was helpless he belonged to her. When he was strong he belonged to his vengeance on Jim Silent; and when she heard Dan whistling softly his own wild, weird music, she knew its meaning as she would have known the wail of a hungry wolf on a winter night. It was the song of the untamed. She never spoke of her knowledge. She took the happiness of the moment to her heart and closed her eyes against tomorrow.

Then came an evening when she watched Dan play with Black Bart—a game of tag in which they darted about the room with a violence which threatened to wreck the furniture, but running with such soft footfalls that there was no sound except the rattle of Bart's claws against the floor and the rush of their breath. They came to an abrupt stop and Dan dropped into a chair while Black Bart sank upon his haunches and snapped at the hand which Dan flicked across his face with lightning movements. The master fell motionless and silent. His eyes forgot the wolf. Rising, they rested on Kate's face. They rose again and looked past her.

She understood and waited.

"Kate," he said at last, "I've got to start on the trail."

Her smile went out. She looked where she knew his eyes were staring, through the window and far out across the hills where the shadows deepened and dropped slanting and black across the hollows. Far away a coyote wailed. The wind which swept the hills seemed to her like a refrain of Dan's whistling—the song and the summons of the untamed.

"That trail will never bring you home," she said.

There was a long silence.

"You ain't cryin', honey?"

"I'm not crying, Dan."

"I got to go."

"Yes."

"Kate, you got a dyin' whisper in your voice."

"That will pass, dear."

"Why, honey, you *are* cryin'!"

He took her face between his hands, and stared into her misted eyes, but then his glance wandered past her, through the window, out to the shadowy hills.

"You won't leave me now?" she pleaded.

"I must!"

"Give me one hour more!"

"Look!" he said, and pointed.

She saw Black Bart reared up with his forepaws resting on the window-sill, while he looked into the thickening night with the eyes of the hunter which sees in the dark.

"The wolf knows, Kate," he said, "but I can't explain."

He kissed her forehead, but she strained close to him and raised her lips.

She cried, "My whole soul is on them."

"Not that!" he said huskily. "There's still blood on my lips an' I'm goin' out to get them clean."

He was gone through the door with the wolf racing before him.

She stumbled after him, her arms outspread, blind with tears; and then, seeing that he was gone indeed, she dropped into the chair, buried her face against the place where his head had rested, and wept. Far away the coyote wailed again, and this time nearer.

CHAPTER XXXIV

THE COWARD

BEFORE the coyote cried again, three shadows glided into the night. The lighted window in the house was like a staring eye that searched after them, but Satan, with the wolf running before, vanished quickly among the shadows of the hills. They were glad. They were loosed in the void of the mountain-desert with no destiny save the will of the master. They seemed like one being rather than three. The wolf was the eyes, the horse the strong body to flee or pursue, and the man was the brain which directed, and the power which struck.

He had formulated no plan of action to free Buck and kill Silent. All he knew was that he must reach the long riders at once, and he would learn their whereabouts from Morris. He rode more slowly as he approached the hotel of the sheriff. Lights burned at the dining-room windows. Probably the host still sat at table with his guests, but it was strange that they should linger over their meal so late. He had hoped that he would be able to come upon Morris by surprise. Now he must take him in the midst of many men. With Black Bart slinking at his heels he walked softly across the porch and tiptoed through the front room.

The door to the dining-room was wide. Around the table sat a dozen men, with the sheriff at their head. The latter, somewhat red of face, as if from the effort of a long speech, was talking low and earnestly, sometimes brandishing his clenched fist with such violence that it made his flabby cheeks quiver.

"We'll get to the house right after dawn," he was saying, "because that's the time when most men are so thick-headed with sleep that——"

"Not Whistling Dan Barry," said one of the men, shaking his head. "He won't be thick-headed. Remember, I seen him work in Elkhead, when he slipped through the hands of a roomful of us."

A growl of agreement went around the table, and Black Bart in sympathy, echoed the noise softly.

"What's that?" called the sheriff, raising his head sharply.

Dan, with a quick gesture, made Black Bart slink a pace back.

"Nothin'," replied one of the men. "This business is gettin' on your nerves, sheriff. I don't blame you. It's gettin' on mine."

"I'm trustin' to you boys to stand back of me all through," said the sheriff with a sort of whine, "but I'm thinkin' that we won't have no trouble. When we see him we won't stop for no questions to be asked, but turn loose with our six-guns an' shoot him down like a dog. He's not human an' he don't deserve—Oh, God!"

He started up from his chair, white-faced, his hands high above his head, staring at the apparition of Whistling Dan, who stood with two revolvers covering the posse. Every man was on his feet instantly, with arms straining stiffly up. The muzzles of revolvers are like the eyes of some portraits. No matter from what angle you look at them, they seem directed straight at you. And every cowpuncher in the room was sure that he was the main object of Dan's aim.

"Morris!" said Dan.

"For God's sake, don't shoot!" screamed the sheriff. "I——"

"Git down on your knees! Watch him, Bart!"

As the sheriff sank obediently to his knees, the wolf slipped up to him with a stealthy stride and stood half crouched, his teeth bared, silent. No growl could have made Bart more terribly threatening. Dan turned completely away from Morris so that he could keep a more careful watch on the others.

"Call off your wolf!" moaned Morris, a sob of terror in his voice.

"I ought to let him set his teeth in you," said Dan, "but I'm goin' to let you off if you'll tell me what I want to know."

"Yes! Anything!"

"Where's Jim Silent?"

All eyes flashed towards Morris. The latter, as the significance of the question came home to him, went even a sicklier white, like the belly of a dead fish. His eyes moved swiftly about the circle of his posse. Their answering glares were sternly forbidding.

"Out with it!" commanded Dan.

The sheriff strove mightily to speak, but only a ghastly whisper came: "You got the wrong tip, Dan. I don't know nothin' about Silent. I'd have him in jail if I did!"

"Bart!" said Dan.

The wolf slunk closer to the kneeling man. His hot breath fanned the face of the sheriff and his lips grinned still farther back from the keen, white teeth.

"Help!" yelled Morris. "He's at the shanty up on Bald-eagle Creek."

A rumble, half cursing and half an inarticulate snarl of brute rage, rose from the cowpunchers.

"Bart," called Dan again, and leaped back from the door, raced out to Satan, and drove into the night at a dead gallop.

Half the posse rushed after him. A dozen shots were pumped after the disappearing shadowy figure. Two or three jumped into their saddles. The others called them back.

"Don't be an ass, Monte," said one. "You got a good hoss, but you ain't fool enough to think he c'n catch Satan?"

They trooped back to the dining-room, and gathered in a silent circle around the sheriff, whose little fear-bright eyes went from face to face.

"Ah, this is the swine," said one, "that was guardin' our lives!"

"Fellers," pleaded the sheriff desperately, "I swear to you that I jest heard of where Silent was today. I was keepin' it dark until after we got Whistling Dan. Then I was goin' to lead you——"

The flat of a heavy hand struck with a resounding thwack across his lips. He reeled back against the wall, sputtering the blood from his split mouth.

"Pat," said Monte, "your hoss is done for. Will you stay here an' see that he don't get away? We'll do somethin' with him when we get back."

Pat caught the sheriff by his shirt collar and jerked him to a chair. The body of the fat man was trembling like shaken jelly. The posse turned away.

They could not overtake Whistling Dan on his black stallion, but they might arrive before Silent and his gang got under way. Their numbers were over small to attack the formidable long riders, but they wanted blood. Before Whistling Dan reached the valley of Bald-eagle Creek they were in the saddle and riding hotly in pursuit.

CHAPTER XXXV

CLOSE IN!

IN that time-ruined shack towards which the posse and Dan Barry rode, the outlaws sat about on the floor eating their supper when Hal Purvis entered. He had missed the trail from the Salton place to the Bald-eagle half a dozen times that day, and that had not improved his bitter mood.

"You been gone long enough," growled Silent. "Sit down an' chow an' tell us what you know."

"I don't eat with no damned traitors," said Purvis savagely. "Stan' up an' tell us that you're a double-crossin' houn', Buck Daniels!"

"You better turn in an' sleep," said Buck calmly. "I've knowed men before that loses their reason for want of sleep!"

"Jim," said Purvis, turning sharply on the chief, "Barry is at Buck's house!"

"You lie!" said Buck.

"Do I lie?" said Purvis, grinding his teeth. "I seen Black Bart hangin' around your house."

Jim Silent reached out a heavy paw and dropped

it on the shoulder of Buck. Their eyes met through a long moment, and then the glance of Buck wavered and fell.

"Buck," said Silent, "I like you. I don't want to believe what Purvis says. Give me your word of honour that Whistlin' Dan——"

"He's right, Jim," said Buck.

"An' he dies like a yaller cur!" broke in Purvis, snarling.

"No," said Silent, "when one of the boys goes back on the gang, they pay *me*, not the rest of you! Daniels, take your gun and git down to the other end of the room an' stand with your face to the wall. I'll stay at this end. Keep your arms folded. Haines, you stand over there an' count up to three. Then holler: 'Fire!' an' we'll turn an' start shootin'. The rest of you c'n be judge if that's fair."

"Too damned fair," said Kilduff. "I say: String him up an' drill the skunk full of holes."

Without a word Buck turned on his heel.

"One moment," said Haines.

"He ain't your meat, Lee," said Silent. "Jest keep your hand out of this."

"I only wish to ask him a question," said Haines. He turned to Buck: "Do you mean to say that after Barry's wolf cut up your arm, you've

been giving Whistling Dan a shelter from the law-—
and from us?"

"I give him a place to stay because he was
damned near death," said Buck. "An' there's
one thing you'll answer for in hell, Haines, an'
that's ridin' off an' leavin' the man that got you
out of Elkhead. He was bleedin' to death."

"Shot?" said Haines, changing colour.

Silent broke in: "Buck, go take your place and
say your prayers."

"Stay where you are!" commanded Haines.
"And the girl?"

"He was lyin' sick in bed, ravin' about 'Delilah'
an' 'Kate.' So I come an' got the girl."

Haines dropped his head.

"An' when he was lyin' there," said Silent
fiercely, "you could of made an' end of him without half liftin' your hand, an' you didn't."

"Silent," said Haines, "if you want to talk,
speak to me."

"What in hell do you mean, Lee?"

"You can't get at Buck except through me."

"Because that devil Barry got a bullet for your
sake are you goin' to——"

"I've lived a rotten life," said Haines.

"An' I suppose you think this is a pretty good
way of dyin'?" sneered Silent.

"I have more cause to fight for Barry than Buck has," said Haines.

"Lee, we've been pals too long."

"Silent, I've hated you like a snake ever since I met you. But outlaws can't choose their company."

His tawny head rose. He stared haughtily around the circle of lowering faces.

"By God," said Silent, white with passion, "I'm beginnin' to think you do hate me! Git down there an' take your place. You're first an' Daniels comes next. Kilduff, you c'n count!"

He stalked to the end of the room. Haines lingered one moment.

"Buck," he said, "there's one chance in ten thousand that I'll make this draw the quickest of the two. If I don't, you may live through it. Tell Kate——"

"Haines, git to your mark, or I'll start shootin'!"

Haines turned and took his place. The others drew back along the walls of the room. Kilduff took the lamp from the table and held it high above his head. Even then the light was dim and uncertain and the draughts set the flame wavering so that the place was shaken with shadows. The moon sent a feeble shaft of light through the window.

"One!" said Kilduff.

The shoulders of Haines and Silent hunched slightly.

"Two!" said Kilduff.

"God," whispered someone.

"Three. Fire!"

They whirled, their guns exploding at almost the same instant, and Silent lunged for the floor, firing twice as he fell. Haines's second shot split the wall behind Silent. If the outlaw chief had remained standing the bullet would have passed through his head. But as Silent fired the third time the revolver dropped clattering from the hand of Haines. Buck caught him as he toppled inertly forward, coughing blood.

Silent was on his feet instantly.

"Stand back!" he roared to his men, who crowded about the fallen long rider. "Stand back in your places. I ain't finished. I'm jest started. Buck, take your place!"

"Boys!" pleaded Buck, "he's not dead, but he'll bleed to death unless——"

"Damn him, let him bleed. Stand up, Buck, or by God I'll shoot you while you kneel there!"

"*Shoot and be damned!*"

He tore off his shirt and ripped away a long strip for a bandage.

The revolver poised in Silent's hand.

"Buck, I'm warnin' you for the last time!"

"Fellers, it's murder an' damnation for all if you let Haines die this way!" cried Buck.

The shining barrel of the revolver dropped to a level.

"I've given you a man's chance," said Silent, "an' now you'll have the chance of——"

The door at the side of the room jerked open and a revolver cracked. The lamp shivered to a thousand pieces in the hands of Bill Kilduff. All the room was reduced to a place of formless shadow, dimly lighted by the shaft of moonlight. The voice of Jim Silent, strangely changed and sharpened from his usual bass roar, shrilled over the sudden tumult: "Each man for himself! *It's Whistling Dan!*"

Terry Jordan and Bill Kilduff rushed at the dim figure, crouched to the floor. Their guns spat fire, but they merely lighted the way to their own destruction. Twice Dan's revolver spoke, and they dropped, yelling. Pandemonium fell on the room.

The long riders raced here and there, the revolvers coughing fire. For an instant Hal Purvis stood framed against the pallid moonshine at the window. He stiffened and pointed an arm toward the door.

"The werewolf," he screamed.

As if in answer to the call, Black Bart raced across the room. Twice the revolver sounded from the hand of Purvis. Then a shadow leaped from the floor. There was a flash of white teeth, and Purvis lurched to one side and dropped, screaming terribly. The door banged. Suddenly there was silence. The clatter of a galloping horse outside drew swiftly away.

"Dan!"

"Here!"

"Thank God!"

"Buck, one got away! If it was Silent—Here! Bring some matches."

Someone was dragging himself towards the door in a hopeless effort to escape. Several others groaned.

"You, there!" called Buck. "Stay where you are!"

The man who struggled towards the door flattened himself against the floor, moaning pitifully.

"Quick," said Dan, "light a match. Morris's posse is at my heels. No time. If Silent escaped——"

A match flared in the hands of Buck.

"Who's that? Haines!"

"Let him alone, Dan! I'll tell you why later. There's Jordan and Kilduff. That one by the door is Rhinehart."

They ran from one to the other, greeted by groans and deep curses.

"Who's that beneath the window?"

"Too small for Silent. It's Purvis, and he's dead!"

"Bart got him!"

"No! It was fear that killed him. Look at his face!"

"Bart, go out to Satan!"

The wolf trotted from the room.

"My God, Buck, I've done all this for nothin'! It was Silent that got away!"

"What's that?"

Over the groans of the wounded came the sound of running horses, not one, but many, then a call: "Close in! Close in!"

"The posse!" said Dan.

As he jerked open the door a bullet smashed the wood above his head. Three horsemen were closing around Satan and Black Bart. He leaped back into the room.

"They've got Satan, Buck. We've got to try it on foot. Go through the window."

"They've got nothing on me. I'll stick with Haines."

Dan jumped through the window, and raced to the shelter of a big rock. He had hardly dropped behind it when four horsemen galloped around the corner of the house.

"Johnson and Sullivan," ordered the voice of Monte sharply, "watch the window. They're lying low inside, but we've got Barry's horse and wolf. Now we'll get him."

"Come out or we'll burn the house down!" thundered a voice from the other side.

"We surrender!" called Buck within.

A cheer came from the posse. Sullivan and Johnson ran for the window they had been told to guard. The door on the other side of the house slammed open.

"It's a slaughter house!" cried one of the posse.

Dan left the sheltering rock and raced around the house, keeping a safe distance, and dodging from rock to rock. He saw Satan and Black Bart guarded by two men with revolvers in their hands. He might have shot them down, but the distance was too great for accurate gun-play. He whistled shrilly. The two guards wheeled towards him, and as they did so, Black Bart, leaping, caught one by the shoulder, whirling him around and around with the force of the spring. The other fired at Satan, who raced off towards the sound of the whistle. It was an easy shot, but in the utter surprise of the instant the bullet went wide. Before he could fire again Satan was coming to a halt beside Dan.

"Help!" yelled the cattleman. "Whistling Dan!"

The other guard opened fire wildly. Three men ran from the house. All they saw was a black shadow which melted instantly into the night.

CHAPTER XXXVI

FEAR

INTO the dark he rode. Somewhere in the mountains was Silent, and now alone. In Dan's mouth the old salt taste of his own blood was unforgotten.

It was a wild chase. He had only the faintest clues to guide him, yet he managed to keep close on the trail of the great outlaw. After several days he rode across a tall red-roan stallion, a mere wreck of a horse with lean sides and pendant head and glazed eye. It was a long moment before Dan recognized Silent's peerless mount, Red Pete. The outlaw had changed his exhausted horse for a common pony. The end of the long trail must be near.

The whole range followed that chase with breathless interest. It was like the race of Hector and Achilles around the walls of Troy. And when they met there would be a duel of giants. Twice Whistling Dan was sighted. Once Jim Silent fought a running duel with a posse fresh from Elk-head. The man hunters were alert, but it was their secret hope that the two famous outlaws would destroy each other, but how the wild chase would end no one could know. At last Buck Daniels rode to tell Kate Cumberland strange news.

When he stumbled into the ranch house, Kate and her father rose, white-faced. There was an expression of waiting terror in their eyes.

"Buck!" cried Joe.

"Hush! Dad," said Kate. "It hasn't come yet! Buck, what has happened?"

"The end of the world has come for Dan," he said. "That devil Silent——"

"Dan," cried old Joe, and rushed around the table to Buck.

"Silent has dared Dan to meet him at three o'clock tomorrow afternoon in Tully's saloon in Elkhead! He's held up four men in the last twenty-four hours and told them that he'll be at Tully's tomorrow and will expect Dan there!"

"It isn't possible!" cried Kate. "That means that Silent is giving himself up to the law!"

Buck laughed bitterly.

"The law will not put a hand on them if it thinks that they'll fight it out together," he said.

"There'll be a crowd in the saloon, but not a hand will stir to arrest Silent till after the fight."

"But Dan won't go to Tully's," broke in old Joe. "If Silent is crazy enough to do such a thing, Dan won't be."

"He will," said Kate. "I know!"

"You've got to stop him," urged Buck. "You've got to get to Elkhead and turn Dan back."

"Ay," said Joe, "for even if he kills Silent, the crowd will tackle him after the fight—a hundred against one."

She shook her head.

"You won't go?"

"Not a step.'

"But Kate, don't you understand——?"

"I couldn't turn Dan back. There is his chance to meet Silent. Do you dream any óne could turn him back?"

The two men were mute.

"You're right," said Buck at last. "I hoped for a minute that you could do it, but now I remember the way he was in that dark shanty up the Bald-eagle Creek. You can't turn a wolf from a trail, and Whistling Dan has never forgotten the taste of his own blood."

"Kate!" called her father suddenly. "What's the matter, honey?"

With bowed head and a faltering step she was leaving the room. Buck caught old Joe by the arm and held him back as he would have followed.

"Let her be!" said Buck sharply. "Maybe she'll want to see you at three o'clock tomorrow afternoon, but until then she'll want to be alone. There'll be ghosts enough with her all the time. You c'n lay to that."

Joe Cumberland wiped his glistening forehead.

"There ain't nothin' we c'n do, Buck, but sit an' wait."

Buck drew a long breath.

"What devil gave Silent that idea?"

"*Fear!*"

"Jim Silent don't know what fear is!"

"Any one who's seen the yaller burn in Dan's eyes knows what fear is."

Buck winced.

Cumberland went on: "Every night Silent has been seein' them eyes that glow yaller in the dark. They lie in wait for him in every shadow. Between dark and dawn he dies a hundred deaths. He can't stand it no more. He's goin' to die. Somethin' tells him that. But he wants to die where they's humans around him, and when he dies he wants to pull Dan down with him."

They sat staring at each other for a time.

"If he lives through that fight with Silent," said Buck sadly, "the crowd will jump in on him. Their numbers'll make 'em brave."

"An' then?"

"Then maybe he'd like a friend to fight by his side," said Buck simply. "So long, Joe!"

The old man wrung his hand and then followed him out to the hitching-rack where Buck's horse stood.

"Ain't Dan got no friends among the crowd?" asked Cumberland. "Don't they give him no thanks for catching the rest of Silent's gang?"

"They give him lots of credit," said Buck. "An' Haines has said a lot in favour of Dan, explainin' how the jail bustin' took place. Lee is sure provin' himself a white man. He's gettin' well of his wounds and it's said the Governor will pardon him. You see, Haines went bad because the law done him dirt a long time ago, and the Governor is takin' that into account."

"But they'd still want to kill Dan?"

"Half of the boys wouldn't," said Buck. "The other half is all wrought up over the killings that's been happenin' on the range in the last month.

Dan is accused of about an even half of 'em, an' the friends of dead men don't waste no time listenin' to arguments. They say Dan's an outlawed man an' that they're goin' to treat him like one."

"Damn them!" groaned Cumberland. "Don't Morris's confession make no difference?"

"Morris was lynched before he had a chance to swear to what he said in Dan's favour. Kilduff an' Jordan an' Rhinehart might testify that Dan wasn't never bought over by Silent, but they know they're done for themselves, an' they won't try to help anybody else, particular the man that put 'em in the hands of the law. Kilduff has swore that Dan *was* bribed by Silent, that he went after Silent not for revenge, but to get some more money out of him, an' that the fight in the shanty up at Bald-eagle Creek was because Silent refused to give Dan any more money."

"Then there ain't no hope," muttered Cumberland. "But oh, lad, it breaks my heart to think of Kate! Dan c'n only die once, but every minute is a death to her!"

CHAPTER XXXVII

DEATH

BEFORE noon of the next day Buck joined the crowd which had been growing for hours around Tully's saloon. Men gave way before him, whispering. He was a marked man—the friend of Whistling Dan Barry. Cowpunchers who had known him all his life now avoided his eyes, but caught him with side glances. He smiled grimly to himself, reading their minds. He was more determined than ever to stand or fall with Whistling Dan that day.

There was not an officer of the law in sight. If one were present it would be his manifest duty to apprehend the outlaws as soon as they appeared, and the plan was to allow them to fight out their quarrel and perhaps kill each other.

Arguments began to rise among separate groups, where the crimes attributed to Whistling Dan Barry were numbered and talked over. It surprised Buck to discover the number who believed the stories which he and Haines had told. They made a strong faction, though manifestly in the minority.

Hardly a man who did not, from time to time, nervously fumble the butt of his six-gun. As three o'clock drew on the talk grew less and less. It broke out now and again in little uneasy bursts. Someone would tell a joke. Half hysterical laughter would greet it, and die suddenly, as it began. These were all hard-faced men of the mountain-desert, warriors of the frontier. What unnerved them was the strangeness of the thing which was about to happen. The big wooden clock on the side of the long barroom struck once for half-past two. All talk ceased.

Men seemed unwilling to meet each other's eyes. Some of them drummed lightly on the top of the bar and strove to whistle, but the only sound that came through their dried lips was a whispering rush of breath. A grey-haired cattle ranger commenced to hum a tune, very low, but distinct. Finally a man rose, strode across the room, shook the old fellow by the shoulder with brutal violence, and with a curse ordered him to stop his "damned death song!"

Everyone drew a long breath of relief. The minute hand crept on towards three o'clock. Now it was twenty minutes, now fifteen, now ten, now five; then a clatter of hoofs, a heavy step on the porch, and the giant form of Jim Silent blocked the door. His hands rested on the butts of his two guns. Buck guessed at the tremendous strength of that grip. The eyes of the outlaw darted about the room, and every glance dropped before his, with the exception of Buck's fascinated stare.

For he saw a brand on the face of the great long rider. It lay in no one thing. It was not the unusual hollowness of eyes and cheeks. It was not the feverish brightness of his glance. It was something which included all of these. It was the fear of death by night! His hands fell away from the guns. He crossed the room to the bar and nodded his head at the bartender.

"Drink!" he said, and his voice was only a whisper without body of sound.

The bartender, with pasty face, round and blank, did not move either his hand or his fascinated eyes. There was a twitch of the outlaw's hand and naked steel gleamed. Instantly revolvers showed in every hand. A youngster moaned. The sound seemed to break the charm.

Silent put back his great head and burst into a

deep-throated laughter. The gun whirled in his hand and the butt crashed heavily on the bar.

"Drink, damn you!" he thundered. "Step up an' drink to the health of Jim Silent!"

The wavering line slowly approached the bar. Silent pulled out his other gun and shoved them both across the bar.

"Take 'em," he said. "I don't want 'em to get restless an' muss up this joint."

The bartender took them as if they were covered with some deadly poison, and the outlaw stood unarmed! It came suddenly to Buck what the whole manœuvre meant. He gave away his guns in order to tempt someone to arrest him. Better the hand of the law than the yellow glare of those following eyes. Yet not a man moved to apprehend him. Unarmed he still seemed more dangerous than six common men.

The long rider jerked a whisky bottle upside down over a glass. Half the contents splashed across the bar. He turned and faced the crowd, his hand dripping with the spilled liquor.

"Whose liquorin'?" he bellowed.

Not a sound answered him.

"Damn your yaller souls! Then all by myself I'll drink to——"

He stopped short, his eyes wild, his head tilted

back. One by one the cowpunchers gave back,
foot by foot, softly, until they stood close to the
opposite wall of the saloon. All the bar was left
to Silent. The whisky glass slipped from his
hand and crashed on the floor. In his face was the
meaning of the sound he heard, and now it came
to their own ears—a whistle thin with distance, but
clear.

Only phrases at first, but now it rose more distinct, the song of the untamed; the terror and
beauty of the mountain-desert; a plea and a threat.

The clock struck, sharp, hurried, brazen—one,
two, three! Before the last quick, unmusical
chime died out Black Bart stood in the entrance
to the saloon. His eyes were upon Jim Silent,
who stretched out his arms on either side and
gripped the edge of the bar. Yet even when the
wolf glided silently across the room and crouched
before the bandit, at watch, his lips grinned back
from the white teeth, the man had no eyes for him.
Instead, his stare held steadily upon that open
door and on his raised face there was still the
terror of that whistling which swept closer and
closer.

It ceased. A footfall crossed the porch. How
different from the ponderous stride of Jim Silent!
This was like the padding step of the panther.

And Whistling Dan stood in the door. He did not fill it as the burly shoulders of Silent had done. He seemed almost as slender as a girl, and infinitely boyish in his grace—a strange figure, surely, to make all these hardened fighters of the mountain-desert crouch, and stiffen their fingers around the butts of their revolvers! His eyes were upon Silent, and how they lighted! His face changed as the face of the great god Pan must have altered when he blew into the instrument of reeds and made perfect music, the first in the world.

"Bart," said the gentle voice, "go out to Satan."

The wolf turned and slipped from the room. It was a little thing, but, to the men who saw it, it was terrible to watch an untamed beast obey the voice of a man.

Still with that light, panther-step he crossed the barroom, and now he was looking up into the face of the giant. The huge long rider loomed above Dan. That was not terror which set his face in written lines—it was horror, such as a man feels when he stands face to face with the unearthly in the middle of night. This was open daylight in a room thronged with men, yet in it nothing seemed to live save the smile of Whistling Dan. He drew out the two revolvers and slipped them onto the bar. They stood unarmed, yet they seemed no less dangerous.

Silent's arms crept closer to his sides. He seemed gathering himself by degrees. The confidence in his own great size showed in his face, and the blood-lust of battle in his eyes answered the yellow light in Dan's.

Dan spoke.

"Silent, once you put a stain of blood on me. I've never forgot the taste. It's goin' to be washed out today or else made redder. It was here that you put the stain."

He struck the long rider lightly across the mouth with the back of his hand, and Silent lunged with the snarl of a beast. His blow spent itself on thin air. He whirled and struck again. Only a low laughter answered him. He might as well have battered away at a shadow.

"Damnation!" he yelled, and leaped in with both arms outspread.

The impetus of his rush drove them both to the floor, where they rolled over and over, and before they stopped thin fingers were locked about the bull neck of the bandit, and two thumbs driven into the hollow of his throat. With a tremendous effort he heaved himself from the floor, his face convulsed.

He beat with both fists against the lowered head of Dan. He tore at those hands. They were locked as if with iron. Only the laughter, the low, continual laughter rewarded him.

He screamed, a thick, horrible sound. He flung himself to the floor again and rolled over and over, striving to crush the slender, remorseless body. Once more he was on his feet, running hither and thither, dragging Dan with him. His eyes swelled out; his face blackened. He beat against the walls. He snapped at the wrists of Dan like a beast, his lips flecked with a bloody froth.

That bull-dog grip would not unlock. That animal, exultant laughter ran on in demoniac music. In his great agony the outlaw rolled his eyes in appeal to the crowd which surrounded the struggling two. Every man seemed about to spring forward, yet they could not move. Some had their fingers stiffly extended, as if in the act of gripping with hands too stiff to close.

Silent slipped to his knees. His head fell back, his discoloured tongue protruding. Dan wrenched him back to his feet. One more convulsive effort from the giant, and then his eyes glazed, his body went limp. The remorseless hands unlocked. Silent fell in a shapeless heap to the floor.

Still no one moved.   There was no sound except the deadly ticking of the clock.   The men stared fascinated at that massive, lifeless figure on the floor.   Even in death he was terrible.   Then Dan's hand slid inside his shirt, fumbled a moment, and came forth again bearing a little gleaming circle of metal.   He dropped it upon the body of Jim Silent, and turning, walked slowly from the room.   Still no one moved to intercept him. Passing through the door he pushed within a few inches of two men.   They made no effort to seize him, for their eyes were upon the body of the great lone rider.

The moment Dan was gone the hypnotic silence which held the crowd, broke suddenly.   Some-one stirred.   Another cursed beneath his breath. Instantly all was clamour and a running hither and thither.   Buck Daniels caught from the body of Jim Silent the small metal circle which Dan had dropped.   He stood dumbfounded at the sight of it, and then raised his hand, and shouted in a voice which gathered the others swiftly around him. They cursed deeply with astonishment, for what they saw was the marshal's badge of Tex Calder. The number on it was known throughout the mountain-desert, and seeing it, the worst of Dan's enemies stammered, gaped, and could not speak.

There were more impartial men who could. In five minutes the trial of Whistling Dan was under way. The jury was every cowpuncher present. The judge was public opinion. It was a grey-haired man who finally leaped upon the bar and summed up all opinion in a brief statement.

"Whatever Whistlin' Dan has done before," he said, "this day he's done a man-sized job in a man's way. Morris, before he died, said enough to clear up most of this lad's past, particular about the letter from Jim Silent that talked of a money bribe. Morris didn't have a chance to swear to what he said, but a dying man speaks truth. Lee Haines had cleared up most of the rest. We can't hold agin Dan what he done in breakin' jail with Haines. Dan Barry was a marshal. He captured Haines and then let the outlaw go. He had a right to do what he wanted as long as he finally got Haines back. And Haines has told us that when he was set free Barry said he would get him again. And Barry did get him again. Remember that, and he got all the rest of Silent's gang, and now there lies Jim Silent dead. They's two things to remember. The first is that Whistlin' Dan has rid away without any shootin' irons on his hip. That looks as if he's come to the end of his long trail. The second is that he was a bunkie of Tex Calder, an' a man Tex could trust for the avengin' of his death is good enough for me."

There was a pause after this speech, and during the quiet the cowpunchers were passing from hand to hand the marshal's badge which Calder, as he died, had given to Dan. The bright small shield was a more convincing proof than a hundred arguments. The bitterest of Dan's enemies realized that the crimes of which he was accused were supported by nothing stronger than blind rumour. The marshal's badge and the dead body of Jim Silent kept them mute. So an illegal judge and one hundred illegal jurymen found Whistling Dan "not guilty."

Buck Daniels took horse and galloped for the Cumberland house with the news of the verdict. He knew that Whistling Dan was there.

24

CHAPTER XXXVIII

THE WILD GEESE

So when the first chill days of the late autumn came the four were once more together, Dan, Kate, Black Bart, and Satan. Buck and old Joe Cumberland made the background of their happiness. It was the latter's request which kept the wedding a matter of the indefinite future. He would assign no reason for his wish, but Kate guessed it.

All was not well, she knew. Day after day, as the autumn advanced, Dan went out with the wolf and the wild black stallion and ranged the hills alone. She did not ask him where or why, for she understood that to be alone was as necessary to him as sleep is to others. Yet she could not explain it all and the cold fear grew in her. Sometimes she surprised a look of infinite pity in the eyes of Buck or her father. Sometimes she found them whispering and nodding together. At last on an evening when the three sat before the fire in solemn silence and Dan was away, they knew not where, among the hills, she could bear it no longer.

"Do you really think," she burst out, "that the old wildness is still in Dan?"

"Wild?" said her father gently. "Wild? I don't say he's still wild—but why is he so late tonight, Kate? The ground's all covered with snow. The wind's growin' sharper an' sharper. This is a time for all reasonable folk to stay home an' git comfortable beside the fire. But Dan ain't here. Where is he?"

"Hush!" said Buck, and raised a hand for silence.

Far away they heard the wail of a wolf crying to the moon. She rose and went out on the porch of the house. The others followed her. Outside they found nothing but the low moaning of the wind, and the snow, silver glimmering where the moonlight fell upon it. Then they heard the weird, inhuman whistling, and at last they saw Dan riding towards the house. A short distance away he stopped Satan. Black Bart dropped to his haunches and wailed again. Dan was staring upwards.

"Look!" said Kate, and pointed.

Across the white circle of the moon drove a flying wedge of wild geese. The wail of the wolf died out. A faint honking was blown to them by the wind, now a distant, jangling chorus, now a solitary sound repeated like a call.

Without a word the three returned to their seats close by the fire, and sat silent, staring. Presently the rattle of the wolf's claws came on the floor; then Dan entered with his soft step and stood behind Kate's chair. They were used to his silent comings and goings. Black Bart was slinking up and down the room with a restless step. His eyes glowed from the shadow, and as Joe looked up to the face of Dan he saw the same light repeated there, yellow and strange. Then, like the wolf, Dan turned and commenced that restless pacing up and down, up and down, a padding step like the fall of a panther's paw.

"The wild geese—" he said suddenly, and then stopped.

"They are flying south?" said Kate.

"South!" he repeated.

His eyes looked far away. The wolf slipped to his side and licked his hand.

"Kate, I'd like to follow the wild geese."

Old Joe shaded his eyes and the big hands of Buck were locked together.

"Are you unhappy, Dan?" she said.

"The snow is come," he muttered uneasily.

He began pacing again with that singular step.

"When I went out to Satan in the corral this evenin', I found him standin' lookin' south."

She rose and faced him with a little gesture of surrender.

"Then you must follow the wild geese, Dan!"

"You don't mind me goin', Kate?"

"No."

"But your eyes are shinin'!"

"It's only the reflection of the firelight."

Black Bart whined softly. Suddenly Dan straightened and threw up his arms, laughing low with exultation. Buck Daniels shuddered and dropped his head.

"I am far behind," said Dan, "but I'll go fast."

He caught her in his arms, kissed her eyes and lips, and then whirled and ran from the room with that noiseless, padding step.

"Kate!" groaned Buck Daniels, "you've let him go! We've all lost him for ever!"

A sob answered him.

"Go call him back," pleaded Joe. "He will stay for your sake."

She whispered: "I would rather call back the wild geese who flew across the moon. And they are only beautiful when they are wild!"

"But you've lost him, Kate, don't you understand?"

"The wild geese fly north again in spring," said Buck, "and he'll——"

"Hush!" she said. "Listen!"

Far off, above the rushing of the wind, they heard the weird whistling, a thrilling and unearthly music. It was sad with the beauty of the night. It was joyous with the exultation of the wind. It might have been the voice of some god who rode the northern storm south, south after the wild geese, south with the untamed.

THE END